LAST WOOL
and
TESTAMENT

PEGGY EHRHART

Kensington Publishing Corp.
kensingtonbooks.com

KENSINGTON BOOKS are published by

Kensington Publishing Corp.
900 Third Avenue
New York, NY 10022

First Printing: May 2025
ISBN: 978-1-4967-4959-8

ISBN: 978-1-4967-4960-X (ebook)

10 9 8 7 6 5 4 3 2 1

Printed in the United States of America

The authorized representative in the EU for product safety and compliance
is eucomply OU, Parnu mnt 139b-14, Apt 123
Tallinn, Berlin 11317, hello@eucompliancepartner.com

MOTIVE FOR MURDER

Pamela fingered the sketch of the hot-pink and turquoise sweater. "Ingrid came up with this design, and all these others"—she waved her hand over the sketches scattered across the table—"but the collection was billed as Nestor Flavin's. The eighties were quite a while ago, and I guess they were a time when women still loyally contributed to men's success with no expectation of credit."

"Ingrid had to be satisfied with reflected glory—reflected from the man her work had made successful." Bettina shook her head slowly, but then the movement stopped with a shudder. "Are you thinking what I'm thinking?" she inquired, echoing Pamela's earlier question.

"Nestor is trying for a comeback, and the last thing he needs is for word to get out that he didn't actually design the first Mariposa collection."

"Exactly!" Pamela nodded. "And how might he imagine he could prevent word from getting out?"

"Convince Eilert to ignore Ingrid's early work in his book . . . but that wouldn't really solve the problem." Bettina took a deep breath and laid her palm on her chest. Her eyes grew large.

Pamela finished the thought. "As long as Ingrid was still alive, Nestor's secret would never be safe."

"Now Ingrid is out of the way . . ." Bettina observed.

Books by Peggy Ehrhart

Knit and Nibble Mysteries
MURDER, SHE KNIT
DIED IN THE WOOL
KNIT ONE, DIE TWO
SILENT KNIT, DEADLY KNIT
A FATAL YARN
KNIT OF THE LIVING DEAD
KNITTY GRITTY MURDER
DEATH OF A KNIT WIT
IRISH KNIT MURDER
KNITMARE ON BEECH STREET
A DARK AND STORMY KNIT
LAST WOOL AND TESTAMENT

Anthologies
CHRISTMAS CARD MURDER
(with Leslie Meier and Lee Hollis)
CHRISTMAS SCARF MURDER
(with Carlene O'Connor and Maddie Day)
IRISH MILKSHAKE MURDER
(with Carlene O'Connor and Liz Ireland)
IRISH SODA BREAD MURDER
(with Carlene O'Connor and Liz Ireland)

Published by Kensington Publishing Corp.

For my readers, with thanks.

ACKNOWLEDGMENTS

Abundant thanks to my agent, Evan Marshall, and to my editor at Kensington Books, John Scognamiglio.

CHAPTER 1

"Everyone was talking about the murder this afternoon at the salon." Despite the serious topic, Holly Perkins's usual ebullience was undiminished, her magnetic charm enhanced by her glowing complexion and raven hair. "It's not every day that we have a murder right here in Arborville, let alone of a well-known artist like Ingrid Barrick."

"News certainly travels fast," Bettina Fraser commented. "The story hasn't made it into the *Register* yet."

"And our salon isn't even in Arborville, but a lot of people from Arborville drive the few extra miles to Meadowside because they like the way Desmond and I do their hair."

Holly's appearance testified to her hair artistry and her aesthetic sense in general. Her raven hair was accented with a dramatic orange streak, a shade of orange that matched her metallic nail polish. Earrings like a silvery cascade dangled nearly to her shoulders.

"The people in the salon were just basing their understanding of what happened on rumors circulating around the listserv," Holly went on, responding to Bettina, "but I'll bet you know the real details. I'll bet you've already talked to Detective Clayborn. Of course he'd want the ace reporter for Arborville's weekly paper to be on top of the story."

Pamela Paterson stifled a laugh. She knew perfectly well that Bettina's access to Arborville's sole police detective depended on his mood, and that more often than not, the Arborville *Advocate* remained unclaimed in people's driveways for days.

Bettina, however, took her work seriously. "I *did* hear something," she said, "though not from Clayborn."

She ventured a glance at Nell Bascomb, who was sitting in a comfortable peach-colored armchair, busily at work on a knitting project. Not far from her, but seated on the hearth, Roland DeCamp was similarly engaged. The other four members of the Knit and Nibble knitting club had lowered their work to their laps in order to focus more attentively on the topic Holly had raised.

Nell met the glance with a glance of her own, made all the more stern by the steely gleam of her pale blue eyes in their nests of wrinkles. When she spoke, however, it was to say, "Don't mind me. I don't see any reason why people have to make shocking events the stuff of social conversation, but I know when I'm outnumbered."

"A neighbor of Ingrid's called the *Advocate* this morning," Bettina said. "She—the neighbor is named Colette Dalrymple—was working in her yard when the mail carrier came around, and she watched him go up to Ingrid's door, then she watched him push the door open. The next thing she knew, he was back outside—though she said Ingrid's yard is such a jumble of random plants that he was hard to see because he was stumbling around. But he was looking kind of frantic and had his phone out."

"Oh, my!" Karen Dowling raised a delicate hand to her mouth. "The scene inside the house must have been quite startling."

"Ingrid was right there in the living room, sprawled out on the floor," Bettina said. "At least that's what the mail carrier told Colette. Then the police came and took him away for an interview, so that's all she knew."

At that, Roland DeCamp ceased knitting and set his work on the lid of the elegant briefcase that rested near his feet. He raised his left wrist and flexed his arm to expose the impressive watch that lurked beneath his flawlessly starched shirt cuff. He seemed about to speak. At the same moment that he opened his mouth, a male figure garbed in a flannel shirt and bib overalls, and with an apron tied around his bulky middle, appeared in the arch that separated the living room from the dining room.

As if in stereo, two voices announced, "Eight o'clock."

One voice was that of Roland, whose self-appointed task it was to remind the Knit and Nibblers that an hour of knitting had passed and the "nibble" portion of the meeting was about to commence. The group was meeting that evening at the Frasers' house, and the other voice belonged to Bettina's husband, Wilfred.

Holly jumped to her feet, followed by Karen, who

was her best friend despite the contrast between shy Karen, with her fair hair and unassertive features, and Holly's vibrant exuberance.

"Let us help!" Holly exclaimed, speaking for both of them. "I can't wait to see—and taste—the treat you've got in store for us tonight."

"Everything's ready," Wilfred said with a contented smile, as he folded his arms across his chest. The aromas wafting from the dining room made that clear—dark and spicy mingled with sweet and fruity. "Come in"—he beckoned—"come in and help yourselves."

Holly and Karen led the way, with Bettina stepping aside to let all the guests precede her.

Wilfred had clearly been busy. An oval baking dish in the center of the Frasers' dining room table held a cobbler, its exact nature hidden by the puffy rumples of its cobbled topping. Next to it was a quart-sized tub of vanilla ice cream on a small tray. A stack of dessert plates from Bettina's sage-green pottery set awaited servings of cobbler, with forks and white linen napkins at hand. A tall chrome carafe held coffee, and a squat teapot held tea, with seven sage-green mugs lined up nearby, along with a matching cream pitcher and sugar bowl.

Wilfred picked up a large serving spoon and scooped a generous portion of cobbler onto one of the dessert plates.

"Ice cream?" he inquired of Nell, who had been steered to the front of the line.

"Yes," she said, "but just a bit—and that's so much cobbler . . ."

"It's mostly fruit," Wilfred responded with a wink. "Very healthful, really."

The fruit in question, from what Pamela could tell based on Nell's serving, was strawberries and rhubarb. The motion of serving had inverted the scoop of cobbler. The ruby-red berries and the deep-pink chunks of rhubarb now lay atop the pale, cobbled crust, which was bathed in their fruity syrup.

Wilfred continued to serve the cobbler, adding spoonfuls of ice cream, as people clustered around the table helping themselves to coffee and tea. Soon the knitters were back in the Frasers' comfortable living room, with the addition of Wilfred, who had perched on the hearth next to Roland. For a few suspense-filled moments, forks hovered in the air, then they dove toward plates and ascended to eager mouths.

"Delicious!" was the first verdict, from Holly.

"Excellent!" Roland gave a judicious nod, as if approving a legal argument. He was a corporate lawyer, and his reaction was in keeping with his pin-striped suit and serious demeanor.

"Local rhubarb?" Nell inquired. "It used to nearly grow wild in Arborville, and I still have a patch in my yard."

"It's from the community gardens." Bettina spoke up. "I did a story on the gardens for the *Advocate* last week, and one of the gardeners I interviewed sent me home with a huge bag of rhubarb."

"*Awesome!*" Holly, sitting next to Pamela on the sofa, gave an excited wiggle. "And Wilfred knew just what to do with it." The smile that accompanied this statement displayed perfect teeth and brought Holly's dimple into play. She positioned her fork for another taste of cobbler.

Pamela, too, was teasing off another bite from the

serving on her plate. She made sure to include a bit of the pillowy crust, a strawberry, a sliver of rhubarb, and a dab of ice cream before she raised her fork to her mouth. Wilfred had used plenty of sugar, but not so much as to cancel the pleasing tartness of the rhubarb or the acidity of the strawberry, which the cool and smooth vanilla ice cream balanced out.

"Are the strawberries from the community gardens too?" Karen asked.

"Not quite," Wilfred responded, "but they *are* New Jersey strawberries. I got them at the Newfield farmers market."

"Such a perfect time of year," Bettina remarked. "Everything's blooming, and the air smells so sweet."

"And the deer are coming around, helping themselves to anything green that they feel like eating." Roland's frown contrasted with Bettina's sunny expression.

"You can plant things they don't like," Karen ventured. "They hate daffodils."

"They've already eaten all of Melanie's lilies, and the buds hadn't even opened yet." Roland's frown deepened. The plate that had held his cobbler was empty but for a few streaks of ice cream and pink dabs of cobbler syrup.

"They were here before we were," Nell pointed out.

"But we're here now."

Nell's melancholy nod seemed a weary acknowledgment that Roland's view was typical.

"And if deer eating our plants wasn't bad enough," Roland went on, "allergy season is starting."

"Are you saying, then, that you prefer winter?"

Bettina's gaze, featuring raised brows and a half smile, implied skepticism.

"Of course not," Roland muttered. "The ice can be dangerous." He pushed his shirt cuff back to reveal his watch.

"And I suppose summer is hot." Bettina's gaze intensified.

Roland met her gaze with an intense gaze of his own. "No need to *suppose*." His scornful tone highlighted the word. "Summer *is* hot, and no rational person would—"

He paused to shift his attention to Wilfred, who had moved a few feet closer and was staring attentively at his neighbor's wrist.

"Look at that!" Wilfred exclaimed in genial tones. "I've been enjoying our chat so much that I've completely lost track of the time." He rested both hands on the hearth to boost himself to his feet. "I'm sure all you knitters want to get back to your knitting."

Watching Bettina from across the room, Pamela wasn't sure whether her friend was pleased or disappointed that Roland hadn't had a chance to explain why fall, too, was a season with nothing to recommend it. Wilfred, smiling to himself and chuckling occasionally, was stacking plates and gathering forks and napkins.

As he edged between the sofa and the coffee table and headed toward the kitchen, Holly hopped up, collected as many mugs as she could manage, and trailed after him. Her voice drifted back as they passed through the dining room, repeating her praise of the cobbler.

Pamela took up her knitting. She was at work on a

new project, a sweater for herself. The shape was to be a simple pullover with a loose turtleneck, like a funnel. But the shoulders, upper chest and back, and the turtleneck would be knit in an ombre yarn that contrasted with the solid color employed elsewhere, creating a dramatically patterned yoke. And the sleeves would be edged with several inches of the same ombre yarn.

She and Bettina had visited the fancy yarn shop in Timberley, and Pamela had picked out a deep cobalt blue for the sweater's body, and an ombre that shaded from orange to yellow to chartreuse for the other sections. Bettina had had her own errand at the yarn shop, coming away with patterns and materials to get started on pullovers destined to be Christmas gifts for her grandsons.

Seated in her armchair across from where Pamela sat on the sofa, Bettina was industriously plying her needles, from which a few inches of bright yellow knitting dangled. That yarn, Pamela knew, had been chosen for the younger grandson, Freddy.

In the companion armchair, Nell was equally busy. Departing from her usual projects, do-good works like knitted stuffed animals for the children at the Haversack women's shelter, Nell was knitting a sweater, also destined to be a Christmas gift, for her husband, Harold. Since it was to be a surprise, she had explained that she would be working on it only during Knit and Nibble meetings and only when the group was not meeting at her house. The color was a bright and cheerful Christmas-appropriate red.

After a second trip to the kitchen with the rest of the mugs, Holly had settled once again into her seat on the sofa. Before taking up her knitting again, however, she turned to Roland.

"Are you going to make another one?" she inquired. Roland's project for the previous several meetings had been a very labor-intensive argyle sock.

Roland looked up, his lean face blank with puzzlement, and said, "Another one what?"

"Another sock," Holly responded cheerily. "You've been making a sock. Will there be a pair?"

"Of course there will be a pair." Roland's tone was withering. "This *is* the other one."

"You've gotten so much faster," Bettina observed, "and so much better. I remember when you first joined because your doctor told you to find a relaxing hobby. I don't think any of us thought you would stick with it."

"Of course I stuck with it, and of course I've gotten better." Roland's expression blended amazement with irritation. "Anyone who applies himself to anything will get better."

Holly and Nell responded in chorus, "*Herself*."

Once again, Roland's lean face was blank.

"Applies *herself*," Holly said. "Anyone who applies *herself* . . . or *themselves*. It's not always a *he*."

Roland had lowered his knitting to his lap while this exchange took place. Now his gaze lingered on it as if he was longing to take it up again. He raised his eyes, scanned the faces of the people regarding him from armchairs and sofa, murmured, "Whatever," and launched a new stitch.

Holly resumed her work as well. Her project, Pamela knew, was a knitted bikini, vibrant lilac in color and undertaken with the coming summer in mind. At present, the bikini top—or rather, half of the top—dangled from her needles in the form of a partial triangle. Emulating her friend, Karen had launched a bathing suit project as well, though more sedate in style.

Pamela was content to be entertained by her own thoughts as she knit, but conversations underway around her provided a pleasingly convivial hum. Holly and Karen were reminiscing about the previous summer's outings to the Jersey Shore and proposing dates for the first shore visit of the current year. Across the room, Bettina and Nell were bending toward each other from their respective armchairs and trading notes on garden plans, though Wilfred and Harold were the chief gardeners in each family.

The rhythm of her needles had such a hypnotic effect that Pamela was surprised when she noticed that Holly and Karen had tucked yarn, needles, and in-progress bathing suits into their knitting bags and were climbing to their feet. Roland, on the hearth, was settling his partial sock, with its four double-pointed needles and dangling bobbins, into his elegant briefcase. She looked toward Bettina, who nodded and mouthed the words, "Nine o'clock."

Some minutes later, Pamela and Bettina stood in the doorway of the Frasers' house waving the other four Knit and Nibblers on their way. Merry good nights echoed through the mild air as Roland veered toward the white Porsche that awaited him at the curb, and Holly, Karen, and Nell headed for Holly's orange VW Beetle.

Pamela's house, with its welcoming porch light, beckoned from across the street, but she was happy to accept Bettina's invitation to stay a bit longer.

"I suspect there's some cobbler left," Bettina said

after she had closed the front door and they had retreated a few steps from the doorway. Without waiting
for an answer, she led the way toward the dining room
and the kitchen beyond.

The remains of the cobbler, an appealing vision of
pale, crumbly crust and richly colored fruit, sat on a
scrubbed-pine table in the Frasers' spacious kitchen.
Their house was the oldest on the street, a Dutch Colon-
ial built by the long-ago proprietors of the apple orchard that had surrounded the house. The orchard was
gone, replaced by more houses that were now themselves old, but its memory remained in the name of the
street: Orchard Street.

The Frasers had added the kitchen when they moved
into the house as newlyweds. It featured a cooking area
and an eating area, separated by a high counter, and it
looked out onto the Frasers' patio and backyard through
a pair of sliding-glass doors.

Bettina darted around the counter and collected a
pair of dessert plates from a cupboard and a couple of
forks from a drawer. Stopping by the refrigerator, she
took the container that held what was left of the vanilla
ice cream from the freezer.

"Oh, no—really." Pamela held up both hands in a
gesture of resistance. "I couldn't begin to eat more."

"Well, I could." Bettina scooped a big spoonful of
cobbler onto one of the plates. Then she opened the
container and added an ice cream garnish to the cobbler. Sinking into one of the chairs that flanked the
table, she picked up a fork. "And that's why I will never
be thin," she said as she lifted a bite of cobbler topped
with a dab of ice cream to her mouth.

Pamela *was* thin, and tall, though her simple wardrobe of jeans and casual tops certainly denoted an absence of vanity. Bettina had long since given up trying to interest her friend in the modish looks that her lanky body might have displayed to such advantage. She herself, however, was a confirmed fashionista, whose ensembles—shoes, handbags, and jewelry included—were coordinated to dazzling effect. Her scarlet hair, of a shade that she admitted was not found in nature, made the effect all the more dazzling.

"It's odd," Pamela commented, joining Bettina at the table, though not partaking in the cobbler, "that everyone jumped to the conclusion Ingrid had been murdered. Maybe she was home alone and had a stroke or heart attack or fell and hit her head . . ."

"The door was ajar," Bettina said. "Otherwise the mail carrier wouldn't have thought to look inside—in fact, he wouldn't have been able to look inside. And he told Colette that the living room had been ransacked, as if the killer was looking for something." She paused for another bite before she spoke again, adding, "Maybe the killer had been ransacking upstairs too, but the mail carrier didn't venture farther than the living room."

"That does sound like it was murder." Pamela nodded.

"You know Ingrid Barrick's house, don't you," Bettina said, "since you walk all over the place? It's in the part of Arborville where that street curves down from Arborville Avenue and disrupts the grid system. The lots are strange shapes and sizes, and Ingrid let her yard go completely wild—but some times of the year, it's full of butterflies."

CHAPTER 2

The white eyelet curtains at her bedroom windows were aglow with morning light when Pamela opened her eyes. She was alone in her large bed except for her cats, and at the moment she could feel one of them making its furry way up from the region of her feet. That cat, a black cat named Catrina, emerged from beneath the edge of the turned-back sheet to greet her mistress with a prolonged amber-eyed stare. Catrina was soon joined by her daughter, Ginger, perching beside her on Pamela's chest.

Pamela had not always lived alone. As newlyweds, she and her architect husband, Michael Paterson, had bought their Orchard Street house as a fixer-upper. Working side by side, they had lovingly repaired the damage and decay that it had suffered in the more than a century since it was built. Then their daughter, Penny, was born, and the small family thrived—until Michael

Paterson was killed in a tragic construction-site accident.

The cats were stirring, clearly eager for breakfast. Pamela gently pushed the bedclothes aside, the cats leaped to the floor, and she sat up. They were at the bedroom door before she had slid her feet into her slippers and halfway to the landing as she tied the belt of her robe. Another cat, a Siamese named Precious, met up with the small procession at the bottom of the stairs, and all together the group proceeded to the kitchen.

The first order of the day was to fetch two cans of cat food from the cupboard. Quite aware of what was in progress, the three cats milled about at Pamela's feet, a shifting swirl of black, ginger, and cream-colored fur. Into a large bowl to be shared by Catrina and her daughter went generous spoonfuls of Feline Feast turkey breast, and into a smaller bowl for Precious went a scoop of salmon pâté.

Once the cats were happily crouched over their breakfast, Pamela filled her kettle and set water to boil for coffee. She arranged a paper filter in her carafe's plastic filter cone and ground a few scoops of beans in her coffee grinder. A dash out into the May morning to retrieve the newspaper brought her back to the kitchen just in time to silence the whistling kettle, tip the contents of the coffee grinder into the filter cone, and pour the boiling water over the fragrant grounds.

As the tantalizing aroma of fresh-brewed coffee filled the little kitchen, Pamela slipped the *County Register* from its flimsy plastic sleeve and laid it, unfolded, on the kitchen table. There, on the front page, a bold headline announced, NOTED ARTIST INGRID BARRICK

FOUND MURDERED IN HER ARBORVILLE HOME. The article beneath the headline bore the by-line of Marcy Brewer.

Before sitting down to read the article, however, Pamela returned to the kitchen counter. There, she slipped a slice of whole-grain bread into her toaster. While the toaster did its work, she took a cup, saucer, and small plate from the cupboard where she kept her wedding china. There was no point, Pamela believed, in having pretty things if one only brought them out on grand occasions. In her view, it was on ordinary days that a person most appreciated the special taste of coffee sipped from a china cup or toast nibbled from a china plate.

Then, with a steaming cup of coffee and a piece of buttered toast before her, Pamela scanned the article about Ingrid Barrick. In essence, the story was what Bettina had already reported—the mail carrier finding the door ajar and investigating to find Ingrid Barrick, age sixty-two, dead on the floor and the room ransacked. Marcy Brewer noted, however, that given the circumstances, the police believed Ingrid's death was due to a break-in gone awry when she unexpectedly walked in on the perpetrator. Marcy Brewer also noted that the exact cause of death wouldn't be known until the medical examiner's work was finished.

Ingrid Barrick, the article concluded, had had a long and varied artistic career focused primarily on the fiber arts. She had lived in the Arborville house for most of her adult life, and she left behind a daughter, Mari Barrick, born during a relationship with the knitwear designer Nestor Flavin.

Pamela browsed through the rest of Part 1 as she finished her toast and coffee. With a fresh cup of coffee at hand, she moved on to the Lifestyle section.

Sometime later, dressed and with her bed made and room tidied, Pamela settled into the desk chair in her office, conveniently situated right across the upstairs hall from her bedroom. As associate editor of *Fiber Craft* magazine, she worked from home most days, starting even before working from home became possible for so many people. Her job was to evaluate articles submitted for publication, copyedit articles chosen for publication, and write the occasional book review. Only now and then did she need to travel into Manhattan for meetings or conferences.

She poked the buttons that would bring her computer to beeping, whirring life and brighten the monitor's screen. Once the icons became visible on that screen, she opened her email program. Not surprisingly, a message from celine.bramley@fibercraft.com waited in her inbox. "Please evaluate these for possible publication in *Fiber Craft*," the message read, "and get your evaluations to me by next Tuesday. I'm sending a book via FedEx for you to review." Lined up across the top of the message were three file names hinting at the articles' topics: "Ancient Espadrilles," "Crocheting Coral," "Doubling Up."

She was just debating which article promised the most interesting read when the faint sound of the doorbell's chime echoed from downstairs. En route to respond, she glanced toward the front door from the landing and recognized her visitor. Pamela's front door, original to the house, featured a large oval window. Years ago, Michael had stripped many layers of paint from the door to reveal its natural oak surface, and Pamela had sewn a lace curtain to stretch over the window. Now, through that curtain, she could see a female figure topped by a pouf of bright scarlet hair.

She continued her descent and opened the door to greet Bettina, who stepped over the threshold bearing a white cardboard bakery box bound with string.

"I've been with Clayborn," Bettina said as she handed the box to Pamela.

The statement, Pamela knew, served as explanation for the bakery box. Arborville's police department was less than half a block from the Co-Op Grocery, whose bakery department kept Arborville's sweet tooth well satisfied.

Bettina had dressed for her meeting with Detective Clayborn in a mid-calf-length sheath, fashioned from a pink-and-white-checked linen perfect for a sunny May morning. She had accessorized it with a bold necklace and matching earrings in green jade, and on her feet were dainty kitten heels in a similar shade of green. A green handbag completed the look.

"I suspect I know what's in here." Pamela tipped her head toward the bakery box. "I *did* just finish breakfast, but . . ."

Bettina interrupted with a laugh. "I know what you consider breakfast—one piece of toast with hardly any butter, and a few cups of black coffee."

She took a few steps across the thrift-shop Persian carpet that hid most of the entry's worn parquet, and

Catrina looked up from her nap in the patch of sunlight that appeared on the carpet every sunny morning.

"Speaking of coffee," she went on. "Is there any left?"

"I could make some." Pamela led the way through the kitchen doorway.

Five minutes later, the aroma of fresh-brewed coffee once again filled the little kitchen. Two cups of coffee had been poured, and two small wedding-china plates waited, one on either side of the kitchen table, for the string on the bakery box to be loosened and the flap folded back. Seated in her accustomed chair, Bettina was sweetening her coffee with sugar spooned from Pamela's cut-glass sugar bowl. After a vigorous stir, she reached for the matching cream pitcher and added a substantial dollop of heavy cream.

Only when the contents of her cup had reached the pale mocha hue she sought did she raise the cup to her lips. After a sip, she returned the cup to its rose-garlanded saucer with a print of bright pink lipstick marking its rim.

"Perfect," she declared, and she leaned forward and tugged at the tails of the string bow atop the bakery box. When the flap was folded back, a large square of crumb cake divided into four smaller pieces was re-vealed. A layer of buttery crumb, pale cinnamon in color, rumpled its top, and its sides were a lemony gold.

Bettina lifted one of the pieces onto each plate. Appreciative silence followed, punctuated by the click-

ing of fork tines against china and hums of contentment. The Co-Op's crumb cake never failed to please,
Pamela reflected. The cake itself was moist and tender,
with a hint of the lemon that its color implied, and the
topping was luxuriously rich.

After a few sips of coffee that offered a pleasingly
bitter contrast to the sweet crumb cake, Pamela focused her attention on Bettina.

"Did Detective Clayborn add anything to what
Marcy Brewer's article in the *Register* reported?" she
inquired.

"He didn't tell her everything." A satisfied smile
accompanied the response. "Or maybe"—the smile
persisted—"he didn't know as much when he talked to
her yesterday as when he talked to me this morning."
The smile faded. "Of course, by the time the *Advocate*
comes out on Friday, the whole story will be old news."

The fact that Marcy Brewer wrote for the county's
daily paper and she herself wrote for Arborville's
weekly was a constant source of irritation for Bettina—
all the more so in that even those who bothered to collect the *Advocate* from their driveways described it
laughingly as containing "all the news that fits."

"What didn't he tell her that he told you?" Pamela
set her coffee cup back on its saucer to signal her attentiveness.

"He confirmed that it seems to be a break-in gone
awry," Bettina said, "but here's the extra thing: the timing. The state of Ingrid's body at ten a.m., when the
mail carrier found her, indicated that she had been
dead at least eight hours. A neighbor saw lights still on
in the house at about eleven Monday night, and a break-

in would likely happen after the house was dark. So that means she was killed around midnight or later."

They were interrupted then by a soft meow. Catrina stood in the doorway gazing at Bettina.

"What is it?" Bettina and Pamela asked in chorus.

With a feline version of a graceful pirouette, Catrina retreated back across the threshold but immediately glanced over her shoulder to focus on Bettina.

"You want me to follow you?" Bettina asked, placing a hand on the table to boost herself from her chair. Her feet in their dainty green heels made their way across the black-and-white tiles of the checkerboard floor.

A moment later she called from the entry. "It's my phone, in my handbag. Catrina heard it."

Pamela interspersed forkfuls of crumb cake with sips of coffee as Bettina's voice drifted in from the entry, by turns cordial, sympathetic, and surprised.

"Colette Dalrymple," Bettina announced when she returned, "Ingrid's neighbor to the east. She's the person who called the *Advocate* after the mail carrier discovered Ingrid's body."

"Complaining about being pestered by Marcy Brewer for an interview?" Pamela asked.

"No. Something else. Something interesting." Bettina paused for a fortifying bite of crumb cake and a swallow of coffee before going on. When she did, it was to say, "Colette—or rather, Coco, as she prefers to be called—doesn't believe the explanation for Ingrid's death is a break-in gone awry."

"Natural causes?" Pamela shrugged. "What about the ransacking?"

"She thinks the intruder was bent on murder and that Ingrid was targeted specifically."

Pamela's fork sat forgotten on her plate. "Why?" she inquired.

"Ingrid was afraid of someone"—Bettina nodded grimly—"and . . . *Coco* . . . wants to show me the evidence. I'm to come over after lunch." She winked at Pamela. "You can come too, but we're not walking."

Coco's house was an old wood-frame house, like Pamela's and like so many houses in Arborville. It was situated just where Serpentine Way began to curve, and so, though the house faced the street and Ingrid's house next to it faced the street, the two houses were not parallel with each other and their yards were wedge-shaped, widening toward the back.

Pamela and Bettina climbed the steps to the rambling porch. In the center of a tarnished brass plate mounted on the door frame was a yellowed plastic doorbell. Bettina pressed it with a manicured fingertip, and a chime echoed behind the heavy wooden door. When no footsteps sounded within and the door remained closed, she pressed again, and again.

"Coco said to come after lunch." Bettina looked at Pamela. "It *is* after lunch. And she seemed so eager to talk to me."

She pressed the doorbell once again. Again, there was no response, and they started down the steps. But as they were nearing Bettina's car, a voice trailed after them, calling "Bettina, Bettina!" They turned to see a barefoot woman wrapped in a flowing, kimono-style robe emerging from around the side of the house. "It's me," the woman added, "Coco."

She caught up to them, panting. A few strands of her wild salt-and-pepper hair clung to her perspiring face. "I was sunbathing in the back, *au naturel*. Such a perfect day—why not? I heard your car, but I had to run inside and grab this robe. Not sure why people are so obsessed with clothes." She paused to fasten the robe's belt. "Anyway, come inside, and I'll make some tea."

Coco led them around the side of the house and up a half flight of steps to a small porch, where a door stood open. She ushered them through the door and into a kitchen whose layout and appliances gave it a vintage appearance.

Sensing that her guests were staring, Coco said, "My parents never got around to updating it. Now they're gone, and it's serviceable. People are too hung up on having new stuff anyway." She pointed to a simple wooden table. "Please sit."

She herself stepped over to the counter, filled a battered kettle at the sink, and set it on the stove. Once the burner was alight beneath it, she vanished through a doorway, only to return in a few moments with a small covered basket, still barefoot. She set the basket on the table, declared, "Here's the evidence," and returned to the counter. There, as steam began to rise from the kettle's spout, she opened a cupboard and extracted three mismatched mugs.

"Tea choices," Coco announced. "Chamomile, ginger, peppermint, hibiscus, or echinacea. Speak up."

"Whatever you prefer," Bettina responded distractedly. She seemed mesmerized by the covered basket, and Pamela suspected she'd have drunk anything put in front of her—even plain black coffee—with little reaction to its taste.

Coco was chattering happily as she worked at the counter, sifting loose tea into a pottery teapot of Asian design. "Ingrid loved my tea," she said. "She was here almost every day, sitting right where you're sitting, Bettina. I'm a very artistic person, and I know Ingrid could sense that about me. It made us very close."

She tipped the kettle over the teapot, releasing a pleasant, spicy aroma. "Steeping, steeping," she murmured, and soon mugs appeared before Pamela and Bettina. Coco joined them with her own mug and pulled the basket toward her.

"Taste your tea," she whispered, as if that was a prerequisite for learning what the basket contained.

Pamela and Bettina obediently took sips, small sips because the tea was very hot.

"Hibiscus," Coco said. "Nice, isn't it?"

The tea tasted the way it smelled, pleasant and spicy, not at all disagreeable.

"Ingrid had been preoccupied lately," Coco explained as her hands hovered over the basket's cover. "And she was constantly drawing, doodling on any surface at hand."

She lifted the cover. "I'm always getting those little notepads that charities send around, even charities I've never donated to." A nod toward a stack of notepads on a section of counter next to the refrigerator illustrated that point. Coco slid the basket toward Bettina, and Pamela leaned over for a look inside.

CHAPTER 3

What she saw was a page torn from a notepad with a holiday theme, featuring holly borders and sprigs of mistletoe in the upper corners. She recognized the design because the very same charitable organization had sent their notepads to her the previous winter. But in the space left for the sort of notes that one commits to a notepad was a large bee.

"I kept the doodles because they were so artistic," Coco explained, reaching into the basket and spreading a handful of the little pages out on the table. "Think of Picasso's doodles—worth so much money now, though I'm not the kind of person who'd trade an artist's doodles for money."

"Bees!" Coco made a dramatic gesture. "So many bees! Lately bees were all she had on her mind. But look, from before—" She shuffled through the pages scattered on the table to point out sketches of butterflies, flowers, a teapot, a cat—all rendered with simple, confident lines.

"She even drew me!" Coco dug around in the basket and came up with a slightly larger sheet of paper.

The likeness was remarkable. Ingrid had captured the lively gaze and easy smile that made Coco's undistinguished features appealing, and the wild hair that straggled halfway to her waist made her seem a figure of romance. After studying that image and making a flattering comment, Pamela sorted out a few pages featuring drawings of butterflies.

"Monarchs," Coco said. "Too bad they're just doodles and not in color. Ingrid's yard is gorgeous when the monarchs come around, but they're not here yet." As Pamela sorted out more butterfly drawings, Coco went on. "Pollinators. Ingrid loved butterflies, bees not so much, but her yard was intended to encourage pollinators of all sorts. You probably knew about it, even before her house became a crime scene, because lots of people in town think everybody needs a manicured lawn, and they complained about Ingrid's yard on the listserv."

After a bit more conversation and rummaging through the doodles, Bettina thanked Coco for her hospitality and the chance to examine Ingrid's doodles.

"Bees, though. That's the important thing." Coco rose from her chair. "Lately it was all bees, and she seemed worried, different, and that's why I think she was murdered. Someone was after her, and she knew it."

Coco escorted them to the front door, and they all stepped out on the porch together. Looking to the west, they could see the yellow tape that marked off Ingrid's house and yard as a crime scene. They could also see butterflies, fluttery white ones, not too large, hovering around spiky shoots bristling with tiny lavender blossoms.

The bright crime-scene tape, in fact, nearly merged into the swirl of color offered by Ingrid's yard. Low, bushy verbena were thickly dotted with small blooms in shades of red, violet, and orange, and poppies rose on delicate stems, their vivid petals contrasting with their dark centers.

"It's just getting started," Coco said. "June, July, August, well into the fall—everything's in flower, including the goldenrod."

"What will happen to it," Bettina inquired, "with Ingrid gone?"

"Someone will buy the house?" Coco shrugged. "Get rid of the wild butterfly garden and put in a lawn?"

"That would be a shame." Bettina sighed. "I wish I'd done an article about the butterfly garden for the *Advocate* while Ingrid was still alive. It's too close to her death now, and by the time it isn't too close, the house's new owner might have replaced all the pollinator plants with a lawn."

"I know one person who wouldn't mind that." Coco's head dipped forward, and her wild hair swayed. "Dorcas Sprain"—she nodded again—"on the other side of Ingrid's house." She turned back to Bettina. "Dorcas was furious about the goldenrod. She thought it was ragweed, and she hated the other things too. She had been hounding Ingrid to get rid of the pollinator plants before the allergy season gets going in earnest."

* * *

"Ingrid didn't die from a bee sting," Bettina remarked to Pamela after Coco had gone inside and they were heading toward the curb, where Bettina's faithful Toyota Corolla waited. "At least I don't think so."

"She *did* seem to have bees on her mind, though."

Neither of them spoke as the Toyota cruised past Ingrid's house and down to County Road, though it was clear that Bettina was thinking. At County Road, a left turn took them to Orchard Street, and another left turn took them home. Only as she was pulling up next to Wilfred's ancient but lovingly cared-for Mercedes did Bettina give voice to her thoughts.

"In Ingrid's mind, the bee could have symbolized someone," she said. "The someone would have had to be someone she'd been in contact with lately, maybe someone she hadn't been in touch with for a while but who had reappeared."

"Or maybe Dorcas Sprain," Pamela suggested, "someone who had been quiet all winter, but now that things are blooming again, resumed her anti-ragweed crusade and became a pest."

"And decided to solve the problem by killing Ingrid?" Bettina twisted the key to cut off the engine and faced Pamela as the car became quiet. "That seems extreme."

"They could have argued. And maybe Dorcas pushed Ingrid, and she fell and struck her head on something."

"The medical examiner's report should be available soon," Bettina said. "It will be interesting to know what actually caused her death."

They pressed down on their door handles in unison and soon were standing on the asphalt of the Frasers' driveway.

"What will you do now?" Bettina asked.

"Walk up to the Co-Op. I'm out of some things."

Bettina laughed. "Why didn't you say something? We could have gone together in my car."

"You don't cook anymore," Pamela said. "Remember? Wilfred took over when he retired."

"Blunt-force trauma," Bettina murmured the next morning, revisiting a topic that Pamela thought they had already exhausted. The *Register* had reported the medical examiner's verdict on the cause of Ingrid's death, and Bettina had paid Pamela an early visit to discuss that verdict in detail. Now she and Pamela were sitting at a small metal table on Pamela's expansive front porch, taking their last few sips of coffee. The wedding-china plates that had held the two pieces of crumb cake left from the previous day were bare except for traces of the buttery topping.

"No clear sense of a weapon," Bettina went on, "but the article mentioned that she fell near her fireplace and her head could have struck the hearth—which doesn't contradict your idea that Dorcas Sprain, or someone, pushed her during an argument."

Pamela and Bettina had been all over this once. Bettina had obviously been pondering the *Register* article silently and now seemed inclined to ponder it aloud. Pamela was gazing at the view of pleasant lawns and flowering shrubs as she enjoyed the gentle breezes that the porch's wide span invited. She was also wondering what could be happening at the church next door on an ordinary Thursday to explain the many cars entering its parking lot or nosing into spaces at the curb.

"*Pamela!*" Bettina rapped on the table when Pamela didn't respond. Startled, Pamela turned to face her friend. "Your idea about Dorcas Sprain, or someone else, pushing her doesn't explain the ransacking."

"Ummm?"

"If Dorcas Sprain, or someone, showed up to argue with Ingrid about ragweed, or something, why would they ransack the house?" Bettina stared across the little table with the satisfied expression of a person convinced that a debate has been won.

It was Pamela's turn to ponder, and she fingered the crease she felt forming between her brows. "Easy," she said after a moment. "To make Ingrid's death appear to be the result of a break-in gone awry, so the police wouldn't look for motives among people who knew her. That could explain the ransacking no matter who the killer was, as well as the fact that the front door was left open."

"Maybe, maybe." Bettina nodded, but her squint and tight half smile made it clear she wasn't convinced. Perhaps at last weary of the topic, however, she changed the subject. "What on earth is going on at the church with all these cars?" she inquired, half-rising to peer down the street. "And all these people?"

A few people were even beginning to arrive on foot, some dressed as if they were attending a somber event, others in jeans, even faded and tattered jeans, or outfits that seemed assembled from forays to thrift shops.

"Bettina . . ." Pamela had risen completely from her chair, had advanced to the porch railing, and was now leaning out as far as she could. "We should have guessed. It's a funeral."

"And people are coming in jeans?" Bettina's usual funeral garb was a black crêpe coatdress accessorized with pearls.

"A hearse is just on its way up from County Road." Pamela sat back down. "It's probably Ingrid's funeral. Who else has died lately in Arborville? You'd know from the *Advocate*, wouldn't you?"

As they watched, the hearse came into view, resembling an elongated SUV with curtains at its back windows. It pulled into a spot obviously saved for it, directly in front of the church, and both side doors opened. From each stepped a man in a discreet black suit. The men proceeded around to the squared-off rear of the hearse, lowered the back door, and extracted a large flower arrangement seemingly assembled from wilder blooms than the usual florist's production.

A slate path led to the church's stone steps, at the top of which heavy wooden doors stood open. One of the men carried the flower arrangement through the doorway while the other returned to the hearse. A small group had begun to assemble on the sidewalk near the hearse, men and women, dressed with varying degrees of formality.

These were the pallbearers, it appeared, as the man who had attended to the flowers rejoined the other man, and guided by four hands, a shelf bearing a simple wood coffin slid into view. The pallbearers arranged themselves three to a side and took hold of the bars along the sides of the coffin.

Pamela and Bettina, however, did not monitor its progress along the slate path and up the stone steps. A voice, rather cheerful given the circumstances, had hailed them from up the street. It took Pamela a moment to recognize the voice's owner, dressed as she was in something other than a robe, wearing shoes, and with her hair tamed into a long side-braid that trailed over her shoulder.

Calling "It's me, Coco!" she advanced up Pamela's front walk, trailed by a tall, slender—almost gawky—man with shaggy gray hair. "And this is Simon, Simon Malbourne," she added when she reached the bottom of the porch steps. The man bowed. He was wearing seriously distressed jeans, Birkenstock sandals, and a leather jerkin with no shirt beneath it.

"You're not coming to Ingrid's funeral?" Coco inquired. "Everyone's welcome."

"We didn't know . . ." Pamela stood and moved to the top of the steps.

"We just now noticed the hearse." Bettina stood too. "And we're certainly not dressed for a funeral."

She looked down at her outfit, which, in fact, was notably more presentable than Coco's gauzy ankle-length skirt paired with a Hawaiian-print shirt and scuffed Birkenstocks. The outfit Bettina had chosen for her morning visit to Pamela involved a sleeveless top in crisp yellow linen, matching wide-legged trousers, orange flats, and earrings of Murano glass swirled with citrusy hues.

"Come on, come on," Coco urged, beckoning.

Pamela and Bettina looked at each other and shrugged. Each picked up her own cup, saucer, and plate. No more than a few minutes later, with cups, saucers, and plates returned to the kitchen, Pamela's purse over her shoulder, and the house locked, they joined Coco and Simon and set off on the brief journey to the church next door.

The sidewalk didn't allow for four people walking abreast, and Coco seemed eager to chat with Bettina. Pamela found herself paired with Simon, and overhearing as Coco eagerly explained Simon's presence. His parents owned the house across the street from her, she said, and he'd grown up there. His parents had now retired to Florida, and he'd been coming down from Connecticut on and off to clear out what they'd left behind and handle the house's sale.

When they reached the church steps, Coco paused and turned slightly so she could address both Bettina and Pamela. "Some of Ingrid's friends are hosting a celebration of her life after the funeral," she said. "Why don't you two come along with Simon and me? It's in Haversack. Simon will drive, and we'll leave right from the cemetery."

Simon's vehicle proved to be an aged SUV nearly as long and boxy as the hearse that had carried Ingrid's coffin to her grave. It was useful, he explained, given the chores involved in making his parents' house saleable—dropping off clothes and household items at donation centers, as well as transporting furniture and other items back to his own house in Connecticut.

Once the brief graveside ceremony at the cemetery had concluded, Pamela and Bettina joined the other mourners straggling back to the gravel parking lot and followed Simon and Coco to Simon's car.

The cemetery was spread out along a cliff overlooking the Hudson River. The back side of the cliff sloped down to Arborville Avenue, and the route that led to Haversack meandered down that slope, crossing Arborville Avenue and then County Road, veering to the right, and then crossing the much-smaller river that had given Haversack its name.

CHAPTER 4

The venue chosen for the celebration of life proved to be located in a section of Haversack zoned for light industry. Simon steered the SUV past low, flat-roofed buildings, nondescript in color and design, and with signage indicating what was manufactured within and/or by whom. Blank, curtainless windows looked out on crowded parking lots or patchy grass uninterrupted by sidewalks.

The SUV slowed as Simon approached a building lacking a sign, and he turned in when he came to a driveway. This building's lot held fewer vehicles than the other lots, but more various. Cars, vans, pickup trucks, and motorcycles were ranged haphazardly over the rutted asphalt.

"Around the back," Coco instructed. "Dell said there's a door next to the loading dock."

The back of the building was even more featureless

than the front, but the door, a faded shade of brown, was ajar as if in welcome. Simon parked the SUV at the lot's edge—painted lines marking spots had long since worn away—and they all proceeded toward the door.

Festive sounds reached them even before they stepped inside, and the sounds guided them down a dim hall-way past closed doors until they reached a door that gaped open. Inside, against a background of mellow jazz, laughter and chatter rose from a crowd of people milling among huge enigmatic objects assembled from what looked like railroad ties.

In the midst of the objects—sculptures, Pamela sup-posed, though they hadn't actually been sculpted—stood a long table covered with a colorful cloth. A cluster of plastic cups and a half-gallon jug of red wine occupied one end of the table, and at the other end was a stack of pizza boxes. In the middle of the table, one pizza box sat open, with one slice remaining. All that was left of the missing seven slices were the grease spots they'd left on the box's cardboard bottom.

"Time to start on the next box," a bearded man in a denim work shirt declared as he picked up the remain-ing slice, folded it in half lengthwise, and aimed the pointed end toward his mouth. His companion stowed the now-empty box under the table and set the top box from the stack in its place.

Judging by their clothing and grooming styles, many people in attendance had moved in the same artistic circles as Ingrid, while others were her friends from Arborville. Like was clustered with like, as tattooed people in jeans communed with other tattooed people in jeans, and people in sedate, funeral-appropriate outfits—suits even—communed with other people in sedate, funeral-appropriate outfits.

"Coco! Coco!" A voice rang out above the hubbub, and a middle-aged woman in a summery cotton dress emerged from a group of Arborvillians. Simon had drifted off toward the end of the table that held the wine jug, and introductions, which involved only Pamela and Bettina being presented to Rose Drury and vice versa, went quickly.

Rose recognized Bettina from events that Bettina had covered for the *Advocate*, and conversation between the two of them flowed easily, so easily that Coco soon followed Simon to the refreshment table.

"Not the typical after-funeral reception, is it?" Rose observed when Coco was out of earshot.

"I guess this is an artist's studio?" Bettina tipped her head toward the nearest assemblage.

"The whole building is artists' studios now," Rose said. "Cheap rent is the appeal. Somebody used to make . . . widgets, or something . . . here, but they moved. Ingrid told me all about it." Rose waved as another Arborvillian passed by. "I got to know Ingrid just by happenstance because of her interest in gardening— though I know some of her neighbors didn't think of her wild yard as a garden." Rose sighed. "Ingrid was a free spirit, but a lovely person, and such a talented artist. She really pushed the boundaries of what can be done with yarn."

"Ingrid had a lot of friends," Pamela observed.

The room had become even more crowded, and two more large jugs of wine had appeared on the refreshment table. The noise level was such that, had the three women not been standing in a tight huddle, conversation would have been impossible. The room throbbed with the hum of many voices, punctuated by occasional shouts or bellows of laughter, some showing the effects of the free-flowing wine.

Bettina and Rose were now discussing the community gardens, and the gardener who had provided the Frasers with a season's supply of rhubarb. Rose had just declared herself seriously envious of Bettina's good fortune in having a husband who baked, when she happened to glance past Bettina into the surging crowd.

"Oops," she commented with a resigned twist of the lips, "I've got to get going."

The Arborvillian at whom Rose had waved earlier, a middle-aged woman dressed in a tan skirt suit, was approaching. Rose introduced her as Sharon Norris and explained that they had arrived together and now Sharon was wanting to go home.

"I wouldn't mind leaving too," Bettina commented after they had gone on their way, "but Coco and Simon look like they're having fun."

She pointed toward the end of the refreshment table that held the wine jugs. Simon had just hefted one of the jugs to refill Coco's plastic cup as two other women held out their cups too. All of them seemed part of a large and boisterous group lingering near the wine supply.

"I'd eat a piece of pizza, though." Bettina's gaze shifted to the other end of the table, where a second stack of pizza boxes had appeared next to a few boxes remaining from earlier.

She led the way, detouring around two of the huge wooden assemblages. One of them, with a nose-like protuberance surmounted by a shelf like a jutting brow, could have been a wooden version of a monumental Easter Island head. At the refreshment table, as before, an open pizza box invited people to help themselves. Two pieces remained, themselves quite inviting—each edged with a puffy ridge of golden-brown crust, layered with mozzarella-streaked tomato sauce, and dotted with lustrous rounds of pepperoni.

"No problem, ladies. There's plenty more," said a man wearing a jaunty fedora.

Bettina and Pamela each took a piece. The man slipped the empty box under the table and set a box from the smaller stack in its place. Then he flipped the box's lid back to release an aroma that combined tomato, garlic, and olive oil with the seductive lure of fresh-baked yeasty dough. Attracted by the sight of a whole new pizza, several people edged closer to the table, and Pamela and Bettina backed off to the side.

Bettina kept backing sideways and Pamela followed until they found themselves standing in the shadow of one of the largest assemblages, which was apparently still in progress to judge by the stack of railroad ties piled near it. This corner of the room, in fact, seemed to be the area in which the artist who rented the studio did his actual work. A tall folding screen had been deployed behind the railroad ties, perhaps to hide tools and other materials when he wasn't actively engaged in a project.

"As Wilfred would say, when in Rome . . ." Bettina commented. She folded her pizza slice lengthwise, gingerly, as if aware of the threat the tomato sauce posed to the yellow linen of her outfit. Then, holding the folded slice at the crust end, which was wider, she aimed the narrow end toward her mouth. The practice of eating pizza without a plate or utensils was well-accepted in Arborville and its environs, especially given the many local pizzerias where pizza was available one slice at a time, to be eaten on the go.

"It's good," she reported after the first bite, but Pamela had discovered that for herself, so the recommendation was hardly needed.

They ate in silence, at least relative silence, given that they'd moved away from the party's main hub—the refreshment table. But as she nibbled her way toward the crusty edge of her slice, Pamela became aware of voices coming from behind the tall screen. She nudged Bettina, who finished chewing, swallowed, and mouthed, "I hear it too."

"You can't forbid me!" The voice was masculine, tense, and the tone was incredulous.

"You'd be wise not to pursue it," came another masculine voice, mild but somehow threatening.

"I intend to pursue it because I've been working on it for a long time, and I'm not going to abandon it now." A hint of an accent—German? Scandinavian?—made the words seem chosen with special precision.

"I'm not telling you to abandon it." The mild voice sounded impatient. "I'm just telling you that you'd better leave that part out."

"I'd *better*?" Laughter. "I don't like it when people tell me that I'd better do something." More laughter. "And besides, you've never explained why that part shouldn't go in the book. It was an important stage in her artistic development."

"I loved her. Her memory deserves respect . . ."

"And including that part in the book is disrespectful to her memory, how?" The tone was even more incredulous.

"You'd be wise not to pursue it."

"Are we going to start back there again? I'm game. I intend to pursue it because I've been working on it for a long time, and I'm not going to abandon it now. And now you're supposed to say—"

The screen trembled as if it was about to fall over, and Pamela and Bettina quickly retreated toward the more crowded part of the room. Coco caught sight of them and darted through the crush of people, arriving at Bettina's side to say, "Having fun?"

"The pizza's great," Bettina responded. "Are you and Simon about ready to leave?"

"Oh, he's . . ." Coco scanned the room. "He's over there by that . . . thing . . . like a lighthouse with a head." Her gaze remained fixed on him for a few moments, then it shifted and she murmured, "Dorcas? I didn't know she was here."

Pamela tilted her head to follow the new direction of Coco's gaze. An imposing woman who appeared to be in her seventies was advancing toward them.

"She's probably here to celebrate Ingrid's death, not her life," Coco whispered, grinning mischievously. "I'll bet she's just itching to see the last of that butterfly garden."

Dorcas, like many of the other attendees, was wearing jeans, but hers were clean and appeared even to have been pressed. Tucked into them was a tidy white shirt, and her hair, dark brown dusted with gray, was trimmed in a precise bob, including bangs.

"*Itching*," she intoned, apparently having heard Coco's whispered comment. "Itching is nothing to grin about, as you'd know if you had an ounce of empathy."

"I'm sorry." Coco raised her fingers to her lips. "That was unkind of me." She was silent for a moment, blinking, before she reached out to nudge Bettina forward. "Dorcas Sprain, meet Bettina Fraser, from the *Advocate*, and her friend Pamela Paterson." Pamela got a nudge too.

The change of subject worked. Dorcas offered her hand and told Bettina how much she looked forward to the *Advocate* every Friday. Focusing on Coco again, she said, "I won't be sorry to see that yard of Ingrid's neatened up, I can tell you that. The butterflies are kind of pretty, but the bees!" She shuddered. "So very many bees, pollinating things, and then the flowers drop seeds, and it all goes on and on and on, not to mention that bees can be dangerous for people who are allergic to bee stings, which I'm not, thank goodness." She sneezed and fumbled a tissue from her jeans pocket.

Perhaps thinking that another change of subject was in order, Bettina remarked, "I suppose the house will be sold, eventually . . ."

"Ingrid's daughter will handle it, I expect." Dorcas nodded in a way that made her neat bob bounce. "And that Realtor, Vivian whatshername, will come sniffing around for a listing. Those details fall to the children so often, legal details, the house sale, clean-outs— sometimes the parents were hoarders—and now the

Malbourne house will be changing hands too, and that Malbourne boy—Buzz, we called him—in my mind, he'll always be a boy, working so hard, with his parents already down in Florida."

She paused, panting a bit, and scanned the room. "Rose Drury was here somewhere, and I want to catch her before she leaves—though I can always talk to her in Arborville, of course. It's just that—oop, there she is!"

"I was always glad Ingrid lived between Dorcas and me," Coco observed as Dorcas strode away, edging between clusters of chatting people. "If I'd been a more conveniently located ear, I don't know what I would have done. Moved, maybe."

Bettina lifted her wrist to consult the pretty face of her bracelet watch. The motion was discreet, but Coco noticed.

"You're wanting to leave," she said, "and I wouldn't mind getting back to Arborville either."

People were beginning to drift toward the door, thinning the crowd and making it easier to see who was where, and the mellow jazz that had provided the soundtrack for the event had been silenced. The refreshment table was visible from where they stood, and all that remained on it were five empty wine jugs and one open pizza box, while the floor beneath it was piled with empty pizza boxes. A young woman in a striped T-shirt was roaming around with an open garbage bag inviting people to deposit their plastic cups. She was also collecting the occasional cup from various assemblages, where cups had been lodged in crevices or perched on ledges or stands.

Pamela and Bettina, anticipating that a reunited

Coco and Simon would soon be joining them, began to move toward the door as well. In doing so, they fell into step with an older man whose dapper appearance made him stand out among the bohemians and suburbanites. His steel-gray hair, thick and precisely trimmed, swept back from his forehead in a smooth wave. He was wearing a cream-colored linen suit set off by a pale peach shirt and a paisley bow tie in the same tones.

"Celebrations of life are a thing now, I guess," he remarked to Bettina, perhaps recognizing a fellow fashionista.

"Did you know Ingrid well?" Bettina replied, always happy to respond to social overtures.

"Yes," the man said. "I did know her well."

They were nearing the doorway, which was quite narrow, and a small bottleneck had developed there. Bettina and the man stepped to the side. Pamela joined them, but she turned back toward the room to search for Coco and Simon. As she listened to Bettina and the man converse, it struck her that his voice sounded familiar—*very* familiar, like a voice she had recently heard. She glanced back to study the man.

Could this well-dressed man, so courtly in his manner, be one of the men whose voices had emerged from behind the screen in the corner of the room as she and Bettina ate their pizza?

"Oh, hey! Here you are!" Coco was surging toward them, pulling Simon along behind her. "And I see you've met Nestor!" she announced when she came to a halt.

"Nestor Flavin," the dapper man said with a half bow.

"Bettina Fraser." Bettina extended a graceful hand for a handshake.

"Pamela Paterson." Pamela extended her hand too.

The bottleneck eased, and soon Pamela and Bettina were following Coco and Simon across the asphalt to Simon's car. Nestor Flavin had hurried off in a different direction.

"How do you know Nestor?" Bettina asked as Coco lagged behind and Simon sped up.

"He was a neighbor ages ago," Coco said, "right there on Serpentine Way. He and Ingrid were housemates, and more. It's too bad he took off so fast. I'd have loved to catch up."

Twenty minutes later, Simon turned off County Road onto Orchard Street, and very soon Pamela and Bettina were standing on the sidewalk in front of Pamela's house.

"Ingrid has a daughter," Pamela said. "Mari. The article in the *Register* mentioned her."

Bettina nodded and her earrings swayed. "I wonder where she was today."

Pamela crossed the street to her own house, noting as she approached that a bulky envelope waited on her porch. Seeing the purple and orange FedEx logo, she realized that the book she was to review for *Fiber Craft* had arrived. She stooped for the parcel, stood to collect her mail, and unlocked her door.

All three cats came padding into the entry to greet her, puzzled perhaps that her sudden exit that morning had led to such a long absence. May days seemed endlessly bright, but when she checked her watch, she saw it was after four o'clock. The nutritive possibilities of the pizza slice eaten at the celebration of life had long since been exhausted, and an early dinner would be welcome.

First, though, she perched on the chair that was the entry's main piece of furniture and peeled back the envelope's flap. The book she extracted was called *Stitches in Time: What Garments from the Past Can Tell Us That History Can't*, and its author was Lynne Ralston, a professor of history at a college in Toronto.

Despite being hungry, she opened the book and was soon engrossed in its first chapter. That chapter focused on a portrait of a British noblewoman, Elizabeth Laidlaw, who was born in the late sixteenth century. The portrait, reproduced in the book, showed the woman in an elaborate gown sewn from finely textured brocade. The gown featured voluminous sleeves, a boned bodice narrowing to an inverted V, and a stiff, lace-edged collar that fanned out behind her carefully coiffed head.

What made the portrait significant from the point of view of the author was that the very gown depicted in the portrait had been preserved through the intervening centuries. "For this," the author commented, "we have to thank the inherited hoarding tendencies of many generations of Laidlaws." The gown was known to be the gown worn by Elizabeth in the portrait because it had been donated to the Victoria and Albert Museum by a descendant, and careful examination of both the gown and the portrait revealed the fabric was identical.

What the gown had to tell us that history could not, the author went on to say, was that even the very wealthy were loath to discard perfectly good clothing just because fashions changed. In an era before industrialization, cloth was made by hand, from the spinning of the thread to the weaving, and it was not to be wasted. She reminded her readers that wills from earlier eras often included clothes among the valuables being bequeathed.

Having had the opportunity to examine the gown on a research trip to England, the author noted differences between the version depicted in the portrait and the version that had survived. The lace-edged collar had vanished—perhaps it had always been detachable— and the neckline of the bodice had been modified to the point that the newly styled gown must have revealed a rather daring décolletage. The voluminous sleeves had been shortened to reach just below the elbow, and a flounce of lace had been added. The gown might even have been passed from Elizabeth to a younger relative who wore it into the mid-1660s and beyond.

The cats had hurried to the kitchen once they had greeted their mistress. Now Catrina and Ginger ventured once again into the entry and stationed themselves at Pamela's feet, clearly ready for their dinner. She used a scrap of paper from the FedEx envelope to mark the page where she had left off reading, set the book aside, and rose.

Pamela had come home from the Co-Op the previous day with an organic chicken, among other things, and she'd roasted it with rosemary from the pot on her back porch for dinner. That chicken would now make many more dinners, and as she headed for the kitchen, she was picturing a chicken salad with romaine and a Caesar-type dressing, and fresh-grated Parmesan over all.

Pamela stayed up late reading *Stitches in Time*, fascinated by details that proved the author's point about the insights into history and historical figures to be gained from the study of clothing. Amazingly, among the garments that survived from Renaissance England was a bodice that had belonged to the first Queen Elizabeth. Not only did the bodice reveal her proportions—smaller than one might suppose, given her significance—but it also confirmed that she was, indeed, right-handed. The stiffening of the bodice was cut shorter on the right side, presumably to allow that arm to move more freely.

CHAPTER 5

The next morning, after feeding the cats, Pamela set water to boil for coffee and hurried out to collect the *Register*—and the *Advocate*, given that it was Friday. Back inside, sitting at the kitchen table with coffee and toast at hand and both papers spread out before her, she noted that, with no new developments in the Ingrid Barrick murder case, the *Register* had nothing to report. The *Advocate*, however, devoted nearly its whole front page to the case, offering no details that hadn't already been hashed over in the *Register*, but appearing under Bettina's byline and giving the story a local slant.

Breakfast finished and the newspapers read, Pamela rinsed her dishes at the sink and climbed the stairs to her bedroom. Fifteen minutes later, dressed and with her bed made, she crossed the hall to her office and sat down at her computer. *Stitches in Time* could be read while lounging on the sofa with cats purring nearby, but copyediting work needed to be done in front of a screen. She brought up Celine Bramley's email again and clicked on the first Word attachment listed across the top, "Ancient Espadrilles."

The article's full title was "Ancient Espadrilles: Ten Thousand Years of Fashion Footwear," and it opened with an illustration, a photograph of what looked like the sole of an espadrille that had seen much wear. The first paragraph explained that the object in the photograph was, indeed, the sole of a sandal, but it was nearly ten thousand years old, as confirmed by carbon dating. It had been found in a cave in northern Spain, where the cool and dry atmosphere had preserved it.

Yes, indeed, the author explained, it was constructed just like a modern espadrille sole, from plant fiber braided into rope and coiled into a flat, foot-sized oblong—and not a symmetrical oblong either, but shaped as if part of a pair and intended for the right foot. Trailing strands of rope suggested that braided straps had anchored it to the foot. The classic canvas espadrille upper was still a ways in the future, the author pointed out.

"Interesting, really interesting," Pamela murmured to herself as she continued reading. Some ideas were so obvious—plant fiber rope used for shoe soles—that it wasn't too surprising to realize that they were very old, and that they were still current. The author traced the modern name of the shoe to the Catalan word for a type of grass used in the making of baskets and shoe soles. Then he went on to make the obvious connection between this ancient cave find and the continuing manufacture and popularity of espadrilles, including many photographs of modern variations on the theme, including wedge-heeled espadrilles.

Pamela sighed. The author could have done so much more with the fiber craft tie-in, but as it was, he had focused on the fashion aspect, to the point that the ten thousand-year-old sandal sole was little more than a footnote. The article would have to be rejected, and she made a note not to include the "footnote" quip in her evaluation. Celine Bramley had never seemed receptive to humor.

She had read nearly half of *Stitches in Time* and finished evaluating one of the three articles. The review and evaluations weren't due until Tuesday morning, and the May day beckoned. After a quick lunch of canned lentil soup, Pamela set out on a walk.

For a change of scene, she walked down Orchard Street instead of up, toward Arborville's commercial district. To the west, along County Road, lay a nature preserve, thickly wooded and crisscrossed with informal trails made by visitors rambling among the trees. Pamela roamed along a path that meandered through thickets of maples and oaks, enjoying the whispers of the breeze-tossed leaves and the play of sunlight filtering onto the new grass below.

She emerged from the preserve onto an unpaved road, little more than a trail itself, that led back up to County Road. She waited for a break in the traffic—County Road was heavily traveled—and crossed, but instead of turning right to return to Orchard Street, she turned left and walked toward the cross street that was Arborville's main east-west artery. A block before she reached it, however, she paused, struck by a magnificent drift of azaleas in the yard of a house on that corner.

Every possible shade of azalea was represented, from creamy yellow, through salmon and lavender, to fuchsia and deepest wine. The display stretched along the front of the house, which faced County Road, and around the side, and she turned the corner and strolled slowly up the street marveling at the variety of colors. The next house, too, offered azaleas, and rhododendrons as well—two huge bushes that were almost treelike, as tall as the house's first story. The saucer-sized blooms, dense clusters of ruffled petals, were an intense shade of ruby red.

The street she was on would eventually cross Arborville Avenue, Pamela knew, and so she continued on her way, admiring each lovely yard she passed. Midway up the block, though, she reached a yard that wasn't like the others. Its owner had eschewed ornamental plantings in favor of the practical. The entire lot from sidewalk to house was devoted to a vegetable garden. The crops were at an early stage, given that the peak growing season was still a month off, but small sprouts lined the parallel furrows. Wire cages were already in place around seedlings recognizable as tomato plants by the spiky lobes of their leaves, and a framework of poles awaited climbing beans and peas.

Someone was moving at the side of the house, someone slim, wearing a curious outfit. Above a white jumpsuit, the person wore a wide-brimmed hat. A fine mesh veil anchored to the edge of the hat brim and gathered into the neckline of the jumpsuit obscured the person's face. The person, Pamela noted after absorbing the details of the outfit, was tending something that resembled a shoebox but was the size of a low filing cabinet. The lid had been removed, and a flat, framed panel with a mottled amber surface had been removed. The air around the person was filled with bees.

A beehive, obviously! Pamela stared. Had the *Advocate* ever run an article profiling a local beekeeper? She wasn't sure.

"Hi there!" The beekeeper's hands were empty now, and she—judging by the voice, the person was a she—was advancing toward Pamela. When she had distanced herself from the hive by several yards, she removed the hat, along with its attached veil.

"They get angry when they think I'm plundering their hive," she explained once she reached the sidewalk. "I can't say I blame them—they work so hard." She pulled off a glove and extended the newly bare hand. "Honey Hurley. Pleased to meet you."

Honey Hurley looked to be about Pamela's age, with blond hair cut in a boyish style, a suntanned face, and a smile unbothered by the gap between her front teeth.

"I never walked this way before," Pamela said, "or maybe just not for a long time. I'd have remembered your garden, and your bees."

"Lawns are a waste." The smile made the statement seem less judgmental.

"Maybe you knew Ingrid Barrick," Pamela commented. Perhaps there was a local sisterhood devoted to lawn disapproval.

"I knew *of* her, certainly," Honey responded. "That's all." A few bees were hovering as if curious as to why she had hurried away. "My bees knew her well." She shrugged. "No accounting for taste."

After slipping the glove back on, she lifted the hat and lowered it carefully onto her head, arranging the veil and tucking it in at the neck.

"No accounting for taste?" Pamela mulled the phrase over as she continued toward Arborville Avenue. Did Honey mean that more discriminating bees would have been less impressed by Ingrid's pollinator garden? Were some pollinator gardens better than others? Or was Honey familiar with Ingrid's art, not a fan, and jokingly implying that her bees were less critical than their keeper when it came to art?

Once Pamela reached the corner and turned, Orchard Street was only four blocks distant. En route, she crossed Serpentine Way and reflected that Honey's bees could, indeed, have included Ingrid's wild yard in their quest for nectar and pollen.

Soon she was headed down Orchard Street. But when she reached the spot where the Frasers' house faced her own, she veered toward the Frasers' driveway and followed it to the little path that ended at their porch. Just as she was about to ring the doorbell, the door opened, and Bettina popped out.

"Pamela!" she exclaimed. "I was just coming to see you!"

"And I was coming to see you," Pamela responded. "I've discovered the most interesting thing."

Ignoring that news, Bettina seized Pamela's arm. "Coco called," she said as she tugged Pamela over the threshold. "She was snooping around Dorcas's yard and peeked into a garden shed. The lots in that part of Arborville are so irregular that nobody knows where their own stops and their neighbor's starts—at least they pretend they don't."

She leaned past Pamela to close the door. "Anyway, she thinks she saw things, clothing and books and things, that could have come from Ingrid's house. Like we were saying, if someone killed Ingrid on purpose, ransacking the house the way a burglar would could be intended to make the killing look less targeted."

"*We* weren't saying that," Pamela pointed out. "*I* was."

"Whatever. The ransacked things would then be discarded, and now they're sitting in Dorcas's garden shed."

Bettina guided Pamela to the sofa, sat down, and pulled Pamela down next to her. Punkin, the ginger cat who was one of Catrina's daughters, leaped to the floor and scurried away.

"Coco described exactly what she thinks happened, and I can see it all so clearly," Bettina said. She stared ahead, and her hazel eyes opened wide, as if watching the scene unfold. "Dorcas pays a call on Ingrid to raise the pollen issue. 'It's May,' she says. 'Now's the time to get rid of the ragweed before it really becomes a problem.' Ingrid says, 'It's not actually ragweed. It's goldenrod, and I like it, and so do the pollinators.'"

Bettina swiveled to face Pamela and appeared to search for signs of agreement. A furrow came and went between her carefully shaped brows. "Dorcas says, 'Goldenrod has pollen too, and so do your other annoying plants.'"

Pamela nodded and chimed in. "The argument escalates. Ingrid shoves Dorcas. Dorcas shoves her back. Ingrid falls and cracks her head against the hearth, and Dorcas scrambles around picking things up at random to make it look like a break-in has occurred."

"Exactly!" Bettina's features took on the pleased expression of a well-fed cat.

"Coco should tell Detective Clayborn. The things in the garden shed could be important evidence."

"Coco thinks I should tell Clayborn, since I'm in contact with him for the *Advocate*."

"Are you going to?" Pamela asked.

"He doesn't like to get tips from residents, not even me. I told her that." Bettina was still studying Pamela's face. "Maybe *we* should look at the things in the shed . . ."

"How would *we* recognize them as coming from Ingrid's, especially if they're just clothing and books? Everybody has clothing and books. They could be things Dorcas is getting rid of. And ransacking doesn't even have to mean things were taken. It can just mean things were disarranged."

"Ummm." Bettina shifted her gaze to the carpet. She no longer looked pleased.

"Besides," Pamela added, "if the things in the garden shed really are evidence, our poking around in them could compromise their usefulness to the police."

"Ummmmm." Bettina turned back to Pamela. "What were you going to tell me?"

"Did you ever know there was someone right here in Arborville with a hive?" Pamela described her walking adventure. She concluded by saying, "It sounded like her bees are very familiar with Ingrid's pollinator garden, and you'd think a beekeeper would be happy that people are creating yards that invite bees—but Honey sounded lukewarm, especially about Ingrid herself."

"Maybe she doesn't like artists." Bettina shrugged. In a change of subject, she asked, "What are you doing for Mother's Day?"

"Penny's coming over from the city." Pamela smiled. "Didn't I tell you?"

"You're telling me now. Come for brunch. We're going to Wilfred Jr.'s for dinner, but we'd love to see Penny while she's here."

Back at home, Pamela climbed the stairs to her office. She settled into her desk chair—after first removing Catrina, who waited a moment and then climbed into Pamela's lap. Once the monitor had awakened from its sleep, she clicked on the file for the next article to be evaluated for *Fiber Craft*, "Crocheting Coral." Its full title, revealed when the Word document opened, was "Crocheting Coral: Science Meets Art."

She began to read, fascinated to learn about a project that had attracted thousands and thousands of crochet aficionados, from every corner of the world, to illustrate the process by which coral reefs grow. The article explained that the organisms responsible for the reefs' growth generated curving structures that allowed for maximum exposure to the seawater containing the nutrients they needed—and given the ability of crochet to create almost any imaginable form, it was the perfect medium to replicate coral.

The project had an ulterior motive—to call attention to the environmental factors threatening the survival of coral reefs—and the beauty of the creations wrought with yarn and crochet hooks brought home the aesthetic dimension of that loss. The article's author made sure to point out, however, that more than aesthetics was at stake, given the coral's role in the ecology of the sea.

The article was accompanied by photographs of representative contributions to the project, some in varying shades of . . . coral . . . from a pale salmon coral to vermillion coral to a deep coral verging on wine. Others were multicolored as a reminder that coral isn't always . . . coral. Additionally, some were wall-mounted, like richly textured tapestries, while others were freestanding, like fantastical, twisty fiber sculptures.

Pamela lingered over the photographs, marveling at the fact that, indeed, more things were possible with a crochet hook than with knitting needles. Then she wrote an enthusiastic recommendation that the article be published, with a suggestion that perhaps other articles with an ecological focus could be grouped with it in an issue of *Fiber Craft* devoted to that topic.

She checked her email in case there was an update on Penny's plans for the next day, deleted a message offering her coupons at the hobby store, and then allowed her mouse to rest on its mouse pad.

Catrina led the way into the hall and down the stairs. By the time Pamela reached the kitchen, she and Catrina had been joined by Ginger and Precious, and all three cats congregated expectantly in the corner where their meals were accustomed to arrive.

Once they were happily crouched over their bowls— one larger, shared by Catrina and Ginger, and one smaller, for Precious alone—Pamela contemplated her own dinner. All the cats were having chicken tonight, chicken pâté, which had looked almost appetizing as Pamela spooned it from the cans, pink and with a texture that suggested it could be spread on crackers. About half of a roast chicken waited in the refrigerator, along with the makings of Italian sausage lasagna, which Pamela planned to serve Penny the following night.

Leftover chicken offered so many possibilities . . . like creamed chicken on toast, a satisfying comfort food in the winter, but just as good all year round. She removed the chicken from the refrigerator, collected the makings for white sauce, and busied herself at the counter.

CHAPTER 6

The next morning, Pamela ate a quick breakfast and then set to work cleaning the house in preparation for Penny's arrival. The first order of business was Penny's bedroom. The door stayed closed when Penny wasn't visiting, and opening it was like opening a door to the past. It was the first part of the house Michael and Pamela had focused on in their efforts to fix up their fixer-upper.

Glossy white paint had freshened the dreary woodwork and a thrift-shop dresser, and pale blue paper sprinkled with pink rosebuds had been applied to the walls, despite the budget-straining expense it represented. Pamela had sewn curtains from white eyelet, the same white eyelet that, as the improvements continued room by room, curtained the windows in the bedroom she and Michael shared. In time, a twin bed had replaced the crib, and a desk and chair, also glossy white, had been added when Penny started school. Art, from Penny's own hand, appeared on the walls.

Ginger had followed Pamela up the stairs to the door of Penny's room. As soon as Pamela opened the door, Ginger scurried between her feet and began to dart about the floor, perhaps recognizing traces of the room's usual occupant. Pamela stripped the quilt, made by her grandmother, from the bed to reveal a mattress clothed only in a mattress cover. Fresh, lavender-scented sheets would be fetched from the linen closet, but first the dust mop would be deployed under the bed and all around the room, and the surfaces of the furniture would be dusted too.

Ginger watched, fascinated, as these operations were performed, and she chose to stay behind when Pamela moved on to clean the bathroom and then vacuum and dust the downstairs. The final step was to scrub the kitchen floor. While it dried, Pamela retired to a wicker chair on her porch for a welcome break.

She was dreamily contemplating the climbing roses that patterned the side of the brick house next to Bettina's, reaching nearly to the roof, when a familiar voice called from the front walk. She refocused her gaze and recognized her daughter, Penny, a small figure with dark, curly hair, advancing toward her. Penny was accompanied by another young woman, much taller, and with loose blond hair that flowed in a careless tumble past her shoulders. It was Sibyl Larkin, Penny's roommate in the city and the daughter of Pamela's neighbor, Richard Larkin. Each carried a roomy canvas duffel bag. Pamela rose and descended the steps to meet them, greeting Penny, and then Sibyl, with a hug.

Pamela examined her daughter, surreptitiously, and decided she looked like herself. She was living just across the river, working for the architecture firm where her father had worked before his tragic death, and thus she was definitely among friends—and Sibyl was a sensible young woman. Still, a mother worried, and since Penny hadn't inherited Pamela's height, Pamela had never been able to see her as truly ready to set out on her own.

Penny's blue eyes were bright, though, and her skin was fresh and rosy. She was wearing jeans, sneakers, and a black-and-white-striped T-shirt that gave the outfit a Parisian flair. "We got an earlier bus," she said, "and there was no traffic, so here we are."

The three of them chatted a bit, about the park-like yards all up and down Orchard Street and the contrast with the city's urban landscape. "And your family?" Pamela inquired of Sibyl when that topic had been exhausted.

"My mom's loving the city," Sibyl said, "after so long on the West Coast, and my dad is fine, though you probably see him more often than I do." She nodded toward his house, which was immediately next to Pamela's. "He's doing his volunteer work with Recycle, Renew in Maine again this summer, leaving pretty soon, I think."

"Are you hungry?" Pamela glanced from Sibyl's face to Penny's and back.

"I told my dad I'd pop in to say hello before we head for Haversack."

"We've got plans," Penny explained. "There's a

great thrift shop in Haversack. We heard about it at a vintage place in our neighborhood."

Sibyl turned and went back down the front walk, duffel bag in hand, and Pamela and Penny climbed the steps to the porch.

"I *am* hungry, Mom," Penny said as they crossed the threshold.

"Grilled cheese?" Pamela closed the door behind them. "With Vermont cheddar?"

"I make them too," Penny replied, "but mine never taste as good as yours, and I miss the Co-Op's cheese counter."

Penny veered toward the stairs with her duffel bag, en route to her bedroom, and Pamela continued on to the kitchen. There, she took the cheddar and a stick of butter from the refrigerator and the loaf of whole-grain bread from the bread drawer. It was quick work to carve off several slices of cheese, butter four pieces of bread, and get the griddle started heating on the stove.

When Penny reappeared, she was accompanied by Ginger, draped around her shoulders like an animated fur piece. The tabby stripes on the cat's orange coat echoed the stripes on Penny's T-shirt like a purposeful fashion statement.

"I am definitely going to adopt a cat when I'm settled next year," Penny commented as she stroked Ginger's flank.

"Have you decided yet *where* you're going to be settled?" Pamela spoke without turning from the counter, and she tried to keep her tone conversational. Penny's job in the city was a temporary one, taken while she applied to graduate schools and waited for their responses.

"Mom?" The plaintive note in Penny's voice made Pamela turn around. "It's not going to be Columbia, though I did get in . . ."

"It would have been nice to keep you close . . ."

"I'll be close to Grandma and Grandpa," Penny said. "The architecture program at the University of Illinois is exactly what I'm looking for."

The meaning of Penny's words sank in only slowly, despite her reference to Grandma and Grandpa, who, indeed, lived a third of the way across the country. The University of Illinois was in . . . Illinois.

Pamela's face must have reflected her momentary confusion, then her realization when the words really did sink in. Penny would genuinely be gone, off on her own, on the adventure of the rest of her life. College in Boston had been one thing, but this was different.

"It's not really that far . . ." Penny's voice was hesitant, and she studied her mother's face as if looking for subtle reactions to the words she was uttering. "You grew up in Illinois, and you came here, and you left your parents there . . ."

"My parents were my *parents*," Pamela said. "There were two of them, and I wasn't their only child . . ."

"Oh, Mom!" Penny lurched toward Pamela, and Ginger dove off her shoulders, landing on all four feet and scampering from the room.

Pamela reached out to welcome Penny with a hug. Neither said anything for a few long minutes, but they seemed to vie with each other as to who could squeeze tighter.

"I don't have to go there," came Penny's voice, muffled, at last. "I got into Columbia. I could even live at home . . ."

"No." Pamela disentangled herself and stepped away, but with her hands resting on Penny's shoulders. "I'm glad, really." She even mustered a smile. "Illinois was your first choice, and you got in—and I'm glad. Really, really glad."

Penny mustered a smile too. When she spoke again, it was to change the subject.

"I think the griddle is hot enough now," she said. "Maybe almost too hot."

In fact, it was radiating heat, in an almost-frightening way. Pamela clicked off the flame beneath it and shifted it to another, unlit, burner.

Pamela returned to her cooking task, monitoring the griddle until it was in a fit state to toast the sandwiches without incinerating them, moving it back to the original burner, and reigniting the flame. Then she lowered two slices of bread butter side down onto its surface, arranged half the cheese slices on one and half on the other, and covered the cheese with the other two bread slices, butter side up.

"Grandma and Grandpa will like having you nearby," Pamela said, looking at the sandwiches as she spoke. "And I'll come out there with you when you move, and maybe we can even find a cat for you together."

A few minutes later, the sandwiches were done, golden-toasty, with dribbles of melted cheddar escaping from the gap where the top slices of bread met the bottom.

*   *   *

Sibyl rang the doorbell to collect Penny just as the last bites were being consumed, and soon the two were off on their thrifting expedition. Pamela tidied up the few dishes and rinsed the griddle, then climbed the stairs to her office, where "Doubling Up" waited for its evaluation.

The article proved to be about a technique called twined knitting, or, more enigmatically, two-end knitting. It involved two strands of yarn, the second of which was twisted around the first after every stitch, so that while the right side appeared to be worked in the traditional stockinette stitch, the reverse had a ridged texture. The two strands were often the two ends of the same skein of yarn—thus the technique's alternative name.

It was a very old technique, the author—an authority on Swedish folk crafts—explained, and was documented as far back as the sixteenth century in both Sweden and Norway. She made the obvious point that inhabitants of cold regions like Scandinavia would seek ways to make their woolen garments as warm as possible, and a technique for doubling up the yarn so a mitten or stocking was twice as thick would be a welcome development.

The article included step-by-step photographs of the twined-knitting process, as well as of a mitten the author had produced while studying the technique. But most importantly, it also included photographs of objects discovered in archeological digs, identifiable as garments or parts of garments, and clearly examples of twined knitting.

Twined knitting, Pamela realized as she read, wasn't

unknown to modern knitters. In fact, she recalled a YouTube video in which a yarn influencer demonstrated the technique—though the article's author noted that Scandinavian knitters who still practiced the twined-knitting technique were few in her experience. But a substantial portion of "Doubling Up" was devoted to the historical evidence for the technique's age, and readers of *Fiber Craft* would hopefully be encouraged to see modern practitioners of the technique, like the YouTube yarn influencer, as performing a vital service by keeping an old craft alive. She wrote a brief summary of the article and concluded by recommending it for publication.

Back downstairs, Pamela collected from pantry and refrigerator the ingredients she would need for her lasagna sauce: a large can of San Marzano tomatoes, an onion, several cloves of garlic, and a plump mound of uncooked Italian sausage. The spicy sausage would provide the sauce with most of its flavor, but, given the season, fresh herbs were available in pots on her back porch as well.

She stepped out the back door to fetch them, scissors in hand. The basil seedlings, which had been brought home from the garden center only a few weeks ago, were still too small to spare more than a few leaves, but the rosemary and oregano were winter-hardy and already green and flourishing once again. As she was bending over the rosemary plant, deciding which of its spiky shoots to choose, she heard a voice calling from the yard to her left, Richard Larkin's yard.

The voice, in fact, belonged to Richard Larkin, who was standing near the perennial border that stretched across the back of his property. It dated from the era before he bought the house, but he had taken it over and tended it faithfully.

The warm spring had hastened its rebirth. The irises' blade-like leaves were tall and vigorous, and the peonies were already in bloom, their heavy pink blossoms drooping on slender stems. Spears of lupine, with their tightly clustered blossoms in shades of purple and blue, rose above the lower, bushier foliage, which included bleeding hearts, whose delicately arched stems dripped rows of deep pink teardrops. Low bushes speckled with magenta flowers marked off the perennial border from the lawn.

Richard was dressed in what Pamela recognized as his gardening clothes, though on his tall, athletic body, distressed jeans and a faded T-shirt could just as well have been a fashion statement. He called again—the message was simply "hello"—and waved.

Pamela responded with a wave and a hello, then descended the steps. From her driveway, she added, "Your perennial border is looking good."

He crossed his lawn until he was standing at the very edge of his lot. His angular features and strong nose made his resting expression almost fierce as he gazed at her. Then she realized he was puzzled. Her comment about the perennial bed mustn't have carried across his yard.

"Your perennial border is looking good," she repeated.

He didn't respond right away, but continued gazing. His expression was, if anything, even more fierce, or maybe desperate, as if he were longing to introduce a subject more serious than the state of his perennial border. Long ago, when he'd first moved next door, he had made his interest in her clear, and she had been attracted to him too, but unwilling to commit—then. She was still attracted, powerfully so, but her earlier reluctance had made things so awkward . . .

As the silence lingered, Pamela searched her mind for a fresh conversational topic, aware that her breathing had sped up, along with her heartbeat.

"Are you enjoying your visit from Sibyl?" she asked at last.

"We . . . haven't visited too much yet . . ." A smile came and went, reminding her that she'd noted before how unaccustomed to smiles his stern features seemed.

"No . . . true," Pamela responded. "They've gone to Haversack."

Nodding in mutual agreement, both were silent until Pamela spoke again. Aware that she was holding her scissors, she raised them aloft. "I was just cutting some herbs, for dinner," she said.

"You're busy." Richard took a few steps backward with his eyes still on her. "Have a nice evening," he added as he turned.

Pamela returned to her porch, and her herb pots, but she found herself staring at the rosemary plant as if uncertain of the errand that had brought her outside. Her mind seemed blank, or nearly blank. Her busy plans—the herbs, the lasagna sauce, then the noodles and cheese—had been supplanted by the image of Richard Larkin. *Why didn't you invite him to dinner?* inquired an exasperated voice in her mind. *It was the perfect op-*

portunity, because Sibyl's here and they'd both come over, and it would be so natural and casual. Not like having just him, like you're wanting him to . . .

With a snip, she claimed a sprig of rosemary and moved on to the unruly tangle of oregano in the neighboring pot.

By the time Penny returned, the sauce was bubbling on the stove, fragrant with garlic and herbs. Pamela heard the front door open and stepped through the kitchen doorway to greet her daughter.

"We were there for ages," Penny said. "There were so many treasures to sort through." She paused. "And that smells delicious." She displayed a shopping bag. "Do you want to see?"

"Most definitely."

Penny followed Pamela back into the kitchen, rested the shopping bag on a chair, and reached inside to pull out a bulky knitted garment.

"Very 1980s!" she exclaimed, shaking it out and holding it up in front of her.

It was a sweater and, with its wide, wide shoulders, indeed very 1980s. It hung straight down from those shoulders, halfway to Penny's knees, but even on a tall person, it would have been long. It was knit from hot-pink yarn, mostly, with irregular horizontal bands of turquoise.

"Isn't it amazing?" Penny said. "The weather is much too warm to wear it now, but it was too interesting to pass up." She held it at arm's length and switched hands so the front of the sweater was facing her. "I'll wear it with leggings, or maybe just tights. It's plenty long."

She laid it out on the kitchen table and pushed the neckline down in front to expose the label, saying, "Here's the most fun part of it." The label read "Mariposa," and it featured a little stylized butterfly.

Penny gathered the sweater back into the shopping bag and headed upstairs. Alone in the kitchen again, Pamela returned to her lasagna project.

She'd started the water boiling for the lasagna noodles before Penny came in. She believed water came to a boil faster if the pot was covered, and now she removed the cover to discover a throbbing riot of huge bubbles. She counted out six of the noodles, which resembled wide, ripple-edged ribbons, and slid them into the pot.

Once the noodles were cooked, the lasagna came together quickly. The rectangular Pyrex baking dish wasn't quite as long as the noodles, so they had to be trimmed, but being a frugal cook, Pamela didn't waste the trimmed-off scraps. A layer of noodles was followed by a layer of the vividly colored, sausage-rich sauce, which was dotted with spoonfuls of ricotta and slices of mozzarella and sprinkled with Parmesan. The process was then repeated, starting with another layer of noodles and the noodle scraps, and the third and final layer of noodles was topped with the remains of the sauce and a sprinkling of Parmesan.

* * *

"I bought something else while I was out with Sibyl," Penny said with a sly smile as she approached the dining room table. Pamela was in the act of setting it with pretty place mats and napkins, pink to match the rose garlands on the wedding china, in honor of Penny's visit. Penny held her hands behind her back but brought one hand forth to display a bottle of wine.

"It's red," she pointed out, though the color was obvious. "We don't have to drink it all, but I knew you were making lasagna."

Vintage wineglasses from a tag sale joined the wedding china, and soon the table was ready. The lasagna was resting on the stovetop until it was cool enough to serve without dislodging layers slippery with olive oil and sausage fat, and a crisp romaine salad waited in a wooden bowl in the refrigerator. Ice cream waited, too, the old-fashioned kind called Neapolitan, with its wide stripes of chocolate, strawberry, and vanilla.

CHAPTER 7

Pamela was so used to sharing the kitchen with three breakfasting cats while she prepared her coffee and toast that the sight of only two crouched over their bowls had been disconcerting. But Ginger, she knew, had become Penny's bedmate for the weekend, and Penny was sleeping late after a long evening out with old Arborville friends.

Part 1 of the *Register* had been set aside in favor of Lifestyle, and Pamela had just refilled her coffee cup when she heard footsteps on the stairs. The next minute, Ginger appeared in the doorway followed by Penny. Penny was still in her pajamas, and her hair showed more recent contact with a pillow than with a comb, but she was carrying a prettily wrapped box.

"Happy Mother's Day," she sang out as she placed the box on the kitchen table.

Ginger, meanwhile, was investigating the empty bowls

left behind when Catrina and Precious finished their
meals and departed.

"I'll do it, Mom," Penny said as Pamela started to
rise. "Moms get to rest on Mother's Day." She stooped
toward the cupboard where the cat food was stored.

"I made extra coffee." Pamela sank back into her
chair and pointed at the carafe. "It's still pretty hot."

Soon Ginger was in the corner nibbling at a serving
of liver tidbits, and Penny had joined Pamela at the
table with toast on a wedding-china plate and coffee in
a wedding-china cup. With the aid of cream from the
refrigerator and sugar from the cut-glass sugar bowl,
she had transformed the dark brew into the pale and
sweet concoction that she, like Bettina, preferred.

Pamela had abandoned the newspaper, happy just to
enjoy Penny's company, even if in silence. But sensing
her mother's eyes on her, Penny spoke up.

"You can open it, Mom. You don't have to wait for
me to finish breakfast."

The Mother's Day gift was wrapped in paper that
featured violets, and the ribbon was the dark green of
the violets' leaves. Pamela slipped the ribbon off and
gently loosened the tape that anchored the paper in
place to reveal a plain white cardboard box. She lifted
the lid of the box and folded a flap of tissue aside. Beneath the tissue was a silky garment in shades of green
that rippled across the fabric from dark to light and
back to dark again.

Pamela lifted the garment from the box and held it
up. It proved to be a blouse, with a wide, rounded collar and flowing sleeves gathered into wide cuffs.

"Oh," she sighed. "It's beautiful."

Penny had been watching Pamela's face attentively. Now she smiled. "Do you really like it?" Pamela nodded, continuing to hold the blouse aloft. "It was old," Penny said, "but now it's new."

She explained that the garment, at least in its new form, had been created by a woman who browsed thrift stores and tag sales for light-colored silk blouses and shirts, which she then dyed, using tie-dye and other techniques.

"I'll wear it today." Pamela folded the blouse and nestled it into its box. "When we go to the Frasers'."

Bettina opened the Frasers' front door and pulled it back in a sweeping motion. "Welcome, welcome," she chirped, "and Happy Mother's Day!"

She was dressed for the bright May Sunday in wide-legged pants and a scoop-necked top belted at the waist and flaring out below like a peplum. The fabric was sky-blue linen, and the neckline was accented with an elaborate turquoise-and-silver necklace. Matching earrings dangled from her ears.

"Miss Penny . . . *and* Miss Pamela!" She paused to survey them. "What a pair of fashionistas!" She gave careful scrutiny to Pamela and added, "You have a new blouse."

"I know you're surprised." Pamela laughed.

"It must be a gift. You never buy anything for yourself."

"From Penny," Pamela said, "for Mother's Day." She nodded as Penny described the blouse's origin.

Penny herself was wearing a summery dress that, as she explained, had stayed in her Arborville closet when she moved into her city apartment. It was simple and flirty, knee-length, with cap sleeves, in an old-fashioned print that featured poppies. The white sneakers she had paired with it gave the ensemble an up-to-date flair.

The aroma drifting in from the kitchen offered a preview of the meal to come: something with a pastry component was baking, or had baked, and sugar was being caramelized. And, as if aware that the guests' attention had been drawn to the food, the chef appeared in the arch between the living room and the dining room, the apron tied around his bulky middle making his role clear.

"Welcome, welcome, welcome!" he echoed Bettina's greeting. Behind him, the dining room table beckoned, with a setting that looked festive even from a distance. "Please take your seats," he urged. "We'll be eating in no time at all—and I can serve coffee right now, or later."

Later, was the decision, and Pamela, Penny, and Bettina took their seats. The head of the table was reserved for Wilfred, mostly because it put him closest to the kitchen. Bettina always sat at the other end, and Pamela and Penny faced each other from the sides. In the center of the table was a low vase containing roses, open wide and in a spectrum of colors that brought to mind a dramatic sunset. The place mats echoed the deep coral tones of some, while the napkins picked up the golden yellow of others.

From the kitchen came the sound of an oven door opening, and the aroma of caramelized sugar became intense. A clatter of dishes was heard, and in a moment, Wilfred stepped into the dining room carrying two small plates from Bettina's sage-green pottery set, with matching bowls centered on them. He placed one before Pamela and one before Penny and returned to the kitchen.

Pamela inspected the contents of her bowl. It was half a pink grapefruit, with a sugary glaze making its pastel surface shimmer. Wilfred was back then, with two more servings. He slid one in front of Bettina then took his own seat. Raising his spoon, like a conductor about to launch a symphony with the wave of his baton, he gave the signal to dine with a hearty "*Bon appétit!*"

"It's broiled," he explained, after the first few bites of the grapefruit had elicited both praise and amazement. "With brown sugar and a little cinnamon. And after I took it out from underneath the broiler, I sprinkled on a few grains of coarse sea salt."

The flavor was noteworthy for its contrasts: citrusy, slightly bitter, overlaid with the dark sweetness of scorched sugar and a pop of salt.

"This was the perfect start to a summery brunch," Bettina declared after she had scooped out the last juicy segment, and only an empty, half-collapsed grapefruit shell remained in her bowl. "Not too filling, because I know you have something amazing in store for us next."

Wilfred beamed at his wife, his ruddy face aglow, as Pamela and Penny added their praise. The dishes were cleared away then, Wilfred insisting that the other diners remain seated while he made quick work of it. In no time at all, he was back, delivering two larger plates from the sage-green set, one to Pamela and one to Penny. Each plate held a wedge of quiche, creamy golden custard with a toasty fluted rim of crust at the wide end.

The quiche was decorated with squiggly slivers of pimento, and a curly cluster of arugula was tucked along the side. Two more plates arrived, Wilfred took his seat again, and with another hearty "*Bon appétit*," invited the diners to commence.

The first taste of the quiche revealed an unexpected dimension. Based on its appearance, Pamela had been expecting a classic quiche Lorraine, despite the pimento strips, but there was no hint of cheese or bacon in the rich custard. Her expression was question enough, and Wilfred responded: "Crab meat, and tarragon." The mild taste of the crab meat blended perfectly with the custard, and the pimento and tarragon added just enough zip.

After everyone had had a few bites, and signaled their appreciation with compliments and hums of satisfaction, the focus turned from the chef to the guests, most specifically to Penny.

"How are your plans for next year shaping up?" Bettina inquired, her light tone identifying the query as nothing more than a conversational gambit.

With a glance at Pamela, Penny said, "University of Illinois."

Now it was Bettina's turn to glance at Pamela, who did her best to look pleased.

"That's quite a ways away," Bettina commented.

"Not so far." Pamela spoke up, determinedly cheerful. "When we first moved out here, Michael and I used to drive it in a day to visit our families. If you leave at dawn, you can get to Chicago by midnight. It was a lot cheaper than flying."

"Sounds grueling." Penny glanced at Pamela again.

Was she, Pamela wondered, pondering the idea of her mother as a young married woman, not much older than Penny herself? Or was she just wondering whether the cheerfulness was an act?

The quiche provided a welcome distraction. Pamela's plate still held the rim of flaky crust, and she used the side of her fork to detach a bite-sized morsel. Meanwhile, Penny was doing her part to keep the conversation flowing.

"I'm sorry I didn't get to see Betty while I was home," she said.

"She's walking now, and she has dolls and they all have names . . ." Bettina's voice trailed off. She closed her eyes, and her lips curved into a contented smile, imagining, Pamela supposed, the many joys that lay ahead as grandmother and granddaughter bonded over girly things. Bettina's other granddaughter was the daughter of Boston academics who had declared they were raising a *person*, not a *girl*, and had forbidden all gender-specific gifts.

Penny listened happily as Bettina went on to recount Betty's latest exploits, which were numerous. After a slight interruption, during which Wilfred supplied the diners with second helpings of quiche, the conversation veered onto the related topic of the dollhouse Wilfred was building for Betty in his basement workshop.

Several minutes later, all that remained on the sage-green plates were flaky shards of piecrust and a few curly arugula leaves. Wilfred surveyed the diners, who returned his gaze with the satisfied contentment of the well fed.

"Yogurt?" he asked. "Just a bit, to finish things off? And then we'll have coffee."

He accepted help, Penny's help, in clearing away. When Penny returned, she was carrying two elegant, stemmed parfait glasses from Bettina's collection of Swedish crystal. The creamy yogurt that filled them partway up was topped by a layer of sliced strawberries, glowing deep red against the yogurt. A moment later, Wilfred joined them, bearing two more servings of yogurt and strawberries.

The yogurt was vanilla flavored, not too sweet, but a smooth and mellow contrast with the acidic strawberries. As the contents of the parfait glasses disappeared spoon by spoon, Bettina and Wilfred were happy to chat about Penny's life in the city, and her adventures on the job, which could involve delivering architectural plans and paperwork by cab, subway, or even on foot.

Bettina seemed eager to move on, though, once her parfait glass was empty.

"Let me do the coffee," she said, and before Wilfred could object, she seized her parfait glass, and Penny's. Leaning toward Pamela, she added, "Come on. You can help."

Pamela obediently climbed to her feet, collected Wilfred's parfait glass and her own, and followed Bettina into the kitchen. Once they were well away from the dining room, the ulterior motive behind Bettina's offer was clear.

"Coco called me," she whispered, taking no chances of being overheard. Penny highly disapproved of Pamela's and Bettina's involving themselves in matters best left to the police, and she was alert to any hint.

"Oh?" Pamela had taken the kettle from the stove

and was standing at the sink. She paused before launching the *whoosh* of water that would muffle their speech.

"She said if I'm not going to use my connections with Clayborn to report the suspicious find in the shed, she's going to do it herself."

"What did you tell her?" Pamela's hand rested on the faucet handle.

"What I told her before. He doesn't like to get tips from residents."

Footsteps from the far side of the high counter announced the entrance of Penny. "I came for the cream and sugar," she said. "And I might as well get the mugs out as long as I'm here." She edged around the high counter and opened a cupboard.

Wilfred had already arranged the filter cone, supplied with a paper filter, atop the carafe and measured in enough of the Guatemalan coffee that the Frasers preferred. Pamela quickly filled the kettle and set it to boil.

The group relocated to the living room for coffee, displacing Woofus, the shelter dog, who had been sprawled out on the sofa. The infusion of caffeine stimulated conversation, which returned to the theme of Betty and thence to the dollhouse under construction in Wilfred's basement workshop.

"I'd love to see it," Penny said, "from an architectural point of view and . . . just because."

"No sooner said than done!" Wilfred boosted himself from his armchair, and he and Penny headed for the kitchen, where a door opened onto the basement stairs, as he chuckled and remarked, "Hard hats not necessary."

"More coffee?" Bettina asked after they'd gone.

"I'm fine." Pamela shielded her mug with her hand, though the carafe was far away in the kitchen.

"Did you get a chance to talk to Sibyl? Rick told Wilfred that she came out from the city with Penny."

"We talked a little," Pamela responded, "but she and Penny were out all yesterday afternoon, and then she was with her dad."

"I wonder how Laine is doing. Does Rick ever mention her?" Laine was Richard Larkin's other daughter. Bettina's tone was offhand, but Pamela raised a suspicious eyebrow.

"I know what you're up to," she said.

"What? What am I up to?" Bettina drew back, raised a hand, and laid it palm-down against the crisp blue linen of her top.

Pamela frowned and tightened her lips. "You're curious to know if I've talked to him lately."

"He *is* your next-door neighbor, and your daughter and his daughter are roommates."

"I just talked to him yesterday, as it happens . . . and sometimes we wave."

"Nothing more?" Bettina's expectant look seemed to demand an assurance that there had been more.

But there hadn't been more, and she'd already chastised herself for that, so she didn't respond. Anyway, voices were echoing in the kitchen, one deep and one higher-pitched. A moment later, Wilfred and Penny were stepping through the arch that separated the dining room from the living room.

CHAPTER 8

"To be opened on Friday." Pamela handed Penny a card and a little package wrapped in paper featuring kittens and tied with a festive bow. "No sooner." The Friday in question was Penny's birthday, May 16.

Penny had descended the stairs with her duffel bag. Now, as Ginger watched, she set it on the entry's parquet floor and stooped to unzip it. The gift—though Penny didn't yet know the contents of the package— was a family keepsake that had come down from Pamela's grandmother, a leather-bound book with an edifying comment for each day of the year. In case edifying comments, despite the book's provenance, didn't seem an impressive enough gift, Pamela had enclosed a generous check in the accompanying card.

Penny checked her watch and said, "If the bus is on time, I shouldn't have to wait more than a few minutes, and I'll be back in the city in less than an hour. Sibyl texted me that she got back in plenty of time for lunch with her mom. No traffic in the tunnel at all."

Penny was on her way then, with a kiss and a hug, and a head-scratch for Ginger, and Pamela was suddenly left feeling at loose ends. She could read *Stitches in Time*—a few chapters remained before she could begin to draft her review. Or she could knit, but with summer looming and months to go before cold weather returned, there was no need to rush a sweater. She decided to go for a walk, down to the nature preserve again.

She stepped out onto the porch, convinced, as she scanned the cloudless sky and surveyed the verdant yards, that being outdoors on a day like this was the best choice. Everything was so *alive*. And, on that subject, she decided to detour into the backyard to check on the tomato seedlings she had launched only a few weeks ago.

As she made her way down her driveway, she heard whistling, melodious, though not a recognizable tune. It was coming from Richard Larkin's backyard, obscured just then by the tall hedge that ran along the property line, but coming into view as she proceeded south. She stopped as she took in the sight that greeted her: Richard Larkin, in his distressed jeans but shirtless. The flesh revealed by the missing shirt was already tan, as if this wasn't the first time this season he had made a shirtless foray into the outdoors.

Stepping gingerly among the plants in his perennial border, he was pruning a tree with a set of long-handled clippers. The muscles in his shapely back and shoulders flexed as he reached overhead, and as he stooped to nudge the leafy trimmings into a pile. The whistling was phrased in a way that accented his rhythmic movements, and to judge by the size of the pile and the sweat that filmed his muscular torso, he'd been at it for some time.

Pamela realized she had stopped breathing. She closed her eyes and inhaled deeply, then opened them. She tried to picture the man she saw before her . . . tamed, sitting at her dining room table, chatting about neighborhood doings. She realized it was impossible, even if she pictured Sibyl and Penny there to domesticate the scene, and that she had once more stopped breathing.

A small branch swished as he cut it loose, and as it fell, he ducked and spun around. Now he was facing his house rather than his back fence, and he caught sight of Pamela. He dropped the clippers and uttered the word, "Pamela." Then he snatched up a small cloth bundle that proved to be a T-shirt and pulled it over his head, further disarranging his shaggy dark-blond hair.

"I was just . . ." He advanced, peering intently at her face. "These trees get big, then other things can't grow because there's too much shade."

She nodded wordlessly.

"This tree shades your yard too." He came closer. "I know you like to grow things that need sun. I'm just finishing up here, but I could cut it back on your side too, some time, if you'd like that."

"Yes . . . yes," she said. "I would."

"I'm . . ." He paused and shifted his gaze from her face to the ground. "You're . . . probably busy and I'm . . ." He paused again. "Right now I really need a shower."

* * *

The next morning found Pamela, breakfasted and dressed, sitting at her computer. She'd opened a new Word file, titled it "Stitches Review," and keyed in a provisional opening paragraph: "We often imagine that if the walls of buildings where history-making events took place could talk, they'd reveal secrets not found in the history books. In *Stitches in Time: What Garments from the Past Can Tell Us That History Can't*, Lynne Ralston shows us that garments preserved from the past can speak quite volubly about their wearers and the worlds they lived in."

She was staring at the second sentence, wondering if it was clear that "they" referred to "wearers" and not "garments"—though, in a sense, the garments had lived in those worlds too—when the telephone's ring interrupted her thoughts. It was the landline, and she spun her chair sideways to pick up the handset.

"Hello?" said a masculine voice. "Have I reached Ms. Pamela Paterson of *Fiber Craft* magazine?"

"Yes?" she responded, curious about the nature of the call. Then she added, "This is Pamela Paterson."

"Eilert Kroll here, calling from Wendelstaff College." The voice was clipped and precise, and sounded somehow familiar. "I hope this is appropriate, my calling you," he went on. "I've been working on a study of Ingrid Barrick's work, a retrospective, and so far I've produced an article about her early fiber art. What I'm wondering is whether it's too soon to submit it to *Fiber Craft*, given what happened . . ."—his voice faltered— "so recently."

"Uh, no," Pamela said. "That is, you could submit it.

We could hold off publishing it until a decent amount of time has passed. I'd be interested in taking a look at it."

"Are you a fan?" His voice quickened.

"I feel that I knew her," Pamela said, "though I didn't actually, but after her death, I realized she had been a neighbor. Did you know her?"

"I was fortunate enough to, yes," came the response. "I was totally in awe after seeing an exhibit of her fiber sculptures in Berlin, and then I was offered a visiting-professor appointment at Wendelstaff and I jumped at the chance. She was so gracious—she even loaned me all kinds of material for my book."

"That *does* sound gracious," Pamela said.

"I have a bit of a problem now, though." He sounded worried. "What do I do with the material she loaned me when I'm finished?"

"There will be a will, I imagine, and heirs. I don't think you have to worry about what to do with it all just yet."

"Good. Yes, good," he responded. "The book is such a big project, and I believe there will be many more articles along the way. In fact"—he paused—"maybe you would like to come out to the campus and take a look at the interesting sketches and documents and photographs she loaned me? You might have some ideas about parts of her oeuvre that would be of particular interest to your readers."

"Yes," Pamela said. "I think I *would* like that."

She arranged to rendezvous with Eilert on the Wendelstaff campus later that morning, and before hanging up, she mentioned that she would most likely be bringing a friend.

* * *

Eilert Kroll's visiting-professor appointment was in Wendelstaff's art history department. Pamela found a place in the visitors' section of the main parking lot, and she and Bettina set off toward the building that housed that department. The route passed through a grassy quadrangle surrounded by the college's older buildings, some classic brick, others ivy-covered gray stone. Narrow paths crisscrossed the quadrangle's lawn, which was freshly green now that spring was well advanced. At half past ten, classes were in session, and only a few students were outside, most dressed in shorts, sandals, and T-shirts or skimpy tops, with heavy-looking backpacks slung over their shoulders.

When Pamela and Bettina reached an impressive brick building with white columns, they veered away from the quadrangle and toward a recent addition to the campus, a modern building of glass and steel. Expansive concrete steps led up to double doors of heavy glass, which opened onto a high-ceilinged foyer bright with sun.

They entered one of the elevators ranged along the foyer's back wall and soon were stepping out into a fluorescent-lit hallway with doors at intervals along each side. Some were open, allowing glimpses of office desks and bookcases, while some were closed, decorated with clippings and cartoons hinting at the personalities of their occupants.

Halfway down the hallway, one of the closed doors suddenly swung back, and a striking male figure stepped through it.

"Hello!" he called, with a wave. "Right on time."

When Pamela and Bettina got closer, he offered effusive handshakes, murmuring, "Eilert Kroll, so nice to meet you," twice, once for Pamela and once for Bettina.

Eilert Kroll was young, maybe in his thirties, tall, and very thin—an effect accentuated by his outfit, which consisted of a long-sleeved black turtleneck T-shirt, tight black jeans, and sleek black-leather boots. Glasses with dark, angular frames lent drama to his otherwise unassuming features.

"Come in, come in!" He retreated from the doorway and gestured for Pamela and Bettina to enter.

The office was unremarkable, with white walls, a pale wood floor, and a wide window. A side wall was totally given over to bookshelves, and a large L-shaped desk with a metal frame and a laminate top dominated the room, with a swivel chair parked nearby. An open laptop occupied the short leg of the L. The rest of the desk was strewn with . . . things. There were bulging manila envelopes, tattered file folders, booklets, leaflets, sketch pads, photographs, and loose papers. A cardboard box tucked under the desk looked to contain more of the same.

"I'm just starting to get it sorted," Eilert explained as they stared. "She kept everything, but she was not very organized—and why should she be? She was an artist." He picked up a large booklet and said, "Catalog from the Berlin show." Displaying the cover, which showed an object that resembled a cactus, but with faces on each of its lobes, he commented, "You wouldn't realize it was made of yarn unless you saw it in person."

He replaced the catalog more or less in the spot it had come from. While he was turned away, Bettina nudged Pamela. When Pamela responded with a glance, Bettina mouthed something unintelligible.

Pamela shrugged and squinted. Eilert was rummaging among the piles of things, still turned away, and Bettina tried again. Eilert turned back just as Pamela was repeating the shrug and squint, but more forcefully.

"Are you all right?" Eilert asked.

Bettina stepped forward with a flirtatious smile. "We were just wondering," she chirped, "where we've met you before. Your voice sounds so familiar."

He responded to the smile with a smile of his own. "It's the accent."

Bettina lifted a finger. "Wait a minute," she said, and added a suspense-inducing pause. "I'll bet you were at the celebration of Ingrid's life last Thursday."

"I was." Eilert nodded. "But I didn't see you there, either of you."

"We didn't actually *see* you . . ." Bettina studied his face.

Pamela knew her friend was adept at gauging how nosy she could be without provoking a refusal to divulge anything—and in the process alienating an interviewee who could be useful. Eilert's expression was receptive, despite the dramatic eyeglasses.

"We *heard* you . . ."

"Arguing with that obstinate fool, Nestor Flavin"— Eilert slapped the desk—"though I suppose he thinks *I'm* the obstinate fool. But my book has to be *complete*, of course, if it's to be a true retrospective, and so I can't omit any part of Ingrid's life or any of her work—especially not her early work. That's where you can see her genius taking shape."

He picked up a manila envelope stuffed so full that its flap couldn't be fastened.

"Look here, for example." He eased a sheaf of papers out onto a bare section of the desk's surface. "Designs for women's clothing."

Artful pencil and watercolor sketches showed models with idealized bodies wearing outfits that featured full mid-calf-length skirts paired with long, boxy jackets. Other sketches were renderings of pantsuits whose jackets were equally boxy.

"But then"—Eilert extracted some photographs from another manila envelope—"around the same time, she was also experimenting with fiber art."

The top photo had apparently been taken at a gallery exhibit, perhaps on the opening night. A young fair-haired woman wearing a skirt and jacket combination that resembled those in the sketches stood in front of a wall hanging that appeared to be woven from some coarse natural fiber. The fiber had been dyed, but unevenly, and the uneven color, combined with variations in the fiber's texture, made the surface of the wall hanging seem to undulate.

"This is her." Eilert pointed at the image of the young woman. "She was barely in her twenties then, but she didn't look all that different when I met her here—still slender, almost girlish. She hadn't changed much over the years." He slipped the photos back into their envelope. "Once she got going with the fiber art, she realized that was how she wanted to express herself, and the fashion design work fell by the wayside."

Bettina had picked up one of the sketches and was studying it. "I was a teenager in the eighties," she said, "but even I wore things like this. Ugh! Those jackets were so unflattering."

She set the sketch down and turned her attention to Eilert. "Did Nestor tell you specifically which things he didn't want you to include in your book?"

"Early things, like I said." Eilert had glanced at his watch and was now gathering up the sketches. "Things from the first half of the eighties, but whether it was the fashion sketches, the wall hangings, or some whole other thing . . ." He shrugged and widened his eyes behind his glasses—a comical effect with the imposing frames. "Nestor was evasive. It was like he had something specific in mind, but for some reason didn't want to say what it was."

He checked his watch again. It was a large, impressive watch that reminded Pamela of Roland's.

"I have a class," he said in explanation, "but you can take some of this material with you if you like." Pamela and Bettina looked at each other. As if he interpreted the look as hesitation, Eilert added, "And return it, of course, but please take it."

He went on, addressing his next comment specifically to Pamela. "I hope to get some of my work published in *Fiber Craft*. It would help my career—a lot." His gaze was so beseeching that Pamela patted his shoulder, which seemed to encourage him. "There's the article I told you about on her early fiber art, but maybe you could let me know if an article on her excursion into clothing design would be of interest to your readers."

Without waiting for an answer, Eilert stacked a few more manila envelopes on top of the bulging one, to which he had returned the sketches of the outfits featuring the long, boxy jackets. To the pile he added some file folders so tattered they appeared on the point of disintegrating, along with a small printed brochure.

"Here you are, here you are." Smiling now, he lifted the pile from the desk, and Pamela held out her arms to receive it.

Wendelstaff College was located to the north of Arborville. The route back to Orchard Street lay along County Road, which happened to cross Arborville's main east-west artery. As Pamela, who was driving, neared the intersection with that artery, Bettina consulted her watch.

"It's almost noon," she said, "and we haven't had lunch at Hyler's for an age."

"Are you craving one of their tuna melts?" Pamela inquired without taking her eyes from the road.

"Maybe—but maybe that 'chef recommends' feature will have an interesting suggestion. We order tuna melts all the time."

Pamela switched on her turn signal and prepared to turn left onto the cross street. A few minutes later, they were cruising toward the entrance to the parking lot that served the library and the police station. From that lot, a narrow passageway between Hyler's Luncheonette and one of Arborville's hair salons led to the sidewalk that paralleled Arborville Avenue. Hyler's entrance was just a few steps away from the passageway's end.

Thus, in no time at all Pamela and Bettina were heading toward one of the capacious booths, upholstered in burgundy Naugahyde, that lined the side walls of Hyler's.

"We beat the lunchtime rush," Bettina commented as she settled into place. "I'm always happy when we can get a booth. It's so much more private."

The booth's worn wooden table was already set with paper place mats, paper napkins, and silverware, and a server appeared almost instantly to provide the over-sized menus that had been part of the Hyler's experience as long as Pamela could remember. The printed card clipped to the menu and headed "The chef recommends . . ." was, however, a recent development.

"Today is Monday," Bettina murmured from behind the huge menu. Only the top of her head, with its pouf of scarlet hair, was visible. "The chef recommends the Monte Cristo sandwich." She lowered the menu. "He's never recommended that before. What is it?"

The server had been hovering nearby, the restaurant not yet being too busy. "Like a cross between French toast and a grilled cheese sandwich," she said, "with ham and turkey too."

"I'll have it!" Bettina said decisively. "And a vanilla milkshake."

"Make that *two* Monte Cristos and *two* vanilla milk-shakes," Pamela amended, and they relinquished their menus.

"Now we know," Bettina commented once the server had gone on her way, "the identities of both the men who we overheard arguing at the celebration of Ingrid's life."

Pamela nodded. "Nestor Flavin and Eilert Kroll. One is a former housemate—and more—who is apparently the father of her daughter, and the other is a young visiting professor at Wendelstaff who is researching her for a book."

"Nestor wants to keep something hidden, but we don't know what—and neither does Eilert." As if to express kinship with Eilert in his puzzlement, Bettina raised her brows and tightened her lips into a knot.

"Not specifically, at least," Pamela said. "I can see why Eilert was arguing with Nestor. Of course he can't skip five or more years if he wants his book to be complete—and there's obviously a lot of material from that period, judging by the pile of envelopes and file folders he gave me to look through."

Bettina's gaze shifted from Pamela to a spot past her head. Pamela slid to the edge of her Naugahyde-covered bench and turned toward the back of the room. The server had emerged from the swinging doors to the kitchen and, bearing two tall, frosted glasses, was heading their way. A moment later, the glasses, which contained the vanilla milkshakes, were sitting on the paper place mats, where dribbles of condensed moisture were already forming damp rings. Straws protruded at a jaunty angle from the froth that rose above the glasses' rims.

Bettina pulled her milkshake close, leaned toward the straw, and took a long sip, leaving the bright imprint of her lipstick on the straw's tip.

"Just as good as ever," she sighed, glowing with pleasure. "Some things never change." She paused, and the glow faded. "But other things do."

"Yes?" Pamela studied Bettina's expression. It seemed

clear that her friend had one particular thing in mind, and soon that thing was revealed.

"Penny is moving to Illinois," Bettina said in the direst of tones.

"Not forever." Pamela sounded more convinced than she felt. "Just a few years. I'm sure she'll want to settle in the Northeast when she finishes."

"What if she meets someone there, and he wants to live there, or . . . what if he wants to move to *California*?"

Longing to soothe herself as well as Bettina, Pamela searched her brain for a response—an old saying, perhaps, like the old sayings Wilfred often invoked. They soothed because they implied that no situation was so unique others hadn't confronted it too. "No use crying over spilt milk" wouldn't really do, nor would "Every cloud has a silver lining."

Even though no soothing words had been uttered, Bettina's expression had suddenly changed yet again—to delight. The explanation came soon enough, as the server appeared at the end of their booth and lowered a heavy oval platter onto each place mat.

The Monte Cristo sandwiches did indeed resemble French toast, even to the sprinkling of powdered sugar, but they were not alone on their platters. Each was accompanied by a golden and glistening mound of French fries and a small portion of coleslaw in a pleated paper cup.

With a cheery, "Enjoy it, ladies," the server departed.

"I definitely think I will," Bettina declared as she seized a French fry with thumb and index finger and transported it to her lips.

The Monte Cristos had been sliced on the diagonal and each half speared with a frilled toothpick. Pamela took up her knife and fork and cut off a corner from one of the halves. As she lifted the fork bearing the potential bite, she could see a cross section of the sandwich: the pink ham layer and the paler turkey layer bordered on each side by a strip of melted Swiss cheese.

The bite did not disappoint. Rather than simply tasting like the bread had been buttered and toasted on a grill, the sandwich's effect was indeed like thin layers of ham, turkey, and Swiss cheese enclosed between two slices of French toast, rich with milk and beaten egg. The powdered sugar added a contrasting hint of sweetness to the sandwich's savory interior. Bettina seemed pleased with her sandwich as well. One half was already gone, and she was just sampling a forkful of coleslaw.

When she finally spoke again, it was first to praise the chef, and she added, "I know that when Hyler's got this new cook and he started calling himself a 'chef,' I was one of the ones who laughed, but I'm a convert now."

The conversation then drifted into channels more cheerful than Penny's graduate school plans. Pamela was happy to listen to Bettina's description of the many online sources for dollhouse furnishings, sharing her friend's joy in finally having a granddaughter she could shower with girly gifts.

* * *

"My turn to pay, I think," Pamela said sometime later, as she surveyed platters bare of all but the pleated paper coleslaw cups, now empty, and the discarded toothpicks with their cellophane frills.

Bettina tilted her milkshake glass and angled the straw to capture the milky, melted dregs before handing it over to the server. The check appeared then, and Pamela reached for her wallet. She extracted a few bills and tucked them and the check under the bowl that held packets of sugar substitute. Then she and Bettina went on their way.

Most of the afternoon lay ahead, but Pamela had work to finish for *Fiber Craft*. Back at home and upstairs in her office, she looked over her evaluations of "Ancient Espadrilles," "Crocheting Coral," and "Doubling Up." Deciding they sounded clear and fair, and even skimming the "Ancient Espadrilles" article to make sure it really deserved to be rejected, she sent them off to Celine Bramley, attached to an email message in which she explained that the book review would be on its way soon.

The two sentences she had drafted that morning, right before she got the phone call from Eilert Kroll, had proved to be a good start. It was the work of only an hour to complete her review of *Stitches in Time: What Garments from the Past Can Tell Us That History Can't* and send it, too, on its way to Celine Bramley.

CHAPTER 9

The next morning found Pamela sitting at her kitchen table with the material she had brought home from Eilert Kroll's office spread out before her. She and the cats had breakfasted, the kitchen had been tidied, and she had dressed. No new assignments for *Fiber Craft* had appeared in her inbox—and this morning seemed as good a time as any to follow up on Eilert's request that she let him know whether the contents of the manila envelopes and tattered file folders could be shaped into a worthwhile article.

She had opened one of the file folders to discover a sheaf of sketches fastened together with an oversized paper clip and labeled, with a sticky note, "Mariposa." The top sketch showed, half-hidden by the sticky note, a tunic-like garment with long sleeves and a turtleneck. The shoulders were wide, but the garment narrowed toward the bottom in a way that suggested a cocoon. Parts of the sketch had been shaded with colored pencil, suggesting stripes of vivid orange and deep green against an aqua background.

Pamela removed the paper clip and set the top sketch aside to reveal another garment of similar shape, but featuring a V-neck and three-quarter-length sleeves. Other sketches carried out the same theme, but with a few variations in sleeve length and neckline. The focus of the sketches seemed more on the designs on the fronts of the garments, however, and the garments—Pamela now realized—were sweaters.

As she paged through the sketches, the designs became more and more complex, in a way that could be realized only in a knitted garment. There were undulating stripes, splotches of color, images that suggested abstract flowers—even bugs.

The doorbell's chime interrupted her as she gazed at a sweater whose entire front was taken up with a swirling spiral, deep indigo against daffodil yellow. As the spiral grew too wide for the sweater's front, the coiling stripe of indigo turned into a fanciful doodle that ended only with the sweater's hem.

Once Pamela reached the entry, any mystery about her visitor's identity was dispelled. Bettina's scarlet coif was visible through the lace that curtained the oval window in the front door. Her first words as she stepped across the threshold were, "I can't stay," and she thrust a canvas tote bag into Pamela's hand as testimony that her visit was not a mere social call.

"Asparagus from the Newfield farmers market," she explained. "Wilfred went out first thing, and he's back already. It's just come into season at the local farms."

Pamela peeked inside the bag to see a neat pile of asparagus spears, all the same length, thicker and pale green at the bottoms, narrower and brighter green at the delicate budded tips.

"You should eat it soon," Bettina added, "but meanwhile it can go in the refrigerator."

"I'll wrap it in a kitchen towel and give you your tote back."

Pamela edged toward the kitchen doorway with Bettina following. She set the tote bag on the counter and continued on to the laundry room in quest of a fresh kitchen towel. When she returned to the kitchen, she found Bettina seated at the table poring over the colorful sketches from the group that the sticky note had identified as "Mariposa."

Pamela laid the kitchen towel out on the counter and reached into the tote to gather the loose spears into a bundle. They were cool and smooth against her fingers. In the background, she could hear the shuffle of papers at the table and Bettina's admiring murmurs. She laid the bundle of asparagus at one end of the towel and gently rolled it up.

As she turned to head for the refrigerator, Bettina exclaimed, "Look at this one!"

The sketch in question showed another one of the long, cocoon-like sweaters. It was a striking shade of hot pink, accented with horizontal turquoise stripes. The stripes were irregular, however—some wider, some narrower, some wider at one end but narrower at the other, in a way that made them seem to dance across the sweater's front.

Pamela halted midway to the refrigerator and set the

asparagus bundle on the table among the sketches, the bright kitchen towel wrapped around it adding to the colorful display.

The sweater looked very familiar. She lowered herself into the chair across the table from Bettina. Of course, of course. She picked up the sticky note and read aloud: "Mariposa." Into her mind there came the image of the label on the sweater Penny had brought back from her thrifting expedition to Haversack. It had read "Mariposa," and a little, stylized butterfly had accompanied the word. The sweater had been very 1980s in shape, like this sketch, *and* it had been hot pink with irregular turquoise stripes.

Mariposa actually meant "butterfly" in Spanish, she thought. She had come across that somewhere. The asparagus remained on the table as Pamela hurried from the kitchen to fetch her phone.

Bettina watched curiously as Pamela took a seat in the chair she had vacated and pressed the button that would bring her phone to life. She then touched the icon that summoned a keyboard to her phone's screen and keyed in "Mariposa sweaters." By the time the internet had brought up a string of possibilities occasioned by that prompt, Bettina had left her chair and was hovering over Pamela's shoulder. Pamela clicked on "Mariposa sweater collection," and together they scanned the small screen.

The Mariposa sweater collection, it seemed, had appeared in 1985, the debut collection of the knitwear designer Nestor Flavin. It had been greeted with much acclaim, and orders had been placed by buyers from the likes of Bergdorf and Neiman Marcus. Nestor's future in the world of fashion seemed assured, but that assurance was short-lived. Subsequent collections were panned as more of the same, and not even that. "He's lost the spark" was a frequent refrain.

"Poor man," Bettina murmured, and she left her post at Pamela's shoulder to return to her chair.

Pamela, however, continued to browse the internet, staring at the screen as her fingers alternately stroked and poked.

"He's trying for a comeback," she said, looking up after a bit. Focusing on the screen again, she quoted, "Citing the cyclical nature of fashion, Flavin believes that the ideas expressed in the Mariposa collection are once more relevant, and he's looking forward to unveiling Mariposa II come fall."

Pamela set her phone down and addressed Bettina. "Are you thinking what I'm thinking?" she inquired.

"Big shoulders never really go away, no matter how unflattering they are?"

Pamela laughed. "No—something more sinister."

"That's sinister," Bettina replied. "I hated that look, and now the fancy stores at the mall are full of it again."

Pamela rested her elbows on the table, leaned toward Bettina, and said, "Nestor Flavin owes the success of the 1985 Mariposa collection to Ingrid Barrick." She picked up a few of the sketches. "This material proves it."

"Oh, my!" Bettina's indignation at the thought of big shoulders returning was replaced by shock at this revelation. Her mouth sagged, and her eyes stared. "Ingrid and Nestor were living together in the early eighties, so collaborating on the collection could have seemed natural. They were two creative people having fun sharing ideas."

"He didn't give her any credit, though." Pamela fingered the sketch of the hot-pink and turquoise sweater. "Ingrid came up with this design, and all these others"— she waved her hand over the sketches scattered across the table—"but the collection was billed as Nestor Flavin's. The eighties were quite a while ago, and I guess they were a time when women still loyally contributed to men's success with no expectation of credit."

"Ingrid had to be satisfied with reflected glory— reflected from the man her work had made successful." Bettina shook her head slowly, but then the movement stopped with a shudder. "Are you thinking what I'm thinking?" she inquired, echoing Pamela's earlier question.

"Nestor is trying for a comeback, and the last thing he needs is for word to get out that he didn't actually design the first Mariposa collection."

"Exactly!" Pamela nodded. "And how might he imagine he could prevent word from getting out?"

"Convince Eilert to ignore Ingrid's early work in his book . . . but that wouldn't really solve the problem." Bettina took a deep breath and raised a hand to her chest. Her eyes grew large.

Pamela finished the thought. "As long as Ingrid was still alive, Nestor's secret would never be safe."

"Now Ingrid is out of the way," Bettina observed, "but right here on your kitchen table is evidence that Ingrid deserves credit for that collection."

"Nestor doesn't know it's here," Pamela pointed out,

"but he knows Eilert intends to go ahead with his vision for the book."

Bettina lifted her wrist to check her watch and seemed startled after a glance at its face. "I was just going to drop off the asparagus," she said, "but I've been here so long we could have had coffee."

"I can make some"—Pamela started to rise—"and cinnamon toast? You always like that."

"I can't stay." Bettina rose too. "Maxie is bringing Betty over. I bought some new outfits for her favorite doll, and we're going to try them on."

Bettina herself was wearing a new outfit, a blue-and-white seersucker jumpsuit just right for a perfect May day. On her feet were pale blue ballet flats, and a necklace and earrings of bold white beads added extra flair.

Pamela followed her friend into the entry and opened the door. Before she stepped out onto the porch, Bettina paused to say, "Knit and Nibble at Roland's tonight. I'll pick you up at a quarter to seven."

Once Bettina was on her way, Pamela returned to the kitchen, where the bundle of asparagus still sat on the table among the material documenting the early years of Ingrid's career. She transferred the asparagus to the refrigerator, gathered the sketches back into a compact sheaf, replaced the paper clip that had fastened them together, and reaffixed the sticky note. Then she stacked the manila envelopes and file folders, topping the pile with the small printed brochure Eilert had included.

There was a lot of material besides the Mariposa sketches, and she'd look through the rest later. She was puzzled about what to tell Eilert, though. Obviously the sweater designs were an important chapter in Ingrid's artistic development—but what if it was Nestor who had murdered her? And what if that meant Eilert was in danger too?

Pamela was just as glad Bettina hadn't accepted the offer of coffee and cinnamon toast. It was getting on toward lunchtime, and something more substantial was in order. The chicken that had already provided three dinners still had just enough meat left on its bones to make a sandwich-worth of chicken salad, mixed up with mayonnaise and chopped celery. And even the bones still had something to give. After she had made and eaten the sandwich, Pamela lowered them into her largest saucepan, added water, and set the pan, covered, to simmer on a back burner for chicken soup.

Celine Bramley was seldom at rest for long. A premonition drew Pamela up the stairs to her office, where she transferred Ginger from her keyboard to her lap and woke her computer by allowing her mouse to explore its mouse pad at will. As she had expected, a message from her boss at *Fiber Craft* waited in her inbox, complete with the stylized paper clip that indicated attachments.

"Please copyedit these articles and get them back to me by noon next Tuesday," read the message. Ranged across the top of the message were the short titles that previewed the articles: "Ahead of Its Time," "A Far-Flung Clan," and "Woven to Last."

Pamela always kept the shades down in her office,

believing that she concentrated better if her work area was an island of light in a dim room. The shades glowed on sunny days, however, and darkened as evening came on, and she was often well aware that the chance for a pleasant walk had come and gone as she pored over an article for *Fiber Craft*.

Today the shades glowed especially bright, and Celine Bramley had given her a week to accomplish her new assignment. Without opening even one file to discover an article's full title behind its tantalizing file name, she pushed her chair back from her desk, transferred Ginger to the floor, and stood up.

She would not take a walk today, however. An excursion to her own backyard would satisfy the urge to experience the May sunshine and breezes. She headed downstairs, with Ginger in the lead, and made her way through the kitchen and out the back door. A small bed of dark earth interrupted the expanse of lawn. The bed's location was strategic, chosen to avoid the shade cast by several large trees, including a venerable catalpa, because tomatoes required lots of intense sun.

The seedlings were doing well, noticeably larger than they had been when she'd checked them on Sunday. There were four of them, different kinds, including early-bearing and later, chosen with the goal of having fresh tomatoes from mid-summer well into fall. Soon she would fetch her wire tomato cages from the garage. To look at the four little plants now, with their spindly stems and lacy leaves, it was hard to picture the sprawl that she knew would come and that the cages would contain.

A few weeds had already sprouted. They were delicate, too, now, but they would grow, and fast. She plucked them up, trailing crumbs of dark earth from the fine filaments of their roots, and carried them to the compost heap at the back corner of the yard.

Refreshed after her venture into the backyard, Pamela climbed the stairs to her office and sat back down at her desk. She brought up the email message from Celine Bramley and clicked on the first file listed at the top of the page: "Ahead of Its Time." When the article opened in Word, the full title proved to be "Ahead of Its Time: Zero-Waste Fashion in the Indus Valley." Pamela hadn't been the one to evaluate the article for publication, and so it wasn't until she began reading that she realized the subject was the sari, still worn every day by Indian woman on the subcontinent and on ceremonial occasions by Indian women everywhere.

The sari, it appeared, had been worn as long ago as the third millennium BC, and in a form that differed little from modern versions. In essence, a sari was a strip of fabric gathered around the waist to form an ankle-length skirt and then draped over a shoulder or arranged to veil the head. It required woven fabric, of course, lots of woven fabric. Thus the cultivation of cotton and the development of spinning and weaving would have been prerequisites to its development. Illustrations included photographs of ancient bas-reliefs in which female figures wore clearly recognizable saris, as well as photographs of twenty-first-century models wearing remarkably similar garments.

The author, an anthropologist who studied the earliest Indian civilizations but who also described herself as an advocate for sustainable fashion, pointed out that the sari was the original zero-waste design. Not a scrap of fabric was wasted—a great advantage in an era when every step in producing a woven fabric was done by hand, but newly appreciated by advocates for sustainable fashion. "Everything old is new again," she concluded hopefully.

Pamela had been editing as she read, adding a comma here and removing one there, correcting the occasional typo—like "scarp" instead of "scrap," and removing "in my opinion" from spots where the context made it clear that the statement was, indeed, the author's opinion. When she reached the end of the article, she closed her eyes. Then she opened them and checked the clock. Another pass through the article would be a good idea, but not now. It was time to have a quick dinner before Bettina picked her up for Knit and Nibble.

CHAPTER 10

"I see what Roland meant about the deer eating everything," Bettina commented as she and Pamela made their way up the walk that bisected the DeCamps' well-groomed lawn.

The shrubs that bordered the foundation of their spacious house resembled the shrub version of skeletons—just a stark cross-hatching of bare twigs and stems against the pale shingles of the house's façade. The front door was slightly ajar. It opened wider as they approached and Melanie DeCamp appeared in the doorway.

"Yes," she said, but with a smile, "the deer have been eating everything they can find. They ate all my lilies, and now they're going for the shrubbery."

Melanie was dressed for the balmy evening in slim pants and a shirt of cream-colored linen, a color that suited her blond elegance. She moved aside with a welcoming gesture, and Pamela and Bettina stepped into the DeCamps' stylish living room. Nell was already seated in the comfortable armchair always reserved for her. Holly and Karen, being younger and more limber, were perched on the low-slung turquoise sofa. Roland was nowhere to be seen, but the sleek turquoise chair was already occupied by Cuddles, the cat. The briefcase that Roland used for a knitting bag rested on the carpet near the chair.

"People have been complaining about it on the listserv," Holly said, looking up from the partially completed bikini top she had just removed from her knitting bag.

In response to a blank stare from Nell, she clarified. "The deer, eating everything, like Melanie was saying."

"They're complaining about pollen, too, or the potential for pollen." Melanie was not an official member of the knitting group, but she often lingered to chat when the group met at the DeCamps' house. "That woman—Dorcas?—is especially vocal."

Pamela and Bettina made their way to the sofa, which was long enough to accommodate four people easily, and took seats at either end, with Holly and Karen in the middle.

"Dorcas Sprain?" Bettina asked.

"That's her." Holly nodded, and her dark ponytail bounced. "She was a neighbor of the woman who was killed, I gather. Just today she posted a note saying something like, 'Not to speak ill of the dead, but she was growing ragweed on purpose and it was very inconsiderate and the plants are still there.'"

Pamela was listening, but she was focused on her project too. It was still in the early stages, and she was in no rush, given that it would be half a year or more until the weather was conducive to wearing a wool sweater. She'd done a bit on and off at home, but the back—the first section she had tackled—was still in progress, and she had many inches of cobalt to go before switching over to the orange-yellow-chartreuse ombre yarn for the fun part.

"Dorcas doesn't like the bees either," Melanie added. Leaving Cuddles undisturbed, she had perched on the edge of the chair that would soon be occupied by Roland. "Someone in that neighborhood apparently has beehives, and the bees are all over the place."

"Pamela met the beekeeper." Bettina paused in the act of rummaging in her knitting bag.

"Are honeybees the ones that sting?" Karen asked.

Before anyone could answer—assuming anyone actually knew the answer—footsteps on the wooden flooring of the hallway announced the arrival of Roland. He'd evidently been baking, as suggested by a comforting sugary aroma that had grown more intense in the past few minutes, but he had also been listening to the conversation.

"People have a right to do whatever they want in their own yards," he said. "It's private property."

Melanie stood. "The Knit and Nibblers are all present and accounted for now," she observed with a charming smile, as she laid a fond hand on her husband's arm. "So I'll leave you to your knitting."

Roland settled onto the turquoise chair, making sure the cat had enough space to stretch along his pinstripe-

clad thigh, and hefted the briefcase from the floor onto
his lap. Nell's fingers had paused in mid-stitch as he'd
declared the rights of property owners to be incontro-
vertible, and she watched from her armchair as he took
his project, with its four needles and dangling bobbins,
from the briefcase. Then, apparently satisfied that he
had no interest in further developing views so antithet-
ical to her own, she returned to her own work, adding
one more stitch and then another to the bright red
sweater that was to be a Christmas gift for her husband.

Soon Holly and Karen were chatting companion-
ably, about house projects and garden plans, with
Bettina chiming in from her end of the sofa. At the
other end, Pamela was happy to knit in silence, finding
the buzz of conversation nearly as soothing as the soft
touch of yarn against her fingers and the rhythmic motions of her needles. Time passed in this way, with
Bettina describing Wilfred's foray into geraniums and
Karen remarking that she had been very successful
with geraniums in the past.

"I'm not sure if the deer like them," she added, "but
we have them in pots on our deck, and the deer haven't
figured out how to climb steps yet."

"We have them in pots on the patio," Bettina said,
"but so far they haven't been eaten."

Out of the corner of her eye, Pamela could see
Bettina's knitting project, the beginnings of the yellow
pullover for her grandson Freddy, lying untouched on
her lap—and Roland, usually so industrious, was idle
as well. He, however, was not chatting. He was poised
on the edge of his chair staring at his watch as Cuddles,
too, tensed as if prepared for action.

Pamela stole a look at her own watch to see that it was nearing ten minutes to eight. Just as the second hand reached the twelve, Roland sprang to his feet, announced, "Refreshments in ten minutes," and headed for the hallway. The cat's fast-moving feet were a blur as he scurried after his master.

Pamela was in mid-row and kept knitting, as did Nell across the way, but Melanie had returned and perched on Roland's chair, and soon chatting had replaced knitting for everyone else. Melanie was especially interested in Holly's bikini project, of which the entire top was now nearly complete. Holly held it up against her chest, which was clothed at the moment in a vintage T-shirt featuring the logo of an eighties rock band.

There was just time for exclamations of approval before Roland entered, bearing a large pewter tray. On it sat seven cup and saucer sets, pale porcelain, and simple but elegant in design. Five of the cups contained coffee, and two were empty. He lowered the tray to the coffee table and turned back the way he had come. On his second entrance, he carried another tray just like the first but for its cargo: a porcelain teapot, a porcelain cream and sugar set, and forks, spoons, and small napkins.

Melanie poured tea into the empty cups, made sure everyone had coffee or tea close at hand and access to the cream and sugar, then headed for the kitchen with the empty trays.

"He's very proud of his creation," she said as she departed.

From the direction of the kitchen came a voice saying, "I'm just waiting for it to be an exact hour since I took it out of the oven."

"It will be fine," Melanie's voice responded.

"Where are the strawberries?"

"In a bowl in the refrigerator," came Melanie's voice.

The creation made its appearance shortly thereafter, squares of puffy golden cake topped with sliced strawberries rendered syrupy by an infusion of sugar.

"Layers!" Bettina commented as she carved off a bite with her fork.

"It's magic," Roland said with a satisfied smile. "The layers form while it bakes, and it's only four ingredients."

The bottom layer was like a firm custard, Pamela thought. The middle layer was softer, and the top layer had an almost soufflé-like quality. The taste was simple and sweet, the perfect foil for the strawberries, which were at the peak of their tart-sweet ripeness.

"It's certainly the season for strawberries," Nell said, "and this is such a clever way to use them—like strawberry shortcake."

Karen joined the conversation. "That's my favorite of all, and with whipped cream on top too."

"This would be good with whipped cream." Bettina paused her fork to study the bit of cake and the strawberry slice that had been on its way to her mouth. "Or vanilla ice cream." The fork resumed its progress, and she chewed thoughtfully. "Definitely ice cream," she added after she had swallowed.

"What about a little chocolate too?" Holly suggested. "I love the combination of chocolate and strawberries."

"Like those whole ones dipped in chocolate!" Bettina smiled at the thought. "I wonder if a chocolate version of this cake would be possible . . . maybe by putting cocoa powder in the batter?"

"Then it would be like layers of chocolate custard and chocolate mousse and chocolate soufflé." Holly's eyes, always bright, grew even brighter, and her dimple appeared. "And then the strawberries on top, of course. Yummy!"

"Don't forget the whipped cream!" Bettina exclaimed. "Or maybe ice cream!"

Roland had relinquished his chair to Melanie and fetched a chair from the dining room, which he had pulled up to the end of the coffee table. He had been concentrating on his cake and coffee, but suddenly he returned his fork to his plate with a *clunk*.

"I thought it was quite good the way it was," he said, addressing no one in particular.

"Definitely." Nell spoke up. "And not too sweet."

"But I wanted it to be sweet." Roland half-turned to face the armchair where she was sitting.

"I just said it wasn't *too* sweet." Nell could look stern even when she didn't mean to, with the intense focus of her pale eyes in their nests of wrinkles.

"Desserts are supposed to be sweet." Roland made this statement as gravely as if he was citing a precedent while arguing a legal case. "My cake turned out exactly the way it was supposed to."

A prolonged silence followed, during which people made a show of finishing the last bits of cake and strawberries on their plates, even to the crumbs and shreds of berry that might otherwise have been overlooked. When the plates were as clean as they could be and the silence threatened to become awkward, Holly leaned forward.

"The planters along Arborville Avenue are such a good idea," she chirped. "Petunias and snapdragons are so colorful."

A number of heads nodded in agreement, and possibly relief that the silence had been breached, but it was Roland who spoke: "No one asked me if I wanted them."

Bettina's "At least it's not ragweed" was greeted with a few titters.

"I'm not the one who complains about ragweed." Roland surveyed the group lined up on the sofa and then tilted his head to include Nell.

"Use of your tax dollars?" Bettina inquired. "Let me guess."

"People can plant their own flowers in their own yards, whatever they want, even ragweed—but don't spend my money that I pay in taxes to plant flowers that I don't want or even like along Arborville Avenue."

"The planters along Arborville Avenue were discussed at the last town meeting," Bettina said. "Everyone was invited, and afterward I wrote an article about it for the *Advocate*."

"I'm a busy person, and I don't have time to go to *town meetings*." Roland pronounced the words as if they named something vaguely distasteful. "And as for the *Advocate*—"

"Roland and I love it!" Melanie sprang up from the low-slung turquoise chair, demonstrating the athletic prowess of her well-toned legs.

"How could anyone not like snapdragons?" Karen whispered to Holly.

Roland rose to his feet too. "And I'll make my desserts just as sweet as I want," he declared before bending over to collect the empty plates.

From the armchair came Nell's quiet murmur. "I only said it wasn't *too* sweet."

After clearing the coffee table and collecting Nell's cup and saucer and plate, Roland reclaimed the turquoise chair. Cuddles joined him, and the knitters took up their projects again. For a time the only sound in the room was the quiet *click* of knitting needles. When conversation resumed, it was limited to subdued exchanges between Holly and Karen or Holly and Bettina as Pamela knitted on, relishing the freedom to say nothing at all.

CHAPTER 11

The next morning, Pamela returned to her office after breakfast to respond to an email message from her mother. Not feeling quite in the mood yet to craft sentences, despite two cups of coffee, she let her mouse stray to the upper margin of the screen and thence to "Favorites," and soon found herself scrolling through the latest posts on the town's listserv, Access-Arborville.

Dorcas Sprain had been very busy. Here was a post from just this morning, asking if anyone knew whether Ingrid's house was going to be put on the market and hoping that, if so, the new owners would replace the wild butterfly garden with a lawn "like normal people have." Responding to the post, someone else seconded the wish for a new owner and new landscaping, and remarked that the butterfly garden was not only a hazard for people with allergies, but also an "eye sour."

Don't people proofread? Pamela often wondered. Or did this person think that the expression actually was "eye sour"? It did make sense, though, in an odd way, as a description of an unsavory spectacle.

Here was a message asking if anyone had found a green hoodie after canasta at the rec center and providing a phone number to call if so. It was immediately followed by one with the heading "Killer Bees."

"Yes," the writer had posted, "the ragweed is a menace, and it's ugly, but even the pretty plants are dangerous because they attract BEES. I personally do not believe that people should be allowed to put BEEHIVES in their yards that encourage BEES to TAKE UP RESIDENCE and fly all over the town scaring people. Where are our elected officials?"

Still chuckling about "eye sour," Pamela closed AccessArborville and returned to her email program, where she applied herself for the next half hour to filling her mother in on her and Penny's recent doings.

After sending the message on its way, she headed for the kitchen, where she plucked from the front of the refrigerator the ongoing shopping list normally held in place with a magnet shaped like a mitten. The gift of asparagus from the Frasers deserved accompaniments that would show it to best advantage, so to the list she added salmon and a potato suitable for mashing.

An hour later, Pamela's Co-Op errand had been accomplished, and she was heading home along Orchard Street, lugging two over-full canvas tote bags and eager to set them down. As she neared her house, she noticed

Bettina across the street, dressed in a colorful sundress and checking her mailbox. But no sooner did Bettina catch sight of her than she scurried back inside her house. Odd, Pamela thought. No greeting or even a wave.

She continued on her way, however, up her front walk to the steps, and up the steps to her porch. There, she rested the tote bags while she retrieved her own mail and fished her keys out of her purse. She unlocked her door, collected the tote bags, and stepped inside.

She was just storing away the new cans of cat food, observed by all three cats, when a subtle shift in the orientation of Ginger's delicate ears indicated that something interesting was happening in the direction of the front door. A moment later, the doorbell's chime drew all three cats to the entry, with Pamela following. On the porch stood a figure so very familiar that she was instantly recognizable even through the lace that curtained the oval window in the front door.

Pamela opened the door to admit Bettina, who stepped across the threshold carrying a platter whose contents were hidden by aluminum foil. Barely stopping, she said, "I was here before, but you weren't home," and continued on to the kitchen.

Pamela entered her kitchen only a few moments later to find Bettina at work emptying the tote bag that still rested on the table.

"You do this," she instructed, waving at the assorted groceries, which were now sharing the table's surface with the foil-covered platter. "You know where things go better than I do. I'll make the coffee."

As if to offer a preview of the pleasures in store once the groceries were put away and the coffee made, she peeled the foil from the platter. On it lay a flat roll of golden pastry, glistening with a sugary glaze. The pastry had been scored at intervals down its length, allowing glimpses of a rosy-red, syrupy filling.

"Strawberry strudel," she announced as she headed for the stove, where the kettle waited. "Wilfred came back from the farmers market with so many strawberries that he made some into refrigerator jam before they got too ripe. Then he got the idea to use the jam in this strudel."

Some minutes later, the table had been cleared of groceries and set with cups, saucers, and small plates from Pamela's wedding china. Pamela supplied forks, spoons, and napkins as the aroma of brewing coffee began to fill the little kitchen, while Bettina transferred the cut-glass sugar bowl to the table, along with the matching cream pitcher, filled with heavy cream.

"You can serve it," Pamela said, with reference to the strudel, after they had taken their seats. She popped up again to fetch a knife.

Knife in hand, Bettina sliced off two generous servings of the strudel and eased them from the platter onto the small, rose-garlanded plates. Her next order of business was to add sugar to her coffee, stir vigorously, and follow with dollops of cream as the contents of her cup grew more and more pale.

After a first bite of strudel and a first sip of coffee, she glanced across the table at Pamela, who had tasted her own strudel and was nodding vigorously as she chewed. The flaky puff pastry was the perfect complement to Wilfred's syrupy, homemade jam. But once the strudel's excellence had been agreed upon, the conversation took a less-comforting turn.

"I looked at AccessArborville this morning," Bettina commented. "What Holly was saying last night reminded me that the listserv can often point me to ideas for articles. If people are posting about something, it might be newsworthy."

"Did you find anything . . . newsworthy?" Pamela looked up from carving off another bite of strudel.

"A woman on Larch Street is trying to rehome a groundhog."

"Rehome?"

"In a forest, or something, far away from her garden." Bettina took a sip of coffee.

"I looked at the listserv this morning too," Pamela said. "I didn't see the post about the groundhog, but Dorcas Sprain has been very busy posting, going on and on and on about the ragweed—at least she thinks it's ragweed—and asking whether, if Ingrid's house is sold, the new owner will be more considerate to allergy sufferers. And somebody else—not Dorcas Sprain—thinks that the butterfly garden is an 'eye sour.'"

She paused for a bite of strudel and went on. "I don't suppose Detective Clayborn looks at the listserv, though he should. It's pretty obvious that Dorcas Sprain bore a real grudge against Ingrid Barrick."

"He still thinks Ingrid's death was the result of a break-in gone awry." Bettina shook her head, as if lamenting Detective Clayborn's stubbornness. "I don't, but I think Nestor Flavin is a more likely suspect than Dorcas. If Dorcas is the killer, it's awfully dumb of her to keep reminding everyone of her feelings about Ingrid's yard."

Pamela shrugged. "Maybe she's posting on the listserv for exactly that reason. People assume a guilty person wouldn't keep bringing up their conflict with the victim, so if she keeps bringing up her conflict with the victim, she must not be guilty."

"Maybe," Bettina said, "but when it comes to motives for murder, Nestor's would have been awfully strong, stronger than Dorcas and the ragweed. He's worried about his creative reputation, especially now that he's trying to make a comeback."

"I *do* agree." Pamela nodded as she felt her forehead contract into a frown. "He stole her ideas, and he passed them off as his own, and now it looks like that might catch up with him."

Bettina nodded sadly. "And he's not the first man who ever stole a woman's ideas and took the credit!"

"If he's really the killer, we can't let him get away with it, or with stealing her ideas," Pamela said. "I wonder where he was the night Ingrid was murdered."

"Night?" Bettina asked. "The break-in gone awry theory placed the killing at night—but if Nestor was the killer, he could have come at any time, as if he was paying a social call. He was someone she knew."

"If he killed her before it got dark, who turned on the light the neighbor saw?"

"So"—Bettina regarded Pamela over the rim of her coffee cup—"if Nestor Flavin did it, she was killed some time after it got dark, but at least eight hours before the mail carrier found her body at ten the next morning—because the medical examiner said she'd been dead at least eight hours."

She raised her cup to her mouth and tipped her head back to drain the last inch of coffee. Then she tucked the foil around what was left of the strudel, leaned on the table to boost herself to her feet, and dashed to the entry. When she returned, she was holding her phone and fingering its already-illuminated screen.

"Nestor Flavin isn't the most common name," she observed as she lowered herself into her chair. "You can keep the rest of the strudel, by the way. Wilfred made two."

Intuiting that Bettina was eager to launch the investigation into Nestor's whereabouts on the night of Ingrid's murder, Pamela hurriedly finished the last few bites of her strudel and drained her coffee cup. While Bettina focused on her phone, murmuring to herself from time to time, Pamela cleared the table and rinsed the wedding china.

"I've found him," Bettina announced just as Pamela was drying her hands. "This has to be him: Nestor Flavin on Dimity Court in Weecaucus." She poked at the screen, it went dark, and she stood. "I'll drive."

"What if he's not home?" Pamela inquired.

"*Duh!*" Bettina laughed. "We're not going to knock on his door and say, 'Hi, Nestor. We're wondering if you were in Arborville the Monday before last, killing Ingrid Barrick.' We're going to talk to his neighbors."

Weecaukus was some distance to the south. It was reached via the Turnpike, with its harrowing multilane traffic, and Pamela was relieved when they arrived at their exit. The spiraling exit ramp turned into a busy street that led east toward the Hudson River, and ten minutes later, that street intersected with a road that meandered along the river's shore. On this bright May day, the river reflected the deep blue of the sky, a blue interrupted only where the breeze tossed up lacy wave-lets.

Dimity Court turned off the meandering road and curved around to parallel the river. Along it, a row of town houses clad in shingles weathered to silver offered unobstructed views of the river and of Manhattan, on the opposite shore. It ended in a cul-de-sac, which enabled Bettina to circle back past the town houses and follow a sign pointing to visitors' parking nearer to the main, meandering road.

Once she had parked, they set out on foot along the sidewalk that served the town houses. Nestor Flavin's was number 12, but a neighbor at number 14 had just begun to pull into her driveway. In obedient response to her BMW's arrival, the garage door was slowly rising. Bettina, however, sped up and waved to catch her attention before the BMW carried her into the garage's depths.

"Hi there," Bettina called when the woman braked and turned. "Do you see your neighbor Nestor Flavin around much?"

Bettina seldom had trouble getting answers to her questions, and the woman seemed happy to respond.

"Nestor? He spends a lot of time in the city," she said. "There's a ferry, right from Weecaucus, so he zips back and forth."

"How about the Monday before last? Did you see him then?"

"The Monday before last?" The woman screwed her lips into a puzzled knot and stared at Bettina. "That's a long time ago. Why that day in particular?"

Bettina, however, was undeterred. "Night, actually," she clarified. "The Monday night before last."

"I don't have a clue," the woman said. "You could ask him yourself, but he went dashing out about an hour ago. I was on my way out too. He was in quite a state, muttering 'Wendelstaff, Wendelstaff.'" She shrugged, and a comical expression transformed her attractive features. "He talks to himself a lot. It's the creative gene, I guess."

Having said that, she faced forward and accelerated, adding, "Have a nice day!"

Pamela and Bettina looked at each other. Pamela had never suggested to Bettina that Nestor's desire to hide the fact that Ingrid was actually responsible for the Mariposa Collection could endanger Eilert. But Bettina had apparently come to that conclusion on her own just now.

"Eilert knows Nestor is an impostor," she whispered. "And Nestor needs to silence him."

They proceeded back toward the visitors' parking lot, each deep in thought and neither speaking. When they reached the Toyota, however, Pamela broke the silence.

"It seems preposterous to imagine that Nestor would drive up to the Wendelstaff campus and kill Eilert outright," she observed, "and yet . . . if he was capable of killing Ingrid . . ."

"As Wilfred would say, 'Might as well be hung for a sheep as a lamb.'" Bettina unlocked the passenger-side door, and Pamela lowered herself into her seat.

"Wendelstaff?" Bettina asked.

"Wendelstaff." Pamela nodded.

"We still don't know whether Nestor has an alibi for the night Ingrid was killed," Bettina commented as she steered the Toyota toward the main road.

* * *

Much to the relief of Pamela and Bettina, Eilert Kroll was alive. As they approached his office door from one end of the long hallway, he appeared at the other end, having just turned the corner from another corridor. He was dressed in black again, a slim and striking figure against the hallway's white walls, which were rendered all the whiter by the fluorescent lights overhead.

"Ladies!" He greeted them with a courtly bow as he drew closer. "This is an unexpected pleasure." His slight accent made the greeting seem even more charming. He bowed again when he reached the door. Opening it, he gestured for them to enter. "Business call or social?" he inquired once everyone was inside and seated, Eilert behind his desk and Pamela and Bettina in chairs facing it.

"We're wondering," Bettina said, "whether you've seen Nestor Flavin today."

"Should I have?" Eilert appeared taken aback, but in a genial way. He blinked a few times behind the lenses of his dark-framed glasses. "I've been away from my office all morning." He laughed, but briefly, as if laughter were a luxury to be rationed. Then his expression grew serious. "If he was here, I'm just as glad to have missed him. I'm not eager to explain—again— why I plan to include *all* of Ingrid's work in my book."

A tap on the door interrupted then, and Eilert called, "Enter. It's open."

The door swung inward and a head peeked around the edge. The head belonged to a middle-aged woman with graying hair pulled into an austere twist.

"Oops!" she said, spotting Pamela and Bettina. "I don't mean to intrude, but somebody was here a few hours ago looking for you. Quite a dapper gent, about sixty or so? Bow tie?"

Eilert nodded. "I know who it was. Did he say he was coming back?"

"Not really." The woman stepped far enough into the room to make her shrug visible. "He was quite excited, though, and very disappointed when he couldn't find you."

The woman backed out and pulled the door closed.

Eilert laughed again and said, "Apparently he won't take no for an answer."

"There's a reason." Pamela leaned forward. Studying Eilert's face as she spoke, she explained what she had discovered about Nestor's debt to Ingrid for the sweater designs that had launched his career.

"Very good sleuthing," Eilert murmured. "Very good, indeed."

"Now he's trying for a comeback," Bettina added, "so he especially would want to take full credit for the earlier designs."

Eilert half-stood and leaned forward as if mesmerized by what he was hearing. "What if Nestor is the person who killed her?" he whispered.

"Very good sleuthing," Bettina responded with a wink.

"The police—"

Bettina interrupted, "—have their own ideas. But meanwhile, *you* might not be safe."

Eilert sank back into his chair. "As I understood it from the reports of Ingrid's death, she died because there was a struggle and she fell, or she was struck on the head with a blunt object. The killer didn't necessarily show up with a deadly weapon."

"Ingrid died all the same," Bettina observed.

"I'm not worried. I think I could hold my own against Nestor."

Eilert *was* quite sinewy, Pamela reflected, as well as being about half Nestor's age, so perhaps he *could* hold his own.

"Thank you for the warning, though." Eilert stood. "And thank you for what you discovered about the sweater designs." He nodded at Pamela. "I look forward to giving Ingrid the credit she deserves, no matter what effect it has on Nestor's career. And I hope that somewhere in all that material, there are the seeds of at least one more article for *Fiber Craft*."

He stepped out from behind the desk, and Bettina moved toward the door. Pamela was about to follow her, but something on the desk caught her attention. It was a card, a glossy photograph of a tapestry, abstract in style but hinting at natural forms like flowers and insects. The colors were deep and vivid, juxtaposed in such a way that they seemed to vibrate. Eilert noticed Pamela lagging behind and paused on his way to the door.

"Oh, yes," he said. "I should have mentioned this— of course you'd be interested. Too bad it's not going to happen."

Pamela picked the card up and turned it over. "Ingrid Barrick—Recent Work," read the caption. "Nonesuch Gallery, May 6 to 18. Opening Reception May 6 at 6:00 p.m." The gallery's address placed it on a street in Timberley's commercial district.

"It's not going to happen?" Pamela inquired as she replaced the card on the desk.

"Everything has to be 'trendy' now, even—or especially—in the art world." Eilert's narrow lips twisted into a sarcastic smile. "The show of Ingrid's tapestries was canceled at the last minute in favor of something more 'trendy,' by a young man."

Bettina was interested now too. "When did the cancelation happen?" she asked. Her gaze had become intense, and a vertical crease had appeared between her brows.

Eilert responded, "As the card says, the show was supposed to open on May sixth. But it was canceled at the last minute, which was very inconsiderate, if you ask me!"

He explained that he had been in touch with Ingrid on the Sunday before her death, and she was furious because she had just heard from the gallery. The tapestries were going to be delivered back to her house the next day. He'd been planning to photograph the gallery show for his book, but she'd told him that, in view of the cancelation, he could come to her house sometime soon and photograph them there.

Eilert was lingering politely, but it seemed clear he needed to be on his way, perhaps to a class. The three of them stepped out into the hallway together, he headed to the left, and Pamela and Bettina headed the other direction, toward the elevators.

CHAPTER 12

"We missed lunch," Bettina commented as the elevator doors opened onto the building's sunny foyer. She checked the face of her pretty watch. "It's one o'clock."

"Timberley isn't far from here." Pamela led the way toward the monumental glass doors that led to the wide sweep of the building's steps.

Bettina responded with a question. "Are you thinking what I'm thinking?"

"That depends on what you're thinking."

"I'm thinking that Timberley has a lot of restaurants and we could grab a late lunch."

They pushed through the doors, against the flow of students heading in, and proceeded down the steps, dodging more students. As the grassy quadrangle came into view, and the small parking lot that served the student union, another solution to the lunch question presented itself.

At the edge of the parking lot was a food truck, a snub-nosed van painted bright turquoise. Emblazoned on the truck's side in block letters were the words "Tacos Burritos Enchiladas." A wide window in the side, shaded by a red-and-white-striped awning and furnished with a counter, gave a view of a small kitchen in the truck's interior. A man wearing a white apron was moving about inside, and a few students were waiting to be served.

Consultation was scarcely necessary. As if reading one another's minds, Pamela and Bettina followed the wide concrete path that led to the quadrangle and then the narrower path that cut across its end. By the time they reached the food truck, the students were moving away from the window bearing Styrofoam containers and paper cups, and the cheerful proprietor turned his attention to them.

The aromas coming from the compact kitchen were a tantalizing blend of frying meat tinged with spice, and warm corn tortillas. Rice and beans were a given. The only question was tacos, burritos, or enchiladas—and what should they contain?

Five minutes later, two sectioned Styrofoam containers appeared on the counter. Yellow rice occupied one section of each, and black beans another. The third section of Pamela's container held two enchiladas, neat rolls filled with chicken and blanketed with a sauce of tomato and chiles. The third section of Bettina's container held a plump burrito, also blanketed in sauce.

"Looks good?" the proprietor asked. Satisfied that

their enthusiastic nods meant yes, he lowered the hinged lids of the Styrofoam containers to enclose the food, then snapped the lids into place. The meal price included a paper cup of soda—both opted for orange drink—and Bettina insisted on paying.

"I know you'd have gone all day on nothing but your morning toast and that strudel we ate ages ago, but I need my lunch," she commented as they stepped away from the window carrying their Styrofoam containers, paper napkins and plastic knives and forks, and their drinks.

Bettina was veering toward where the Toyota was parked, but Pamela had another idea.

"There are picnic tables down by the river," she said. "That would be much more pleasant than eating in the car."

She led the way across the parking lot and along the side of the student union to several picnic tables that occupied a patch of grass where the Haversack River marked the western edge of the Wendelstaff campus. A few of the tables were in use, and students in outfits that approached beachwear also lounged on towels on the grass, soaking up the May sunlight. Only the backpacks abandoned nearby gave a clue to the context.

Pamela and Bettina put their lunches on an empty table and settled across from each other on the wooden benches. The first order of business was food, and Pamela realized as soon as she lifted the lid of her Styrofoam container that she was very hungry, Bettina's estimation of her ability to go all day without eating notwithstanding.

The plastic utensils were unwieldy but serviceable,

and the meal was well worth the effort of managing
them. The rustic taste of the corn tortillas comple-
mented the shredded chicken filling of the enchiladas,
and the combination was enlivened by the chili-infused
sauce, with its chunks of tomato fresh from harvesting.

"The beans are good," Bettina commented. "Made
from scratch with dried beans, I'm sure."

The beans did, indeed, have the earthy quality that
results from long simmering. Pamela and Bettina ate in
silence for a time. Even the students around them,
lulled by the mellow sun and the soft breezes, were
silent but for occasional murmurs. The river was high,
responding to the tide and the April rains, and only a
narrow border of mossy rocks was visible along the
nearest bank.

"Eilert seemed pretty convinced that Nestor posed
him no threat," Pamela commented as the food remaining in the compartments of her Styrofoam container
dwindled.

"Maybe, maybe not." Bettina looked up and raised a
skeptical brow. She had been using her plastic fork to
capture a last few grains of yellow rice. "Eilert might
be able to hold his own if Nestor lunged for him.
Ingrid, on the other hand, would have been totally
caught off guard. How many people expect murderous
intent on the part of someone apparently paying a social call?"

"We've been assuming that if Nestor intended to
protect his creative reputation by killing Ingrid, he
showed up with a plan to do just that—whereas if
Dorcas killed her, Ingrid's death was the accidental re-

sult of an argument that got out of control." Pamela
glanced at Bettina to make sure she agreed, and Bettina
nodded.

A new idea had begun to percolate in Pamela's mind,
set aside temporarily in the quest for food. She gazed
at the river, appreciating its gently rippling, distraction-
free surface, as she worked out the details. After a few
minutes, during which Bettina finished the last tidbits
of her burrito, she spoke.

"Here's another argument that might have gotten out
of control," Pamela said.

"Oh?"

"An argument arising from Ingrid's desire to protect
her creative reputation."

"The gallery!" At Bettina's exclamation, a few sunbathing students raised their heads.

"Eilert said Ingrid was furious when he spoke with
her on Sunday because she had just heard about the
cancellation, and her tapestries were going to be delivered back to her house the next day."

"That was the day she was killed." Bettina inhaled
deeply, and her eyes opened wide.

"Let's imagine someone from the gallery, maybe the
gallery owner, shows up with the tapestries on Monday. Ingrid is still furious, there's an argument, the argument becomes physical, and she falls and knocks her
head against the hearth."

"How could we prove that?" Bettina inquired.

"Maybe we can't." Pamela snapped the lid of her
Styrofoam container closed, raised her cup to her
mouth to drain what was left of her orange drink, and

stood. "But we're so close to Timberley that we might as well take a look at the Nonesuch Gallery while we're out."

The route to the gallery took them along Timberley's main commercial street for a few blocks, past the florist, the yarn shop, the cheese shop, the purveyor of artisanal chocolates, and the other establishments that made Timberley a destination for Arborvillians seeking wares a bit beyond the ordinary.

"Turn left here," Pamela instructed, consulting the map she had conjured up on her phone. "And then right at the first corner."

The Nonesuch Gallery occupied a storefront between a yoga studio and an antiques store whose window displayed a sharp-angled lounge chair upholstered in black and white pony fur. The gallery's window was partly obscured by a van parked right in front, at a stretch of curb normally off-limits by reason of a fire hydrant. The back doors of the van were ajar, suggesting that loading or unloading was taking place and the van would soon be leaving.

As they sat there, the door of the gallery opened, and a young man walked out carrying a large, flat object wrapped in brown paper. He circled to the back of the van and bent forward to deposit it inside.

"If that's the gallery's van, it would be useful to know whether anyone saw it near Ingrid's house on Monday," Bettina observed, "and if so, what time?"

"She'd been dead at least eight hours when the mail carrier found her body at ten a.m." Pamela watched

Bettina twist around to collect her handbag from the back seat and extract her phone. "'At least eight hours' could be a lot more than eight hours."

"That's what I'm thinking," Bettina said. "If the tapestries were delivered early on Monday, we can forget the gallery connection. Neighbors saw lights on at her house that evening, and she had to still be alive to turn them on. But if the van showed up in the evening . . ."

She waited until the young man had turned and headed back to the gallery, then she raised her phone and took several photos of the van. It was nondescript, except for being an odd shade of faded green.

Simon Malbourne was the first to greet them. He was kneeling in the dirt near the steps leading to Coco's porch, digging a small hole. At his elbow, a flat of impatiens in various pinks and oranges made the purpose of his industry clear. He was in grimy jeans and shirtless, but a jaunty red bandanna looped around his forehead tamed his shaggy gray hair.

"How are you two doing?" he inquired, climbing creakily to his feet while commenting that his knees weren't what they used to be. "Enjoying this beautiful day, I hope."

"Perfect weather," Bettina responded, always willing to do her part when small talk was called for. "And it looks like you've got a good project there."

"If my knees hold out." Simon laughed.

They were joined then by Coco. The front door had been ajar, and she appeared first behind the glass of the storm door, waving and smiling, before pushing that door open and stepping out onto the porch. Like Simon, she was wearing a pair of distressed jeans, topped by a T-shirt that made her braless state quite obvious.

"Can you stay?" she inquired sociably. "I have banana bread in the oven, and I can make hibiscus tea— it's delicious on ice." She continued down the steps, adding, "And while you're here, I can show you the things in Dorcas's garden shed, the things I think the killer took from Ingrid's house. We can sneak over there, and Dorcas will never know."

"Umm." Bettina's expression was pleasant but noncommittal. She reached into her handbag and pulled out her phone. "I'd like to show *you* something," she said as she touched the button that would awaken the phone, and then fingered its screen. She pondered the array of images for a moment and edged closer to Coco, inquiring, "Did you happen to notice a van like this in front of Ingrid's house the Monday she was killed?"

Coco bent down to peer at the screen—she was quite a bit taller than Bettina. "Weird shade of green," she commented. "I can't say for sure, but it may have been around that day. Why?"

"A gallery in Timberley had some tapestries of Ingrid's that it decided not to exhibit."

"You're onto something!" Coco laughed and gave Bettina an affectionate squeeze. "You've got that nose for news, no question. I won't pry. I'll just look forward to the next issue of the *Advocate* to see what you've been up to."

She beckoned to Simon. "Take a look at this. Do you remember seeing a van like this around last week?"

Simon joined them, peering at the phone from over Coco's shoulder. "Not sure," he said after a moment, "but yes . . . in fact, yes. I remember that color. Yes, it was here that Monday . . . around dinnertime."

"I looked at the photo of the van," Coco said after Bettina had tucked her phone away. "Turnabout's fair play. Come along with me and take a peek inside Dorcas's garden shed. *I* still think the stuff piled in there is an important clue, even though Clayborn wasn't receptive at all."

Pamela and Bettina looked at each other. Bettina's expression was the facial equivalent of a shrug.

"Come on!" Coco urged. She was already en route, edging past the shaggy bushes that grew along the side of her porch. Bettina complied, and Pamela joined the procession.

They emerged into Coco's backyard. There, a patch of straggly grass furnished with a few weathered lawn chairs gave way at the back of the property to a dense stretch of glossy-leaved ground cover shaded by trees. The border with Ingrid's yard, to the right, was uncertain, given the untamed nature of Ingrid's landscaping, a sweeping, leafy tangle interspersed with tall stalks bearing tightly packed blossoms.

"This way," Coco instructed, turning to beckon them as she made her way along that uncertain border. "It thins out behind her garage."

They proceeded single file, skirted the clapboard side of the garage, and turned right to squeeze between its rear wall and an ancient chain-link fence that marked the property's back border.

"There's Dorcas's shed," Coco announced after she had emerged from behind the garage and Pamela and Bettina had caught up with her.

She was pointing at a small wooden structure about twenty feet away, just beyond where Ingrid's butterfly garden left off. It was freshly painted, white, and had a peaked roof. The side facing them was featureless, but Coco led them, taking delicate steps among the stalks and tangles in their way, until they reached Dorcas's well-groomed lawn. Now they could see the shed's front and a set of double doors that were closed but evidently not locked—as was apparent when Coco flung them open with a dramatic gesture.

CHAPTER 13

She was looking over her shoulder at Pamela and Bettina as the doors creaked back, her eager expression seeming to anticipate their confirmation that the shed indeed contained a valuable key to Ingrid's murder. That confirmation, however, was not to come, because the small space was completely empty but for garden tools. The wooden floor even appeared to have been swept.

As Pamela and Bettina stared into the shed's shadowy depths, clearly unimpressed, Coco did likewise.

"It was full," she murmured after a bit, still contemplating the interior of the shed, "full of all kinds of stuff that could easily have been grabbed by whoever killed Ingrid—and I think that someone was Dorcas—to make it look like there had been a break-in."

"Big trash day," was Bettina's response.

"Huh?" Coco turned around.

"Monday was big trash day," Bettina clarified. "Did you notice a pile of stuff at the curb, maybe stuff similar to what you saw in the shed?"

"I'd have noticed, for sure." Coco seemed deflated. She sighed, which seemed to deflate her even more. "But the trash truck comes really early. Dorcas could have put the stuff out after it got dark Sunday night, and by the time I got up on Monday, it was long gone."

She swung the shed's doors back into place and set off toward the tract of butterfly garden lying between Dorcas's yard and her own. Pamela and Bettina followed, treading gingerly as they stepped over bushy plants and eased past spiky ones.

Another woman, middle-aged with short blond hair, was making her way through the rampant foliage as well, someone who hadn't been there previously.

"Hello!" the woman greeted them as her path was about to cross theirs. "Lovely day, isn't it!"

Bettina took the sociable lead, responding with a cordial greeting of her own, but it was Pamela who addressed the woman by name: Honey. After momentary puzzlement occasioned by the nagging sense that the woman looked familiar, Pamela had recognized Honey Hurley, the local beekeeper she had come upon some days earlier while walking in an unfamiliar part of Arborville.

"I'm scouting on behalf of my bees," Honey explained.

A glance at Bettina's face told Pamela that her friend had made the connection between this woman and Pamela's report of meeting an Arborville beekeeper. Coco, on the other hand, seemed uninterested in socializing, still downcast from discovering that the shed was empty.

"Lots of flowers here that they'd like, I imagine," Bettina ventured, adding, "I'm Bettina Fraser."

"Honey Hurley," Honey said in return.

Pamela recalled that Honey had seemed less than enthusiastic about Ingrid, remarking "No accounting for taste" after noting that her bees knew Ingrid well. But it was hard to see how bees would be able to resist the inviting pollen and nectar buffet offered by Ingrid's garden. At that very moment, bees were burrowing into the clustered, bell-shaped blossoms atop the stalks of a neighboring plant.

"Penstemon," Honey commented. "Yes, they do like it, and yarrow too." She pointed at a bushy plant with flaring flower heads that shaded from yellow to pink. "Most things they like don't bloom till mid-summer, like coneflowers and black-eyed Susans." She surveyed the yard. "Ingrid's yard has lots of those too. I just hope when the house is sold, the garden stays the same."

They chatted a bit more, Honey and Bettina in particular. Then they took their leave, wishing Honey happy scouting, but not before Bettina mentioned interviewing Honey for a future article in the *Advocate*.

They had noticed when they first arrived at Coco's that the crime-scene tape was gone from Ingrid's house, and that someone had parked in Ingrid's driveway. Now, back in Coco's front yard, where Simon had just lowered an impatiens into one of his holes and was patting the loose dirt around it into place, they turned their attention to the car.

"Ingrid's daughter, Mari," Coco said. "Seems to have recovered from her grief at her mother's death."

Mari, in fact, was the picture of cheer when they met her moments later. She was likely in her late thirties or early forties, given what they knew of her history from the *Register* article reporting Ingrid's murder. She looked much younger, though, and her fair hair, worn in a short bob with bangs, contributed to that effect. Pamela recalled the photo Eilert had shown her of a young Ingrid posing with one of her creations and was struck by the mother-daughter similarity.

She'd apparently been making trips to and from her car, whose trunk had been opened since they first saw it, and she was carrying a large plastic bin, which she deposited in the open trunk. That chore done, she advanced until she was close enough to talk in normal tones to the group standing in Coco's yard.

"Who needs an extra frying pan," she inquired, "or an alarm clock?"

Coco cut in to make quick introductions, and Mari went on. "How about rain boots? An umbrella? A set of flannel sheets?"

"You should have an estate sale," Bettina said. "There are companies that will do all the work for you."

"I'll probably resort to that," Mari replied, "but first, anybody who wants anything can have it for free." She took a few steps back the way she had come, and beckoned them to follow along. "So much stuff to find homes for—take some yarn, whatever you want . . ."

Bettina had joined Mari in the lead, with Pamela and Coco following, while Simon stayed behind with his plants. Snatches of conversation drifted back as Bettina and Mari threaded their way through the patch of butterfly garden between the edge of Coco's yard and Ingrid's driveway.

"Lovely funeral," Bettina commented, "and the celebration of life—what a positive approach to the loss of a loved one! I'm sorry I didn't get the chance to meet and talk with you there. Arborville was fortunate to have your mother as a resident."

"I wasn't there," Mari said quite matter-of-factly. "As far as the celebration of life goes, my mother's friends are . . ." Her voice trailed off. When she spoke again it was to say, "My mother's friends are . . . my mother's friends."

Mari and Bettina had reached the steps that led up to the porch, with Pamela and Coco close behind. At the top of the steps, across the porch's scuffed wooden surface, the front door stood open. Once they were all inside, Mari waved an arm in a gesture that took in the heaps of clothing on the Victorian-style sofa, the large glass coffee table covered with art books, and the cardboard boxes, some half-open to reveal papers or faded magazines.

"There's so much more elsewhere," she said. "Kitchen things in the kitchen, art things in the studio, more clothes upstairs. Please help yourselves."

Coco wandered off toward the back of the house, and Bettina began rummaging through the clothes on the sofa, remarking that there might be some vintage treasures Penny would appreciate. Pamela crouched down near the coffee table. She hardly needed to bring more books into her house, but the cover of a book dealing with medieval tapestries had caught her eye.

She paged through it, admiring the skill with which

the weavers had depicted the elegantly dressed noble-
men and noblewomen enjoying their leisure pursuits
amid realistic flora and fauna, like columbines and
rabbits. She set that book down and picked up another
to discover hiding beneath it a smaller book that was
actually an appointment calendar. The cover featured
an attractive abstract design, with large numerals indicating that the calendar dated from 1985.

Inside, the year 1985 was broken up into weeks,
each allotted one page, with a rectangular space for
each day. Ingrid had repurposed the calendar as a kind
of pictorial journal, however. Leafing through it,
Pamela saw that each space contained a tiny drawing,
sometimes including butterflies, or bees, or both. It
certainly looked like an item that should be added to
the materials documenting Ingrid's artistic career,
rather than left out with the clothing and household
items that Mari was trying to find homes for.

As Pamela was examining the little book, Mari returned from making a trip to her car and pulled a
wooden chair up to the coffee table.

"That looks interesting," she commented, leaning to
the side until her head almost touched Pamela's.

Pamela turned a few pages to make the book's
unique quality clear and said, "I guess you know about
Eilert Kroll's project?"

"Oh, definitely." Mari nodded. "In fact, he's coming
here to photograph the tapestries that were going to be
in the ill-fated gallery show. My mom had invited him,
and I got in touch to say the invitation still stands. The
tapestries are in my mom's studio now, still all packed

up from their trip to the gallery and back. Otherwise, you'd be welcome to take a peek."

"She repurposed this appointment calendar as a journal"—Pamela turned a few more pages—"but with pictures instead of words. You might want to keep it because it's kind of a personal memento of your mother, but I'm sure Eilert would appreciate a chance to study it. And I'd like to study it a bit myself."

"Take it," Mari said.

Before Mari could elaborate, though Pamela wasn't sure she intended to, a cheerful voice hailed them from the doorway. The door had been left ajar from Mari's trips to the car, and the visitor had pushed it fully open and stepped inside. Mari swiveled toward the doorway and then jumped to her feet, nearly upsetting the chair.

"Dad!" she exclaimed as she hopped across the floor.

Alerted by the commotion, Bettina turned away from the clothes she was rummaging through, and both she and Pamela watched as Nestor Flavin and Mari hugged. After he finished the hug, he noticed Pamela and Bettina, acknowledged them with a courtly bow, and inquired, "How are you two ladies today?" He was looking very summery in a lime-green polo shirt and khaki slacks.

Pamela was startled at this evidence that Mari and Nestor were on such affectionate terms, given that Nestor and Ingrid had never married and he had apparently left the relationship not long after Mari's birth. But she certainly couldn't come right out and ask them about the nature of their bond.

Bettina, meanwhile, had responded to Nestor's polite question, stating that she and Pamela were fine and that it would be hard not to be on such a lovely May afternoon. As is often the case, the weather proved to be a serviceable conversation starter, and soon Coco joined them. Her explorations had evidently involved the kitchen, to judge by the large enamel pot she carried.

Mari nodded when she caught sight of it and said, "Yes, please take it. In fact, there are more." She took it from Coco's hands, set it on a chair near the door, and steered Coco back the way she had come.

But the conversation didn't suffer from her departure, because, as the topic of weather led to travel, which led to shopping while traveling, Nestor and Bettina had discovered a mutual interest in Scandinavian crystal and were happily trading notes. Once justice had been done to that topic, however, Bettina glanced at Pamela, as if to alert her that social Bettina was about to be replaced by curious Bettina.

"I think you're acquainted with Eilert Kroll," she said, arranging her features to convey benign interest.

Nestor drew back, his well-groomed elegance giving the action the effect of a rebuke for a social misstep. After a moment, though, he seemed to recalibrate.

"Why, yes." He smiled, though a bit more stiffly than he had when describing his recent acquisition of a vintage crystal vase. "We're actually collaborating on a project dealing with Ingrid's work. He reached out to me, and to Mari, of course, and she's invited him to come and photograph the tapestries that were going to be in the gallery show. Luckily they were spared when Ingrid's killer grabbed things willy-nilly the night of the murder."

"Have you seen Eilert lately?" she inquired.

"I dropped by his office to look for him this morning," Nestor said, "but he was out. I was heading up here anyway to see Mari, and I thought I'd say hello." His voice was grave, and his level gaze, perhaps intended to ensure that Bettina was paying attention, seemed almost threatening. "Why?" he appended after an awkward pause.

Bettina was saved having to answer when a new arrival announced, "Break time!" Simon Malbourne had just entered, still in the grimy jeans he'd worn while gardening, but no longer shirtless. He carried a large plate on which were arranged slices of . . . something. The something was quickly identified when he added, "Banana bread, anyone?" He crossed over to the coffee table and set the plate in a clear space amid the books.

"You're working so hard, Meredith"—he addressed Mari, who had reappeared—"running in and out with boxes. I could have helped if you'd asked me."

"I'm doing fine, Simon," she replied, "and it's 'Mari,' not 'Meredith.'"

"Oh, of course. Sorry." Simon dipped his head, dislodging a few strands of his unruly gray hair. He raised a hand to push them back into place. Noticing that Bettina had given him a curious look, he said, "I've known her since she was a child. Never quite got used to 'Mari.'"

Mari's lips twisted into a skeptical knot, but what she said was, "I suspect Coco is really the person we should thank for this banana bread."

Coco had been hovering behind Mari near the doorway that led to the back of the house. "But he sliced it and carried it over," she said as she darted around Mari. "So thoughtful! And making it was his idea. I only did the work."

She was carrying another enamel pot, dark blue like the one that had been waiting on the chair, but smaller, and she nestled it inside its mate.

"Let's all have some banana bread, shall we?" Coco picked up a piece and lifted it to her mouth.

Simon appeared disinclined to stay, but soon everyone else, including Nestor, was standing around the coffee table. Mari had dashed away briefly and returned with a stack of paper napkins, and people were cradling slices of banana bread in paper napkins and breaking off bits to nibble on. Coco acknowledged the murmurs of "Very good, very good" with a smile, but she insisted that Simon deserved equal credit.

Many more slices were left on the plate, and Bettina and Coco swooped in for seconds. Mari, however, seemed eager to get back to work. She hefted one of the cardboard boxes stacked around the room and headed for the door with it. Taking the hint, Nestor picked up a box and followed her.

When Mari returned, it was without Nestor—she'd been outside long enough that Pamela assumed she and Nestor had said their farewells and he'd gone on his way.

"My car is full," she said, "and I'm finished for now. But you can all hang around and keep rummaging." Focusing on Coco, she added, "When you leave, just make sure the lock on the front door is set and pull the door closed behind you. And thank you for the banana bread."

"Will do!" Coco nodded. "And you're welcome!"

Left alone in the house, the three seemed momentarily at loose ends.

"I'm happy with my two enamel pots." Coco gazed at them fondly. "As for more rummaging, my house is crowded as it is."

"And I found this." Bettina reached for a garment draped over a nearby chair. It was a leather jacket styled like something a small and slender cowboy would wear, but in an improbable shade of aqua. "Miss Penny might like it."

"What about you?" Coco turned to Pamela. "Did you find any treasures?"

"I rescued something," Pamela said. "It belongs with the materials that document Ingrid's artistic career, but I'm looking forward to spending a little time with it first because the drawings are so charming."

She leaned over and picked up the appointment calendar repurposed as a pictorial journal. Opening it at random, she held it out so Coco could see a few pages.

"Bees!" Coco exclaimed, seizing the little book from Pamela's hands. "These are just like the bees Ingrid was drawing before her death—in the doodles I showed you."

They were, Pamela realized, bending closer as Coco flipped through more pages showing bees, and a few butterflies. It occurred to Pamela to wonder whether the bees here and in Ingrid's doodles had been a response to the threat Dorcas posed, with her crusade against the butterfly garden. Would Dorcas have already been a neighbor back in 1985?

"Very cool." Coco closed the book and gave it back to Pamela. "Ingrid was into nature. You could see that, with the wild yard." She picked up the nested enamel pots and took a few steps toward the door.

"What will happen to the banana bread?" Bettina inquired.

"I'll come back for it—or you can take it."

"Let me help you." Pamela tucked the little book under her arm and stooped for the plate with the remains of the banana bread. The three of them proceeded across the floor, Bettina carrying the aqua leather jacket.

A few minutes later, with Ingrid's door locked behind them, they approached Coco's porch. The bed of impatiens was now complete, two rows of seedlings with their cheerful little blooms, and the damp earth around them testifying to Simon's ministrations.

"That's a big job for Mari," Bettina observed as they climbed the steps, "but I expect she's the heir, and maybe there was no one else to do it."

"Yes," Coco said. "She really had to take charge. She arranged the funeral too."

"But then didn't go? Were they on bad terms?" Bettina's conversational tone made the question sound . . . conversational.

They had reached the front door. "Not at all," Coco replied as she twisted the knob—the door wasn't locked. "Mari was at the funeral, but she skipped the celebration of life." Coco laughed. "Mari didn't approve of some of Ingrid's friends."

A note from Simon greeted them, lying on the floor right beyond the threshold, as if placed for maximum visibility.

"See you later," it read. "Impatiens are done. Banana bread was delicious. Love, S."

Coco paused to read the note, smiling to herself, then she set the pots down on a small table already crowded with an assortment of framed photos.

"Shall I take the banana bread to the kitchen?" Pamela inquired. She recalled the house's layout from the visit she and Bettina had made to Coco the previous week.

Coco nodded absentmindedly. She had picked up the note and was studying it, continuing to smile.

"He seems very thoughtful," Bettina commented, "even if it was actually you who baked the banana bread."

"Simon loves my cooking." Coco's expression was that of a trusting child, never mind that the bloom of youth had long since disappeared. "He planted the impatiens for me." The next words came out in a rush. "I think this could be the real thing, after all this time."

"It can take a while to meet the right person," Bettina said. "My Wilfred was already forty when he met me." She raised a hand to her chest and added, "I, of course, was much younger."

"Oh, Simon and I have known each other forever!" Coco picked up one of the photos. She and Bettina were still standing near the table where she had set the pots. "We grew up together, I in this house and he across the street. Here we are home from college one Christmas, with a bunch of his friends." She held out the photo, and Pamela edged next to Bettina to get a look at it too.

The photo, which was in color, showed a small crowd

clustered around an old van decorated with peace signs and hand-painted flowers in Day-Glo colors. Coco was recognizable as a younger version of her current self, but with her wild hair not yet streaked with gray. Other people had wild hair, too, and the men had mustaches and beards, and the winter attire ran to woolly ponchos, berets, oversized mufflers in eye-popping colors, a vibrant black-and-yellow-striped sweater paired with weather-defying sandals, and an army surplus officer's coat.

"That's me"—Coco pointed to the figure that Pamela had already recognized—"and that's Simon's best friend, Knut." Knut was the figure in the army surplus coat, grinning and making a "V for victory" sign. "And then here's—I think her name was Molly, and Simon"— that was the striped sweater—"and I can't remember all the other names, but—oh!—we had so much fun that Christmas, and then he went back to his college, and I went back to mine."

Her voice trailed off, and she returned the photo to its spot. "But now," she added, lively again, "here we are, back together."

They chatted a bit more, about Mari's labors, and Simon's, too, with his parallel job of cleaning out his own parents' house. Then Pamela and Bettina bade Coco goodbye and made their way back to where Bettina had parked the Toyota so much earlier in the day.

"It's getting on toward dinnertime," Bettina said after they had settled into their seats, "and Wilfred's cooking for some of his pals from the historical society or I'd invite you over. But we've got a lot to talk about, so I'll come by first thing tomorrow. Make plenty of coffee."

CHAPTER 14

True to her word, Bettina showed up first thing Thursday morning. Pamela had barely gotten back inside after fetching the *Register*, and the kettle was still whistling on the stove, when the doorbell's ring summoned her to the entry. A few moments later, Bettina was stepping over the threshold bearing a foil-covered platter. In contrast to Pamela, who was still in her pajamas, robe, and slippers, Bettina was wearing a crisp linen sheath, salmon in color, with matching kitten heels. Her green jade jewelry added an interesting contrast.

"I have an engagement," she explained, though Pamela knew that even her friend's casual outfits were carefully considered as well. "The seniors' group is sponsoring a wellness fair this morning, and I'm covering it for the *Advocate*. But it doesn't start till ten, so we have plenty of time." She glanced toward the kitchen doorway and added, "It sounds like the water is boiling and then some."

She set out toward the kitchen, still carrying the platter, but Pamela darted around her. En route, they encountered all three of the cats heading the other way, and had to step gingerly around them. Pamela had already ground coffee beans and prepared the carafe's filter cone, and it took no time at all to tip the kettle over the carafe and send the steaming water swirling over the fragrant grounds.

Bettina worked meanwhile preparing the table, setting out wedding china, napkins, and silverware, as well as the cut-glass sugar bowl and the cream pitcher, which she made sure to supply with plenty of cream. As a final touch, she removed the foil from the platter to reveal another of Wilfred's strawberry strudels.

Noticing that the *Register* was sitting on the counter still tucked into its flimsy plastic sleeve, Bettina said, "I'll save you reading Marcy Brewer's latest article on the 'Arborville break-in gone awry' murder case."

"There's an article?" Pamela had been watching the boiling water disappear into the grounds and reappear below as a dark liquid gradually filling the carafe, but she turned to face Bettina. "Has Detective Clayborn made progress in the case?"

"More like desperation on Marcy's part." Bettina laughed. "She's determined to have a story of some kind, but the story is that there is no story—no progress in finding the person who broke into Ingrid's house looking for things to steal and killed her when she interrupted him." She laughed again. "And there's no progress because that's not what really happened. Clayborn is barking up a blind alley."

"Isn't it 'the wrong tree'?"

"Whatever."

Pamela pronounced the coffee ready then. She filled the cups, and they took their seats. The first order of business was the strudel, apportioning slices onto the little rose-garlanded plates, tasting the flaky and buttery pastry anointed with homemade strawberry jam, and pronouncing it just as good as it was the first time around. The first tastes were followed by swallows of coffee, and then it was time for conversation.

"There seems to be a real bond between Nestor and Mari," Bettina said, and Pamela nodded.

She had been about to make the same comment, but she elaborated instead: "It's hard to imagine that he would kill his daughter's mother, though people, of course, *do* kill estranged partners." She paused for another sip of coffee and went on, "We don't really know if the breakup was acrimonious or amicable."

"But we do know that Nestor stole Ingrid's designs, and now he needs to keep the fact that they were her designs hidden as he tries to make a comeback."

"He's found himself in a bind," Pamela said. "The Mariposa drawings, and Ingrid herself, are and were a potential threat, but Ingrid is the mother of his daughter, and he loves his daughter."

Bettina looked up from nudging a bite of strudel onto her fork. "Could Mari possibly know that Nestor stole her mother's designs?"

"I can't imagine she does!" Pamela pictured Mari's

excited greeting as Nestor stepped through the front door of Ingrid's house.

The strudel occupied their attention for a few minutes, but not *all* their attention—at least not all of Pamela's. She continued to ruminate on the drawings, and their implications for Nestor's career. She waited until Bettina had finished the last crumb of her strudel and even salvaged a few syrupy bits of strawberry before she spoke.

"Even with Ingrid gone, the drawings are still a threat," she said, "as long as they remain in existence—especially with Eilert determined to include them in his book."

"They are." Bettina nodded. "We already agreed that Eilert could be in danger—though if we don't think Nestor would kill Ingrid . . ." Her lips curved into a tight smile that implied uncertainty. "Do we think he would kill Eilert?"

"He admitted he'd been looking for Eilert at Wendelstaff yesterday morning. Wouldn't he deny it if he'd had murder in mind?"

"One of Eilert's colleagues talked to him, so denying it would just seem suspicious." Bettina leaned forward to study the remains of the strudel.

"I'd have another piece," Pamela said.

"You would?" Bettina reared back, staring. "What's gotten into you?"

"I'm frustrated." As Bettina continued to stare, Pamela took up the knife that lay alongside the platter, cut a good-sized slice, and transferred it to her plate. "And confused," she added, picking up her fork.

"Here's something else to be confused about," Bettina responded, "but first . . ." She helped herself to another slice of strudel.

Pamela was on her feet now, moving the carafe from the counter to the stove and lighting a flame under it. Picking up her fork, Bettina continued speaking, "Simon appeared to recognize the van from the Timberley gallery when I showed him the photo on my phone, and he said he saw it on Serpentine Way around dinnertime on Monday."

"What time does Simon eat dinner?" Pamela was standing at the stove, watching lest the coffee reach too energetic of a boil.

"That's exactly the question. Dinnertime could be anywhere from five p.m. to eight p.m. or later. If the van came and went before it started to get dark and neighbors saw lights on in Ingrid's house when it did get dark, that means the gallery owner didn't kill her—because she was still alive to turn the lights on. But if the van was there after dark . . ."

Pamela advanced toward the table bearing the carafe, and Bettina paused while the coffee cups were refilled. That task accomplished, Pamela finished Bettina's thought for her. "The lights in Ingrid's house would have already been on, so their being on doesn't mean the gallery owner didn't kill her."

Bettina applied herself to sugaring and creaming her coffee. When it reached the pale mocha tint that signaled the process was complete, she raised the cup to her lips and took a long swallow. As if the fresh cup of coffee had inspired a fresh thought, she said, "But the gallery owner isn't our only suspect. What do you think it means that Dorcas's garden shed was empty?"

"I think it means that, as you said before, Dorcas keeps Arborville's town calendar handy and pays attention to the days scheduled for big trash pickup." Pamela sampled her coffee and followed up with a bite from her second piece of strudel.

"So we'll never know whether the things Coco saw in the shed came from Ingrid's house as part of an attempt to shift the blame for Ingrid's death to some fictional burglar."

"No," Pamela said. "We'll never know."

They ate strudel and sipped coffee in silence for a few minutes. Then, as the flaky slices of pastry dwindled to nubbins and then just crumbs, the conversation shifted to cheerier topics, like Pamela's expectations for her small tomato patch and Wilfred's upcoming fishing expedition with his cousin John. At length, Bettina drained her coffee cup and lifted her wrist to check her watch.

"I've got to be getting along," she said, "but before I go . . . I've just been thinking. I wonder if Eilert has heard from Nestor. Nestor *said* he dropped by Wendelstaff yesterday to say hello, since he was in the area anyway, but . . ."

Pamela was on her feet. The landline phone was right there, and she'd made a note of Eilert's number when he first reached out to her. She sat back down with the handset. After a few rings, the line clicked, and she heard Eilert's precise voice saying "hello."

He *had* heard from Nestor, it seemed, and Nestor had made an appointment to come back to Wendelstaff that very afternoon.

"I don't know why I agreed," Eilert commented.

"I've made it very clear to him that I have no intention of omitting anything that's relevant to Ingrid's story—and now that I know what he wants me to omit and why, I'm all the more determined."

"Be careful," Pamela said. "That's all—just be careful."

Bettina was on her way then, off to her reporting assignment. Pamela wrapped the small remainder of the strudel in the foil that had covered it and washed the breakfast dishes, including the platter that had held the strudel.

Talking to Eilert had reminded her of the little book she'd brought back from Ingrid's house, the appointment calendar repurposed as a pictorial journal. It would go to Eilert eventually, and she wished she had thought to mention it when she spoke to him. But she'd requested it from Mari with the intention of examining it herself first and, with nothing pressing on her schedule, she settled on the sofa and began to page through it.

The spaces allotted to the days of the week were quite small, but Ingrid had managed, with a few pen strokes and colored pencils, to create lively scenes. The drawings for January documented snowstorms, cozy gatherings around a fireplace, artistic accomplishments—complete with tiny renderings of her work displayed as in a gallery.

Valentine's Day was commemorated with miniature valentines squeezed into the same rectangular space, one signed "Love, Nestor" and one signed "Love, Ingrid." As the year advanced toward spring, minuscule crocuses bloomed, robins hopped about, and Easter was celebrated with an Easter egg hunt.

In June, a particularly striking flower was introduced, like a black-eyed Susan, but deep pink, and with two expressive leaves that suggested arms. The flower recurred from panel to panel, visited at times by a majestic black and gold butterfly that it seemed to beckon with its leafy arms. In other panels, the butterfly was replaced by a bee, its fuzzy, striped body rendered in impressive detail.

With summer came picnics, and visits to the shore, and fireworks—in explosive abundance—filling the Fourth of July panel to the very edges.

Some panels contained sketches of a rambling, wood-framed house, recognizable as Ingrid's house on Serpentine Way, viewed from different angles. The yard had already been given over to natural plantings, and close-ups of goldenrod, coneflowers, Queen Anne's lace, and the like were rendered in charming detail. Interspersed among them was a starker image that recurred from week to week—a bulbous cocoon dangling from a bare stem.

Browsing through to the end of the year, past colorful panels devoted to autumn leaves, followed by evocations of Halloween, Thanksgiving, Christmas, and New Year's Eve, Pamela reached a page headed "Notes." In place of notes, however, Ingrid had filled the page with drawings.

The cocoon dangling from the bare stem had returned, but in the first drawing, part of its exterior had become transparent, allowing a glimpse of a deep orange wing crisscrossed with black veining. Subsequent drawings chronicled the process of a butterfly emerging from the cocoon. Headfirst, it extracted itself little by little, paused as if to catch its breath, then flew away toward the lower right-hand corner of the page.

Pamela was so captivated by this drama that she quickly turned the page, hoping to follow the butterfly's adventures, but the reverse side of the page was empty, and the other pages that had been left blank for "Notes" were empty as well.

Work for *Fiber Craft* awaited, not to mention that Pamela was still in her pajamas and robe with her bed unmade, and so she set the little book aside and headed for the stairs.

"A Far-Flung Clan" proved to be about unexpected evidence of a fair-haired, blue-eyed people living along the Silk Road in western China four thousand years ago. Their mummified remains showed they were more akin genetically to Europeans than Asians and—most relevant for readers of *Fiber Craft*—among the textiles found in the graves were some with a plaid design. The author pointed out that they were unlike anything previously associated with that region at that date but very similar to textiles discovered at sites in Germany and Austria a millennium or so later.

Plaid, Pamela murmured to herself. She knew the tartan plaids of Scotland were a fairly recent development, certainly not a tradition reaching back millennia—and it could occur to any weaver with access to various colors of fiber that it would be fun to alternate them in warp and weft. So the idea that some batch of ancient people who invented plaid broke into groups that wandered as far as the British Isles in one direction and western China in the other would probably always just be an idea. Still, it was gratifying to think that textiles could give tantalizing hints about ancient migrations in eras before people left written records of their adventures.

The article's text included many place names transliterated from Chinese, most of them unfamiliar. Pamela made sure the author had used the most commonly recognized forms for those names, but other than that, the text required little intervention.

The shades at Pamela's office windows glowed bright, in a seductive reminder that May afternoons were limited in number. She saved her Word file and closed it, leaving her mouse to rest on its mouse pad and descending to the kitchen. After a quick lunch of leftover salmon mashed with mayonnaise and spread on toast, she headed for her backyard. A few hours of weeding and other yard work would be almost as enjoyable as a walk, and constructive too.

The next day was Penny's birthday, and as she opened her eyes, Pamela recalled that long-ago morning when she had awakened in this very bed, but with Michael beside her, knowing—though she had never given birth before—that Penny was on the way.

This morning began, however, with an email from the grown-up Penny, thanking her for the card and the check and the keepsake book that had belonged to Pamela's grandmother. And to demonstrate her satisfaction with the book, which contained an edifying comment for each day of the year, she quoted the edifying comment for May 16, her birthday: "Write it on your heart that every day is the best day of the year," from Ralph Waldo Emerson.

Every day can't be *the best*, Pamela murmured, but then she reminded herself that life was not a copyediting assignment. She stood up from her desk and let the cats lead the way to the kitchen while she lingered to slide her feet back into her slippers and knot the belt on her robe.

As she stepped over the threshold en route to collect the *Register*, Pamela caught sight of Bettina holding two newspapers, a fat one and a thin one. On her feet were pink satin mules with marabou trim, coordinating with a pink satin robe. She was focused on extracting the thin newspaper from its plastic sleeve. That task accomplished, she unfolded it to examine the front page.

"Hi!" Pamela called when Bettina was halfway up her front walk.

"You got the right one," Bettina said without preamble. She refolded the newspaper. "The carrier apparently gave half the people in Arborville the same issue of the *Advocate* that they got last week. She had them left over in her garage."

Pamela made an appropriately sympathetic comment, though she suspected many of the people who got the old issue of the *Advocate* wouldn't notice, and many who did notice wouldn't care.

"Whatever." Bettina sighed. "What I really came over for was to invite you to lunch. Wilfred is fishing with his cousin today, and he took along homemade submarine sandwiches for both of them. But there's plenty of ham and salami and cheese left, and yummy rolls, so come over when you get hungry."

* * *

There had been plenty of ham and salami and cheese left, and the rolls had been yummy. Now Pamela and Bettina sat at the scrubbed-pine table in the eating area of the Frasers' kitchen, sipping root beer from tall, crystal glasses, with the remains of their lunch, in the form of crumbs and shreds of lettuce, scattered on the sage-green plates before them.

"Everyone who called the *Advocate* to complain has gotten a copy of today's paper," Bettina said, "and the carrier has assured us that she'll be more careful in the future."

Pamela was about to comment that readers of the *Advocate* certainly deserved to get the most recent issue, but before she could speak, a trill from Bettina's smartphone, which was sitting nearby on the high counter, announced an incoming call.

"Not a complaint about getting the wrong paper, I hope," Bettina said as she climbed to her feet. "Most people have been calling the *Advocate*'s office line, so I've been spared."

But it was clear from Bettina's greeting that the caller was Coco, and it was clear as soon as she spoke again that something very distressing had occurred.

"How is Dorcas surviving?" Bettina asked, and then she added, "Yes, of course. Anyone would be horrified." She listened for a bit, to sounds that reached Pamela's ears only as a kind of scratchy static, then interjected, "I know I said Clayborn doesn't like to get tips about crimes from residents—" She paused, and Pamela heard more scratchy static.

Bettina had been facing the counter, but now she

turned toward where Pamela still sat at the table. Her eyes were wide, and her expression mingled horror with comic desperation.

"Obviously, obviously, obviously . . ." She repeated the word until the voice on the other end was silent. "Obviously calling the police to report that you just found a body is a whole different thing than calling them with a tip. *Of course* you should call them. I'm on my way, but call them right now."

Bettina aimed a decisive finger at her phone's screen and watched the screen go dark. "Honestly!" she exclaimed. "How can people even function?"

"There's a body . . . I guess . . . ?" Pamela remained sitting, though she suspected Bettina's "I'm on my way" actually meant "We're on our way."

"Dorcas found a body in her garden shed, and that was Coco calling to say she heard screaming and went out to see what was going on and it was Dorcas and Dorcas is frantic."

"Whose body is it?" Pamela was on her feet now.

"They don't know." Carrying her phone, Bettina headed for the doorway leading to the dining room and the living room beyond. "Dorcas was too shocked to look closely, and Coco refuses to go inside the shed with a dead person in there."

Bettina paused in the living room to collect her handbag and keys. Woofus glanced up from the sofa, where he was napping, but he seemed unconcerned about his mistress's imminent departure. He went back to sleep, and Bettina continued out the front door, with Pamela following.

CHAPTER 15

Nothing appeared out of the ordinary when the Toyota came to a stop in front of Coco's house. "In the backyard, I expect," Bettina said as she pushed the car door open and swung her feet onto the asphalt.

She and Pamela made their way through the shaggy bushes that edged Coco's rambling porch. As they emerged onto Coco's back lawn, they were confronted by a tableau at the far-right corner of the yard, where Coco's property abutted Ingrid's. Simon Malbourne and Coco were embracing, so completely entwined that they seemed fused together. Dorcas, who, from what Coco had reported, would seem more in need of comfort, was surveying them from the far-left corner of the yard.

"You'll have to come to me," she called when she caught sight of Pamela and Bettina. Bettina veered off in her direction, and Pamela followed. As they got

closer, Dorcas continued, "I've already had enough exposure to the butterfly garden for one day, thank you
very much. Between the agitation of finding a body in
my garden shed and wading through a field of pollinator plants in search of Coco, my histamines are going
crazy. I'll be lucky if I don't break out in hives any
minute."

She stopped talking, turned away, and sneezed ex-
plosively. Then she closed her eyes and took a deep,
raspy breath. If Pamela hadn't known from Coco's summons that she and Bettina would be encountering
Dorcas, she would never have recognized the woman.
The Dorcas she had met at the celebration of Ingrid's
life had been wearing a crisply pressed shirt and jeans,
and her gray-streaked bob with its precise bangs had
hugged her head smoothly. Now her hair was in disarray, with wiry strands radiating in all directions, and a
summery dress that might have started out fresh from
the ironing board was as rumpled as if it had been
slipped on straight from the laundry hamper.

"Someone *did* call the police . . . ?" Bettina's tone
implied she expected yes for an answer. When Dorcas
nodded toward Simon and Coco, now detached from
each other but conversing intensely, Bettina murmured,
"Good." She took Dorcas's arm and tugged her in the
direction of the weathered chairs that occupied Coco's
small patch of lawn. "You need to sit down," she urged.

"Uh-uh." Dorcas resisted and shook her head, setting the wiry strands of her hair in motion. "Too near
the pollinator plants."

Simon and Coco had become aware of their visitors
now, and Simon was loping toward Bettina with Coco

close behind. Coco darted around him and flung herself on Bettina, crying, "Thank you, thank you, thank
you!"

She pulled back, and Pamela could see she had been
weeping. "It's been so distressing—you can't imagine.
Ingrid dead first, and now it's déjà vu all over again.
Another body right next door . . . well, next door to
next door this time."

"No idea at all whose body it is?" Bettina patted at
her linen shirt in an effort to remedy the effects of
Coco's impulsive hug.

Coco shuddered, theatrically. "I could not go in
there. The negative vibes are so strong I can feel them
even from here, like a black hole, sucking energy."

Simon, meanwhile, had moved the two lawn chairs
to a spot far removed from the border with Ingrid's
yard. Dorcas had settled into one of them, and he was
perched on the other. Pamela was about to take her
chances with the negative vibes and venture through
the butterfly garden to peek inside the garden shed, but
she lingered for a moment when she heard Simon ask
Dorcas whether she saw or heard anything in the time
leading up to her discovery of the body.

"I try not to go outside this time of year," Dorcas
replied as Pamela set out across the lawn.

She made her way among the thicket of stalks and
stems that lay between Coco's property and the garden
shed. Viewing it in profile, she could see that the doors
had been left ajar, presumably as Dorcas recoiled in horror and dashed to consult Coco. Soon she had stepped
into Dorcas's tidy yard and was approaching the shed,
focused on its shadowy interior.

A figure was visible in its depths—quite visible, in fact—given that while still alive, the deceased had taken from his closet a summer-weight suit made from creamy white linen.

"Nestor?" Pamela heard herself whisper. "Who would kill you?" As if in response, a voice in her mind chimed in with, *At least Eilert is safe now.*

"Pamela! Pamela!" The summons came from nearby. Pamela backed away from the shed's entrance to see a small contingent of people bearing down on her.

It was Bettina who had called her name, but leading the charge were two uniformed police officers, burly Officer Keenan and Officer Sanchez with her sweet, heart-shaped face. Pamela drew back even farther as the two officers switched on their flashlights and approached the shed's wide doorway.

The rest of the group had arrived too, Bettina and Simon and Dorcas, and even Coco—though she hovered several yards away. The officers had disappeared into the shed at this point, and Bettina eased her way past the shed's entrance to join Pamela. Her expression was question enough, and perfectly clear without words.

"It's Nestor Flavin," Pamela whispered.

"Why?"

Before Pamela could answer—though her answer would have been that she didn't know—Officer Sanchez emerged from the shed, looking as serious as her youthful features would allow.

"I need you all to follow me back to Ms. Dalrymple's yard," she said, "where I'll take your statements."

"Pamela knows who it is," Bettina ventured.

"Detective Clayborn has been summoned," Officer Sanchez responded. "He'll be interested, I'm sure."

Bettina's features were impassive, but for an amused glance from the corner of her eye.

Despite Bettina's announcement that Pamela could be consulted about the identity of the victim, Officer Sanchez was more interested in talking to Dorcas—presumably because it was she who had discovered the body and because the garden shed was on her property. Dorcas led the way to where the lawn chairs waited at a good distance from the offending pollinator plants, and Officer Sanchez followed, taking out a small notepad and a pen.

As Officer Sanchez interviewed Dorcas, Simon and Coco stood on the other side of the yard, watching, with Coco's head snuggled against Simon's T-shirted chest.

"Very bad timing in terms of the *Advocate*," Bettina confided to Pamela. "The next issue is a whole week from now. By then, this will be old, old news."

She turned and glanced toward the garden shed. Pamela glanced too, and the glance revealed that Detective Clayborn had arrived. In fact, he had already inspected the crime scene and was just emerging from the shed. Officer Keenan, meanwhile, was standing at the shed's entrance in a pose that suggested praiseworthy vigilance. Detective Clayborn paused to confer with him for a moment, Officer Keenan pointed toward Coco's house, and Detective Clayborn waded into the wild meadow that was Ingrid's backyard.

Pamela and Bettina were the first people he encountered after making it to the other side. He greeted them with a nod and a curt, "Officer Sanchez will take your initial statements."

"We know who the victim is," Bettina volunteered, but he had already stepped away, heading for Simon and Coco.

He conferred with them for somewhat longer, then made his way across the lawn, where he took Officer Sanchez's place in the lawn chair. As if Coco's backyard was the setting for some kind of parlor game, Officer Sanchez circled around to Pamela and Bettina. Turning to a new page in the notepad, she recorded their names and addresses and the fact that Coco had called Bettina to ask what to do about the body Dorcas had discovered.

"I'm the police liaison for the *Advocate*, you know," Bettina added—though Officer Sanchez certainly knew this already—"so people consult me about . . . things."

As Pamela recalled, Bettina herself had found it incredible that anyone would need advice about whether to call the police about a dead body, but Officer Sanchez simply nodded and said, "Detective Clayborn will want to talk to you too." Her next stop was Simon and Coco, and no sooner had she left than Detective Clayborn was striding toward them, notepad at the ready.

His garb, as usual, was nondescript: a sports jacket— lightweight in acknowledgment of the warm weather— a dress shirt, and a tie with a pattern that suggested something glimpsed through a microscope in biology class. His face was nondescript as well, but for the slight tension around the eyes that sharpened his melancholy glance.

"It's Nestor Flavin," Bettina said, before he could

speak. "Pamela looked in the shed before you got here, and she recognized him. He was Ingrid's romantic partner for a while."

"I know who Nestor Flavin is," Detective Clayborn said as he made a notation. "I read the *Register*, and the *Advocate*." The tension around his eyes increased to the point that he seemed to be squinting. "The shed— as well as the yard, and possibly the house—is now a crime scene. You didn't go inside the shed, did you?"

"Of course not," Pamela replied. "I watch the BBC crime dramas."

"How was it that you recognized . . . Nestor Flavin?"

"His clothes," Pamela said. "He likes, or *liked*, linen suits. The body in the shed is wearing a white linen suit."

Detective Clayborn took a deep breath and let it out slowly. "What I meant was, where do you know him from?"

Bettina spoke up. "Pamela and I went to Ingrid's funeral—she was, after all, an Arborville neighbor. Afterward there was a celebration of her life at an artist's studio in Haversack, and we tagged along . . . with Coco and Simon, actually." She nodded toward where Officer Sanchez, notepad in hand, was interviewing the pair. "We both met Nestor there."

Detective Clayborn grunted and made another notation. Looking first at Bettina, and then at Pamela, and finally back at Bettina, he asked, "And why did you come here today?"

Bettina repeated what she had told Officer Sanchez about being summoned by Coco, and Detective Clayborn grunted again. Closing his notepad and returning it to an inner pocket of his sports jacket, he said, "Don't leave town."

Meanwhile, further developments were taking place in Dorcas's backyard. The county's crime-scene unit had evidently arrived, and three figures in white jumpsuits complete with hoods were moving toward the entrance to the garden shed, where Officer Keenen was still standing guard. Detective Clayborn repeated the admonition not to leave town and set off to join them. Officer Sanchez, too, had completed her interview work. She followed him as he waded through the flowery underbrush of Ingrid's wild garden.

Coco was stirring, gliding across the lawn with the breeze lifting her hair and setting her gauzy skirt afloat. "Hibiscus tea for everyone!" she called as she advanced toward her back porch. Hibiscus tea sounded like as good a plan as any, so after a glance that confirmed agreement, Pamela and Bettina joined the small procession that already included Dorcas and Simon.

Soon everyone but Coco was seated in Coco's living room. Dorcas and Bettina were on the sofa, which was covered with an expanse of light cotton fabric, like a bedspread, that featured a paisley design. Simon was sitting cross-legged on the scuffed wooden floor, next to a shaggy potted plant so large that it towered above him, and Pamela was in a beanbag chair. No one spoke, as if waiting for their hostess to serve the tea that would lend an aura of sociability to the gathering.

The tea was not long in coming. Coco emerged from around the corner bearing a tray that held five mugs, various in color and design. She set the tray on the coffee table, a makeshift construction consisting of cinder blocks topped by a plank of wood that looked like it had been salvaged from a demolition project.

She retraced her steps and soon returned with the pottery teapot Pamela recognized from the previous hibiscus-tea occasion. Once the tea had been poured and tasted, Coco lowered herself onto the sofa, at the end closest to Simon's spot on the floor.

"Shocking," she commented, speaking more to her steaming mug of tea than to the assembled group. "First Ingrid, and now this."

Dorcas was sitting between Coco and Bettina, but instead of acknowledging Coco's comment, she turned to Bettina. "Will I be able to go home?" she inquired with a woeful expression.

"Clayborn, or someone, will let you know," Bettina said.

Dorcas nodded and concentrated on her tea. The tea *was* comforting, Pamela thought, with its faint spiciness and rosy color and even the warmth of the mug as she cradled it in her hands. Silence prevailed then, until it was broken by the sound of footsteps on the front porch. The footsteps were followed by the doorbell's chime, and Coco hopped up from the sofa as if eager for distraction.

The voice that drifted in from the front door was that of Detective Clayborn. A moment later, Coco peeked around the corner from the entry and beckoned for Dorcas to join her. Three sets of eyes watched Dorcas rise from the sofa to make her way past the coffee table, the beanbag chair, and the towering plant until she disappeared around the corner. Fragments of conversation in which two female voices alternated with one male voice could be heard, and then the front door closed with a *thud*, and Coco returned to the living room alone.

"Dorcas has gone home. Her house isn't part of the crime scene," she announced, "but everybody is supposed to stay out of the backyard—and especially the shed—though the crime-scene unit has taken the body away. There might still be clues."

Simon unfolded himself and stood, teetering a bit and complaining about his knees. "I've got packing to do across the street," he said, "and I guess everybody's okay now?"

He surveyed Pamela and Bettina, and let his eyes linger when he got to Coco. She nodded, and after pausing to give her a quick hug and kiss, he went on his way, with her following him around the corner to the door. When she returned, she was smiling.

"It's coming, it's coming!" she sang, wrapping her arms around her chest in an embrace. "He's going to propose, really soon. I can feel it! Oooh!" She hopped from one foot to the other. "Simon, Simon, Simon!"

Bettina watched with a smile of her own, a tolerant one. Then she leaned forward and began to gather the mugs and the teapot, setting them on the tray.

"Let's just see how much of Dorcas's yard is marked off with crime-scene tape," Bettina said as they prepared to take their leave. They were in Coco's kitchen, having deposited the tray with the tea things on the counter. Coco escorted them to her back door and stepped out onto the back porch with them. From that vantage point, the extent of the crime scene was clear. The bright yellow tape stretched from the back border of the lot past the side of the shed and halfway to the rear of the house, sagging a bit along the way. It turned a corner then, and another corner, and headed back toward the shed, where it disappeared around the far side.

Coco's porch also gave a view of Ingrid's backyard—and Pamela was surprised to see that a figure was moving about among the flowers and errant butterflies.

"That's that bee woman, isn't it?" Coco edged close to the porch railing and leaned over. "She was around on Wednesday too. Remember?"

"Honey Hurley." Bettina edged in next to her. "She was checking on what was in bloom already that her bees might be interested in."

It *was* Honey Hurley. Pamela recognized her blond hair with its boyish cut—but why would she be back again so soon? "Wednesday was the day before yesterday," she said. "I can't imagine much has changed since then. Ingrid's yard certainly looks the same."

"She's not really looking at the plants," Bettina observed. "She's more interested in Dorcas's yard."

Indeed, Honey Hurley had advanced to the ragged border where Dorcas's lawn met the butterfly garden and was scanning the portion of lawn marked off by the crime-scene tape. She cast an occasional glance at the garden shed, but the doors had been securely closed by the crime-scene unit and sealed with strips of sticky tape.

"Just curious, I suppose." Coco turned away with a shrug. "People can be so nosy when something like a murder happens."

"How would she know there had been another murder?" Bettina inquired. "The body was just found this morning. Marcy Brewer hasn't even gotten onto the story yet." She laid a hand on Coco's arm. "She will, though. A word of advice—don't answer the door if she comes around, and warn Dorcas too."

Pamela and Bettina bade Coco goodbye then, with thanks for the hibiscus tea. They followed her back through her house and bade goodbye at the front door again. The Toyota was waiting at the curb.

"I guess this *really* means Nestor didn't kill Ingrid," Pamela commented as Bettina navigated the curving route that would deliver them to County Road at the bottom of Serpentine Way.

"The motive was convincing, though." Bettina's head swiveled to face her passenger, and Pamela held her breath as the intersection with County Road approached. "His creative reputation was at stake—and maybe even more important, financially speaking—his comeback as an important figure in the fashion world."

Once the Toyota had heeded the stop sign, Pamela responded. "We don't have to worry about Eilert anymore. However much Nestor might have wished he could silence Eilert, he's not going to be able to do that now."

Bettina made the turn onto County Road. "His legacy will suffer when the world finds out the designs that launched his career weren't actually *his*."

"The gallery owner probably didn't kill Ingrid either," Pamela said, "if the same person who killed her killed Nestor—and we assumed that if the gallery owner killed her, the death was the accidental result of an argument anyway. Why would the gallery owner seek out Nestor later to kill him on purpose?"

"That leaves Dorcas as a suspect." They were approaching Orchard Street.

"But only for Ingrid's death, again," Pamela pointed out. "Why would Dorcas care about Nestor?"

"We'll sleep on it," Bettina said as the Toyota turned the corner for the last lap of its journey home.

CHAPTER 16

Saturday morning's *Register* did not disappoint. Even before setting water to boil for coffee, but after giving the cats their breakfast, Pamela had hurried to the curb to collect it. Now, as the cats clustered in the spot where they were accustomed to receive their meals, tails radiating out and heads bowed toward the juicy morsels in their bowls, Pamela slipped the newspaper out of its plastic sleeve and unfolded it on the table.

A bold headline, all in caps and spanning two columns, read: NESTOR FLAVIN, INGRID BARRICK'S ERSTWHILE PARTNER, IS SECOND VICTIM IN ARBORVILLE KILLINGS. The article, under Marcy Brewer's byline, began, "Serpentine Way, long one of Arborville's prettiest streets, is once again a crime scene . . ."

Pamela skimmed far enough down to discover that either Coco hadn't warned Dorcas to ignore Marcy's likely request for an interview, or Dorcas had ignored the warning. Marcy quoted Dorcas extensively, along the lines of, "I would never have expected to find a dead body in my garden shed, and with all the pollen in the air at this time of year I was in a bad enough state already."

Coffee would be required before she read further, Pamela decided. Feeling a premonition that Bettina would arrive soon, requesting coffee but bearing something tastier than buttered toast, Pamela measured twice as much water as usual into the kettle and left her loaf of whole-grain bread in the bread drawer.

While the water was heating, she slipped a paper filter into the carafe's filter cone and spooned coffee beans into the grinder. The whirring clatter that resulted when she pressed down on the grinder's cover to launch the grinding process sent the cats scurrying from the kitchen, but leaving clean bowls behind.

Soon Pamela was seated once again at the kitchen table, but with a cup of steaming coffee at hand and Part 1 of the *Register* spread out before her. The preliminary report from the county medical examiner indicated that Nestor had been killed with a blow from a blunt object, which could have been a brick or a stone. No murder weapon had been found, and the killer could have discarded it anywhere in—justifiable— expectation that it would blend into the landscaping. By the time Dorcas discovered the body, Nester had been dead for at least eight hours.

Pamela had just reached the end of the article when the doorbell's chime summoned her from the room. She opened the front door to admit Bettina, dressed for the bright day in a yellow cotton shirtwaist and strappy yellow sandals with wedge heels. Catrina looked up from her nap in the sunny spot that appeared every morning on the thrift-shop carpet, then she nestled her chin down onto her paws again and closed her eyes.

Bettina was smiling in a way that implied great satisfaction . . . with *something*.

"You've been out," Pamela said, nodding toward the white cardboard bakery box that Bettina carried. Its top flap was held in place by a crisscross of string secured with a bow. "Did you speak with Detective Clayborn?"

Bettina frequently detoured past the Co-Op bakery counter on her way home from the meetings with Detective Clayborn that were part of her reporting duties.

She shook her head, and the turquoise pendants on her bold earrings swayed. "No time in his schedule for a reporter based right here in Arborville, but he was certainly happy to provide Marcy Brewer with everything she needed for her story—and in time for the story to appear in this morning's *Register*."

"She doesn't sleep," Pamela commented.

"He told me he'd talk to me at our usual Monday meeting, and he pointed out that the *Advocate* is a weekly and won't be out again until next Friday."

"Then why are you looking so happy?"

"Because . . ." Bettina advanced toward the kitchen, stepping past Pamela but turning to ask over her shoulder whether Pamela had made extra coffee.

"As a matter of fact, yes." Pamela followed her friend through the doorway.

"Because," Bettina repeated, setting the bakery box

on the table, "the Co-Op had—" She tugged at a string end, the bow loosened, and the flap popped up. "The Co-Op had . . . *chocolate croissants*!" She eased the flap all the way back to reveal four flaky and buttery crescents nestled in a bed of waxy paper.

The *Register* was swiftly refolded and transferred to the counter, and a second cup and saucer set joined the one already in use, along with two small wedding-china plates, and napkins and silverware. Bettina fetched the cut-glass sugar bowl and cream pitcher, then poured a goodly dollop of heavy cream into the pitcher.

As Bettina slipped a croissant onto each plate, Pamela filled Bettina's cup and added fresh coffee to her own. She waited to sample her croissant, however, sipping her coffee black. Meanwhile, Bettina methodically sugared her own, dribbled in cream, and stirred until the liquid swirled about by her spoon was nearly as pale as the porcelain of the cup that contained it.

"They don't always have these," Bettina said, taking a fork to her croissant. "I was all set to get the crumb cake, but then . . ." Her voice trailed off as her fork cut through the overlapping layers of the croissant's shell to expose the vein of chocolate within. "And I got the last four," she concluded, spearing the morsel of pastry and lifting her fork to her mouth.

The buttery pastry and the rich, bittersweet chocolate blended perfectly, with some bites more pastry-intensive and others more chocolate-intensive. For a minute or two, the only sounds were forks clinking against china and hums of enjoyment. The silence invited mental activity, free from distraction—but for the seductions of coffee and croissants.

"What if Nestor somehow knew who killed Ingrid?" Pamela inquired suddenly. "And what if the killer knew that Nestor knew?"

"Ummm." Bettina's eyes, gazing at Pamela over the rose-garlanded rim of her coffee cup, widened. "That would mean the killer's motive in murdering Nestor would be to prevent him from revealing what he knew."

"So the killer could be Dorcas, or the gallery owner— but why would the gallery owner leave the body in Dorcas's garden shed? Why not just take it away, in that van we saw at the gallery?"

"But why would Dorcas call the police to report finding Nestor's body if she was the person who killed him?" Bettina sipped at her coffee and returned the cup to its saucer.

"To allay suspicion? Being shocked, and purposely bringing the police to the scene, would seem more what an innocent person would do than a guilty one, but it could all have been an act. And her motive, the pollen issue, is pretty strong—at least as a motive to pay a call on Ingrid that escalated into an argument and then became physical."

Pamela carved off another bite of croissant. She had reached the middle, where the vein of chocolate was particularly thick. As she chewed, another argument in favor of Dorcas's guilt took shape in her mind. As soon as she swallowed, she spoke.

"Dorcas told Simon she tries not to go outside this time of year, so why would she have just randomly been in her backyard, randomly looking in the garden shed— unless the whole just-happened-to-find-a-body story was nothing more than . . . a story?"

Bettina nodded.

"But"—Pamela held up a finger to signal that an important point had just occurred to her—"we're assuming Nestor was on the scene when Dorcas, or the gallery owner, carried out the evil deed. Otherwise, how would he have been a threat?"

Bettina frowned and sipped her coffee. Then she brightened. "We know Nestor and Ingrid were on good terms now, no matter how the long-ago breakup happened. He could have been at her house but in another room, or even upstairs, while the argument was unfolding. He hears angry voices, hurries to the living room. Ingrid is unconscious on the floor, and somebody— let's assume it's Dorcas—is dashing away. Dorcas looks back and sees Nestor and realizes he's got to be eliminated."

She took another sip of coffee and went on. "The crime-scene unit decided Dorcas's house wasn't part of the crime scene—and they must have gone over it pretty thoroughly. So let's assume she summoned Nestor to her yard on some pretext and then lured him to the garden shed. He seemed so gentlemanly, and she's pretty athletic. He might not have fought back until it was too late."

"No." Pamela shook her head. "If he knew Dorcas was the killer, why would he let himself be lured to the garden shed? And if he was on the scene when Ingrid was killed, why wouldn't he have immediately called the police?"

Bettina shrugged and twisted her features into a sad smile. "Don't forget—we decided Nestor had a strong motive for wanting Ingrid dead. Maybe he saw that

Dorcas had just solved his problem for him, but Dorcas, of course, didn't realize that he had a reason for staying mum."

"And the gallery owner?" Pamela inquired.

"The same explanation. He knew Nestor knew that he had killed Ingrid so he had to eliminate Nestor."

"But again, why would the gallery owner put Nestor in Dorcas's garden shed? Why wouldn't he just carry him away in his van?"

Bettina uttered a sound like a backward hiccup and checked her watch. "I've got to get going!" she exclaimed. "I'm meeting Marlene Pepper at the community gardens to do an interview on the composting program." She scooted her chair back and stood, but before she stepped away from the table, she peeked inside the bakery box.

"Two left, and they're both for you," she said. "Food for thought. I don't know about you, but I'm more confused about our puzzle than I was when I arrived. I think somehow it all goes back to Nestor, though—wanting to take credit for work actually done by a woman."

After the mental workout of the conversation with Bettina, Pamela was looking forward to immersing herself in her *Fiber Craft* work as she climbed the stairs to her office. The articles she was tasked with evaluating or copyediting represented a mental workout on the part of their authors, sometimes an arduous mental workout. But by the time they were submitted to *Fiber Craft*, any puzzles presented by the research topic had been solved, and any loose ends tacked firmly into place.

She settled into her desk chair and guided her mouse

around the mouse pad until the monitor's screen brightened. After a quick check of her email, she opened Word and then the file labeled "Woven to Last." Its full title, displayed across the first page to come up on the screen, was "Woven to Last . . . Before There Were Blue Jeans."

The author, a man, was a materials science professor at a university in Texas, and he explained in his introduction that his interest in the topic derived from his own experience working as a cowhand during summers while he was in college. His article dealt with the stresses placed on woven fabric by the act of horseback riding. The rider needed a trouser flexible enough that a leg could be swung over the horse when mounting, without fear that the fabric would tear. The trouser also had to be particularly strong in certain spots, like the knees, because of the way a rider anchored himself on the horse while it was in motion.

The world's oldest pants, he noted, had been created three thousand years ago in China, designed for the warriors and herders whose professions required that they be comfortable, as well as skilled, on horseback. In examining the three-thousand-year-old pants on a research trip, he had discovered that though the entire garment had been woven from the same type of fiber—wool—different weaving techniques had been ingeniously employed in different sections. A technique that allowed flexibility had been used to make areas that would be stressed by the action of mounting more elastic. On the other hand, a technique that created a reinforced effect had been used in the knees and other areas subject to extra wear. The author had actually figured out how to replicate these different techniques, and he included both photographs and diagrams that showed the different effects.

The article required minimal copyediting, except that the author had a tendency to insert apostrophes where they didn't belong and omit them where they did. As Pamela pushed her chair back from her desk after saving and closing her file, her stomach reminded her that it was well past lunchtime. The chocolate croissant had been filling but not sustaining. She mentally inventoried the contents of pantry and refrigerator on the way down the stairs, and decided that a grilled cheese sandwich sounded particularly appealing.

It was quick work to transform two slices of whole-grain bread into a buttery, toasty envelope containing a layer of melted Vermont cheddar, and even quicker work to eat it. She had decided to sit at the little table on her front porch, taking advantage of the perfect day. Looking up from the now-empty plate to admire the flowery bounty in the yards across the street, she noticed Bettina's Toyota making its way toward the Frasers' house and its own driveway.

Once the Toyota was parked, Bettina climbed out—a flash of bright yellow in her summery shirtwaist. Instead of heading for her front door, she advanced to the end of her driveway, waved at Pamela, and proceeded across the street.

"I was going to call you," she sang out when reached the opposite curb, "but here you are." She waited to say more until she had climbed the porch steps and perched on the edge of the metal chair across from the one where Pamela sat. "Coco got in touch with me while I was up at the community gardens. We're invited to Ingrid's house if we want to come. Eilert is going to be photographing the tapestries that were supposed to be in the gallery show."

She paused with an expectant smile and added, "What do you think?"

"I'd like to see them—and Eilert will probably want to interest me in an article about them for *Fiber Craft*." She picked up her plate and climbed to her feet. "So, yes—let's go."

It was Coco who greeted them when they reached Ingrid's front door. "I'm so excited," she said, hugging herself. Her wide eyes and open expression made her excitement obvious. "It was such a disappointment when the gallery show was canceled."

She stepped aside and waved them into the living room, which was empty—of humans and of tapestries.

"Mari and Eilert are in the studio, unpacking the tapestries, but he's going to photograph them in here because the light is good and there's a nice blank wall to display them against." She gestured toward a sturdy picture-hanging hook centered on the far wall.

"We've been wondering . . ." Bettina said, moving close to Coco and speaking in a low voice.

Pamela wasn't sure what "wondering" Bettina was about to implicate her in, but she recognized her friend's tone and manner—often a prelude to extracting information that was actually none of her business.

Coco's excited expression modulated to pleasant attentiveness, and she murmured, "Yes?"

"What do you think made Dorcas decide to look inside her garden shed on Friday morning?"

Coco shrugged. "Checking to see if I returned her shovel, I suppose. She's not a very trusting person."

Bettina looked at Pamela, her features altering subtly. She's pleased, Pamela said to herself. She thinks she's on the trail of something. And she was!

"I borrowed the shovel," Coco continued, "for Simon to use when he planted the impatiens—and yes, I admit I didn't put it back as soon as I could have."

"When *did* you put it back?" Bettina inquired conversationally.

"Thursday night. I remembered right before I went to bed. It was dark, so I took a flashlight and carried the shovel right over there."

"And put it inside the shed?" A hint of excitement had crept into Bettina's voice.

Coco nodded. "Opened one of the doors, went inside with the flashlight, found the hook for the shovel, and put it back where it belonged."

"And there was no body yet . . ."

"Of course not, or I'd have freaked out."

Bettina seemed to teeter, and Pamela stepped forward to steady her, but Coco didn't notice. Mari and Eilert had just emerged from the back of the house, and she advanced to meet them.

Bettina stepped forward too. She took both of Mari's hands in her own and said, "I'm so sorry about your father." She accompanied the comment with a sympathetic puckering of the brow.

Mari indeed looked like a person bereft, with her fair hair untended and her outfit of faded leggings and shapeless T-shirt suggesting she had put on the first things that came to hand. Her mournful eyes enhanced the impression of youthfulness that Pamela had had on first meeting her. Mari nodded at Bettina's words, and Pamela added her own murmured condolences.

Eilert had remained standing next to Mari. The all-black ensemble he'd worn when he met with Pamela and Bettina at Wendelstaff had seemed a modish nod to his artistic interests. Today, the same ensemble seemed an acknowledgment of Mari's bereavement. As Mari and Bettina continued to talk, with Coco joining in, Eilert edged around to join Pamela.

"I'm so grateful to Mari," he said in his precise voice. "The tapestries will go into storage as she continues to prepare the house for sale, but she was willing to let me photograph them for the book, even though they have to be unpacked and then packed back up—to be tucked away again for who knows how long."

He'd been facing her while he spoke, but he paused. His gaze, set off by the dark frames of his angular glasses, intensified. "You would perhaps be interested in an article previewing that section of my book?"

"I don't make the final decisions about what to accept," Pamela responded, "but yes, you should certainly write something up—with the photographs, of course—and submit it."

She hadn't noticed it when she and Bettina arrived, but now Pamela realized that Eilert had come equipped with the photo equipment he would need. A black metal tripod was set up about ten feet back from the wall destined for the tapestry display, and a serious-looking camera, black with bands of muted silver, was mounted atop it.

The tapestries had begun to appear, rolled up or loosely folded, carried out from the back of the house by Mari, Coco, and Bettina and piled on the sofa. This first view of them, of their reverse sides at any rate, revealed swathes of woven, knitted, or crocheted fiber in textures that ranged from fine to ragged. Vivid colors overlapped and intersected, forming chevrons, crosses, even random zigzags.

"Two more to come," Coco announced as she deposited a particularly large and bulky one with the others.

Mari and Bettina entered then, each with arms extended, bearing a rolled-up tapestry. Mari unrolled the one she had been carrying and moved toward the wall to suspend it from the hook. As it unfolded and the full tapestry was revealed, Eilert whispered, "Beautiful." He took his position behind his camera and leaned forward.

"Yes, yes, good," he murmured as his slender fingers adjusted the lens that jutted from the camera's front. A faint but solid click—more like a *chunk*, really—indicated that he had gotten his first shot. He continued to stare through the viewfinder.

The tapestry *was* beautiful, but troubling as well. In the center was a small dress, like a child's dress, that looked as if it had come from a real child's wardrobe or been found at a thrift shop. The fabric was yellow-and-white-checked cotton. The little dress was splayed against a crocheted background, also yellow, but with diagonals of black yarn running through it, like sinister lightning bolts. Ingrid had somehow managed to hook into the cotton fabric of the dress here and there, and then execute her crochet stitches, so it looked as if the dress was dissolving into its background—or being devoured by it.

Eilert snapped a few more photos, changing position slightly, then signaled he was ready to move on. Mari removed that tapestry, rolled it up, and handed it to Coco, who carried it off to the back of the house. Mari then hung another tapestry, and Eilert again whispered, "Beautiful," and concentrated on his photography.

This tapestry, too, incorporated a garment, repurposed from somewhere, into its design. The garment was a tiny, one-piece outfit for a baby, pink, but showing the stains and wear of actual use. Again, it was of a piece with its background, which also seemed distressed. It had been knitted of extra-thick yarn, but stitches had been dropped, and knitting and purling had been interchanged in a way that made no sense. The background started out deep pink at the top, then a blood-red yarn had been grafted in with the red yarn tied onto the pink and the tails left hanging.

Similar tapestries followed, each integrating a garment into a background crafted from wool or some other fiber. Pamela and Bettina had found chairs and pulled them up like spectators at a performance, facing the wall where the tapestries were being displayed.

CHAPTER 17

At last, only one tapestry remained on the sofa, a particularly bulky one bundled into a careless roll. Mari gripped the top edge and—still facing the sofa—let it unfurl. It wasn't until she turned and made her way to where the hook waited on the wall, raising both hands aloft because the tapestry was quite large, that Pamela got a clear look at it.

The garment that had been worked into this tapestry was a yellow-and-black-striped pullover sweater, long-sleeved and crew-necked. It was positioned at an angle in the upper-left-hand corner of the knitted panel, a moody shade of gray, that formed the background. The sleeves angled, too, bent where the elbows would be, as if to suggest the motions of a human body wearing the sweater.

Slashing diagonally across the tapestry, a long twig had been lashed to the background with the same moody gray yarn. Dangling from the twig was the object that had made the tapestry so bulky: a three-dimensional cocoon, a bulbous pod, knit from pale green yarn. It was, however, much larger than an actual cocoon, about a foot long, and it appeared to have been stuffed—perhaps with fiberfill—in the same way one might stuff a knitted toy animal.

None of the other tapestries had included words in their designs, but along the bottom edge of this one, the word *conception* had been embroidered in jagged letters, pale green like the cocoon.

Eilert devoted particular effort to photographing this last tapestry, moving his tripod from one side to the other, as well as forward and backward, trying perhaps to do justice to the tapestry's three-dimensional effect. Finally, with one last *chunk*, he raised his head from his camera and stepped back. He removed his glasses and rubbed his eyes.

"What an experience," he sighed. "What an honor to view and photograph this oeuvre." He replaced his glasses and turned toward Mari, who was now sitting on the sofa where the tapestries had been. With a courtly bow, he added, "I shall be forever in your debt."

Coco asked whether Mari wanted some help in packing the tapestries up again, but Eilert insisted it would be his great pleasure to stay and do whatever was necessary. A few minutes later, Pamela, Bettina, and Coco bade farewell and stepped out onto Ingrid's porch. Basking in the afternoon sun, the yard dazzled with bright dots of color, the flowers and the butterflies hovering over them, and the flowers exhaled their fragrance into the warm air.

As Pamela focused on the garden, and Bettina said a last few words to Mari, who lingered at the door, Coco's attention was drawn elsewhere. Mari said a final good-bye, and Coco led the way down the path that ran from Ingrid's porch to the street.

"This is a surprise," she commented, still moving ahead but looking to her left.

"What's a surprise?" Bettina caught up with her.

Coco stopped and faced Bettina. Her lips quivered, then settled into a mischievous smile. "Dorcas has a boyfriend, but for some reason, it's a secret—or it has been." She nodded toward Dorcas's driveway. "That's his car—the first time I've seen it in daylight, and the wrong day too."

Bettina seemed to freeze. Watching her in profile, Pamela saw her eyes widen and heard her short intake of breath. Something had occurred to Pamela as Coco spoke, and she suspected the same thing had occurred to Bettina. If Dorcas had a boyfriend who came around at night, and if an argument about pollen had led to Ingrid's death, Dorcas might not have been alone when she paid the call that resulted in the argument.

"Does he visit often?" Bettina inquired. It was obvi-ous from her voice that she was trying to control her excitement.

"They're very methodical." The mischievous smile returned. "Her house one night, his house the next—I assume that's where she goes, anyway. Some nights her house is dark and her car is gone. She's always back by the time I go out to pick up the *Register*, though—and I've never seen his car in daylight before."

"She's upset," Bettina said, "about finding Nestor's body. Maybe she needs extra comforting."

"*Everybody* needs 'comforting'"—Coco snickered—"the more often, the better. And in this day and age—*hello!*—nobody cares if a couple of adults who like each other want to spend the night together—assuming they're single, of course." She paused. "But maybe he isn't?" She paused again. "But how could they spend every night together if he wasn't?"

"The wrong day, you said?" Coco nodded. "And methodical? Every other day?" Coco nodded again.

"Ingrid and I used to laugh about that." Coco laughed as if in reminiscence. "And the sneaking around in the dark. Ingrid had her share of male attention, and I don't think she ever found it necessary to be discreet."

Bettina was only half listening. With her right index finger, she was counting off pinkie, ring finger, and middle finger of her left hand. As she did so, her lips moved.

"It's Saturday," she said when she had finished, "and Dorcas is supposed to go to his place then, not vice versa."

"That's right." Coco was watching Bettina's face attentively, obviously wondering what she was getting at. Coco, of course, had no idea that Pamela and Bettina suspected Dorcas of killing Nestor.

"So she would have gone to his place Thursday night—unless they'd already deviated from the schedule."

"I suppose." Coco shrugged. "Does it matter?"

Bettina ignored the question—or was she just at a loss for words, disappointed that she'd reached a dead end just when an alibi for Dorcas seemed at hand?

"The shovel!" Pamela said suddenly, the words surprising even her as they popped out.

She'd halted on the path a yard or so behind Coco and Bettina when they'd stopped to talk. Both turned to her now.

"When you returned the shovel to Dorcas's garden shed, did you notice whether the lights in her house were on or off?"

"Off, now that you mention it. Why?"

"Oh, look at that!" Bettina darted forward, pointing. "A hummingbird!"

"Did you really see a hummingbird?" Pamela asked Bettina after Coco had veered off toward her own yard and they were advancing on the Toyota.

"You missed it?" Bettina tipped her head in Pamela's direction, revealing an attempt to suppress a smile.

"There was no hummingbird, was there? You were just trying to distract Coco so you wouldn't have to explain why you cared whether Dorcas's lights were on or off."

"It worked, didn't it?" Bettina unlocked the passenger-side door, and Pamela lowered herself into her seat.

"Dorcas didn't kill Nestor," Bettina said after she had settled behind the steering wheel. "His body wasn't in the garden shed when Coco returned the shovel Thursday night, which she said was just before her bedtime."

Pamela chimed in, "So he was killed sometime between then and when Dorcas found him the next morning—but earlier rather than later, because the medical examiner said he'd been dead at least eight hours."

"And we know"—Bettina took over—"that Dorcas was at her boyfriend's house all night." She twisted her key in the ignition, and the Toyota's engine came to life with a low rumble.

"What about the gallery owner?" Pamela asked.

"Why would he put Nestor's body in Dorcas's garden shed?" Pamela suppressed a laugh, recalling that she had already posed exactly the same question more than once. "So maybe it really was a break-in gone awry," Bettina concluded.

"Or what if there were two killers? We eliminated Nestor when he became the second victim, but he could have killed Ingrid and then someone else killed him."

"Why?" Bettina had pulled away from the curb, but she swiveled to look at Pamela.

"I'm not going to answer unless you watch the road."

Obediently, Bettina faced forward, and Pamela went on.

"Because they knew he killed Ingrid, of course."

"That means . . ." Bettina was navigating the curve that gave Serpentine Way its name, and she slowed down. "That means it could be Eilert!" The Toyota lurched. "Or that sweet, sweet Mari!"

"Nestor was her father," Pamela pointed out. "So she kills her father to avenge the death of her mother?"

"It's been done."

"But it sounds like the plot of a Greek tragedy."

"Eilert then?"

They were both silent as the Toyota covered the rest of the distance to Arborville Avenue, turned, and then turned again onto Orchard Street. But Pamela had not stopped thinking.

"Maybe it's neither Mari nor Eilert," she said. The Toyota had come to rest in the Frasers' driveway, and Bettina was about to step out onto the asphalt.

"Oh?" She settled back into her seat.

"Let's suppose it *was* Nestor who killed Ingrid, and he ransacked her house to make it look like there had been a break-in and hid the things in the most convenient spot at hand—Dorcas's garden shed. Later he came back and cleared the garden shed out to dispose of the things farther away from the crime scene."

"Okay . . ."

"There's more, though." Pamela's tone was urgent.

"I hope so," Bettina said. "The garden shed was empty on Wednesday, and Nestor wasn't killed until Thursday night."

"He came back Thursday night, to make sure he'd removed everything he'd hidden there—and someone else came upon him in the shed and took him for an intruder."

"Who?" Bettina inquired. "Not Dorcas or her boyfriend, because we know they were at the boyfriend's house Thursday night. Nobody was home at Ingrid's house because she was dead. Some neighbor whose lot backs up to Dorcas's? Wouldn't they just think whoever was in the garden shed had legitimate business there? Coco put the shovel back, and nobody killed her."

Pamela let all that sink in. Then she reached for her door handle. As she and Bettina parted at the end of the driveway, she said, "I wonder if Detective Clayborn has made any progress—on either case."

* * *

He hadn't, as it turned out. Sunday morning's *Register* included, on an inner page of the section devoted to local news, an article with Marcy Brewer's byline. The article, short by Marcy Brewer's standards and with an inconspicuous headline that read ARBORVILLE MURDERS CONTINUE TO FRUSTRATE POLICE, reported that the police had no leads in the murder of Nestor Flavin but were dubious that it was linked to the break-in gone awry that had resulted in Ingrid Barrick's death—for which they also had no leads.

Pamela checked the carafe, hoping to discover a last bit of coffee. She had drunk her usual two cups but still felt as if she was sleepwalking. Her dreams had been vivid, and she had awakened several times, staring at the luminescent numerals on the face of her bedside clock as the night slowly gave way to morning. Images from the tapestries had inspired the dreams, she suspected.

They had featured clothing, on display as if at a flea market or bazaar, and people trying on the clothing, only to assume roles suggested by the clothing—a winsome child in a child's dress, a pretty young woman in a flirtatious frock . . . And everyone posed then for a group photo before dissolving, literally, into the background.

A few inches of coffee did remain, and Pamela lit the burner under the carafe. After a few minutes, tiny bubbles made their way to the surface of the dark liquid, and after a few more minutes, Pamela tipped the carafe over her cup. Upon tasting, she discovered the coffee was now bitter where it had been aromatic, but the extra portion of caffeine was welcome.

Later, the cup empty and returned to the counter along with the plate that had held toast, Pamela wandered into the living room. Precious was lounging on the top platform of the cat climber, totally content to be unproductive. Taking a cue from her, Pamela settled onto the sofa, still in her pajamas and robe. She'd left the little appointment calendar journal on the coffee table after she'd finished looking through it the first time, and now she picked it up again.

She opened it at random and discovered she was looking at a page that recorded a week in mid-June. Delicate sketches rendered scenes of the butterfly garden with flowers in profusion, and a few sketches featured human figures as well. It took only a bit of imagination to see those sketches as studies for tapestries Ingrid later produced.

Among the materials Eilert had entrusted to Pamela, she had noticed photographs of tapestries that resembled flowery fields reproduced in wool. And then there were the tapestries she had just seen in person, the ones that had given rise to the previous night's restless sleep. They hadn't included people, but looking at the little sketches of human figures in the journal, Pamela realized that if one focused on the clothes—which sometimes merged with backgrounds patterned in various ways, these sketches, too, could have been studies for Ingrid's later fiber art.

She turned a few more pages, admiring again the skill with which Ingrid had fit such lively scenes into panels that were only an inch high and a few inches wide. Here came July, with Fourth of July fireworks, and August, and then a different color palette for autumn leaves and Halloween. She skipped ahead to Christmas, admiring a tiny decorated tree, which seemed to be lying on its side unless one rotated the journal clockwise to study it.

With the last week of the year complete, Pamela turned to the "Notes" page at the end of the journal, where Ingrid had documented the process of a butterfly emerging from a cocoon. The cocoon, though two-dimensional and much smaller, brought to mind the one she had recently seen in the tapestry that had provided a dramatic finale to the collection that was to have been exhibited in the Timberley gallery show.

It occurred to Pamela that this cocoon, and the butterfly that had developed within it, represented a sort of finale to one of the storylines chronicled in the journal. She closed the little book and then opened it again near the middle. Paging back a few weeks, she reached June, and the deep-pink flower with its black center and arm-like leaves. It was a popular flower, doing its part in the pollinator garden ecosystem. In some panels, a magnificent butterfly, with the delicate patterning on its wings rendered in black and gold, came calling. In others, it was visited by a fuzzy black-and-yellow-striped bee.

Precious had descended from the top platform of the cat climber and was indulging in a luxurious stretch on the carpet. Taking the cat's action as a sign that she, too, should get moving, Pamela closed the little book and set it back on the coffee table. She was in motion now, but her thoughts still lingered among the images that Ingrid had sketched back in 1985.

CHAPTER 18

Half an hour later, Pamela had dressed, tidied up her bedroom, and checked her email. Still at loose ends, she decided a walk would lend some structure to her day, especially a fine May day with weather too good to waste. She set off down Orchard, crossed County Road, and rambled through the nature preserve, coming out on a side street that led back to County Road. She crossed County Road again and continued north until she came to the lower end of Serpentine Way.

Ingrid's yard, and the butterfly garden, lay halfway up the block, and she headed up the slight hill until the butterfly garden's colorful display interrupted the more conventional landscaping of its neighbors. She continued on, passing Dorcas's house and pausing to admire the butterfly garden up close, as butterflies and bees hovered and buzzed, darting in and out. Aside from the insects, Pamela was the garden's only visitor today—

no sign of Honey Hurley monitoring the offerings available for her discriminating bees.

But as Pamela gazed, a voice hailed her from Coco's yard, and she turned to see Coco advancing toward the property line where her own ragged grass yielded to Ingrid's tangled but colorful vegetation. Looking past Coco, Pamela could see Simon. He'd been stooping toward his recently planted impatiens, but he straightened up with a grunt.

Simon was wearing the grimy jeans that seemed to be his gardening outfit, paired with a faded concert T-shirt, but Coco was quite dressed up, in a summery frock that hugged her trim torso and flared out in a tiered skirt that reached her ankles.

"The impatiens are doing great," she said, glancing back at Simon with a fond smile. He was stooping again, making his way along the row of blooms, patting soil into place here and there. "We're going to the garden center in a bit to buy more plants. He's really taken an interest in the yard, and he has such a green thumb, and it looks like"—she leaned close and whispered—"one day soon, *my* yard will be *our* yard." She seemed buoyant, so filled with joy that she might easily float away. "Of course, we *could* move across the street, into his parents' house . . ." She paused. "But I think he wants to sell it."

"That will be easy, I'm sure," Pamela said. "Serpentine Way is one of the prettiest streets in Arborville."

"Ingrid's house will be on the market too." Coco nodded. "Of course, a new owner could spell the end of the butterfly garden." She blinked, as if suddenly remembering something. "That reminds me—the bee woman was here again this morning, inspecting the flowers. I don't know what her bees will do if the garden disappears."

"I don't expect anything will happen to it before the end of the summer," Pamela commented. "So the bees will have one more season at least—and anyway, the butterfly garden will live on, in a way."

Coco's expression—wide eyes and parted lips—invited explanation even before she added a questioning, "Oh?"

"Ingrid's journal—that appointment calendar I found when Mari invited us to help ourselves to the things that needed to be cleared out of the house. It's a calendar for 1985, and Ingrid made a record of what happened each day of the year by drawing a little picture. Some of the pictures are mysterious, with flowers and butterflies and bees, but the way it all unfolds, I think the flowers and butterflies and bees represent real people."

Pamela hadn't actually thought that until she heard herself say it. Clearly, the act of walking had set her mind free to roam as well, and it had been mulling over the journal images she had studied anew before heading out the door.

"And there's a cocoon," she added. "At the end a butterfly comes out. Mari is probably just about the right age to have been born in 1985."

Simon had finished tending the impatiens and was standing slightly behind Coco with a hand resting lightly on her shoulder.

"Ingrid *did* express herself in pictures," Coco said. "She was drawing all those bees, bees, and more bees, like a premonition, and then . . ." Coco put her hands over her mouth and shuddered as her voice sank to a whisper. "And then . . . she was killed."

"She had secrets"—Pamela nodded—"and the secrets are hidden in the journal, if only a person could figure them out."

Coco nodded but didn't answer. After a bit, Simon broke the silence, saying, "Update on Nestor, by the way."

"Oh, yes." Coco turned and acknowledged him with a smile. "There *is* an update on Nestor, and Pamela might be interested."

"Funeral arrangements," Simon clarified.

"He has a brother," Coco went on, "and the brother and Mari have been in touch. We'll keep you posted, though it may be a while because his body is still with the medical examiner."

As Pamela made her way back to Orchard Street, the realization that lunchtime had come and gone added urgency to her long strides. At home, she discovered that the refrigerator was bare of leftovers, not to mention raw ingredients. The cupboard, however, yielded a can of tuna, and she very gratefully made a tuna salad sandwich, which she ate while sitting on her porch.

A trip to the Co-Op was in order for general provisions, she decided, and with Knit and Nibble coming to her house on Tuesday, it was also time to think about an interesting nibble to serve. She returned her plate to the kitchen, took out one of the little notepads that arrived so faithfully in the mail from charities near and far, and settled at the table to make a shopping list.

Strawberries, she wrote, as ideas for a dessert themed to the season presented themselves to her mind. She paused, studying the word. Strawberries were certainly in season, but Wilfred had made strawberry-rhubarb cobbler when Bettina hosted the Knit and Nibble group, and the following Tuesday, Roland had topped his magic cake with sliced strawberries, and then there had been the yogurt and strawberries as part of Wilfred's brunch menu, and the strawberry strudel he'd made just the other day . . .

She left the word *strawberries* topping the list but added *bananas*, and then *whipping cream*, and *vanilla wafers*. Fish would be on the menu for tonight, and a meat loaf in the near future could provide meals well past the middle of the coming week.

An hour later, Pamela's serviceable compact was back in her driveway, and she was unloading a collection of bulging tote bags from the trunk. After the morning's ramble, walking to and from the Co-Op had seemed daunting, especially the trip home laden with groceries, and she had broken with a long-standing custom of doing local errands on foot.

The car trip had made it possible to stock up on cat food, many more cans than she would normally buy at a time. One whole heavy tote was nothing but cat food, and it was set aside until the perishables had been stored. Once all the totes were empty, and returned to their hook in the entry closet, Pamela fetched a cookbook and sat down at the kitchen table. It was her oldest cookbook, a repository of every basic recipe a person might want, like . . . vanilla pudding.

She nodded as she read through it, reminding herself of the steps, picturing the stage at which the pudding was thick enough to coat a metal spoon. On the counter, the strawberries waited in their cardboard container, glowing red and so fragrant they perfumed the kitchen. Next to them sat the bananas, four of them, streaked with pale green but sure to become fully ripe in time.

Ginger had been sitting in the entry, visible through the kitchen doorway. She stirred, and the motion caught Pamela's eye. A moment later, Pamela heard footsteps on the porch, and then the doorbell chimed, once, twice, three times. Ginger whirled and darted through the doorway and across the kitchen's black-and-white tile floor as Pamela headed the other direction.

The figure visible through the lace that curtained the oval window in the front door was tall and slender, dressed in a flowing, light-colored garment that contrasted with the green tones of lawn and shrubbery. Pamela opened the door to discover that her visitor was Coco Dalrymple.

The flowing, light-colored garment was the same dress Coco had worn earlier that day, but her serene buoyancy had been replaced by agitation. She'd walked from Serpentine Way, apparently, and fast—her face glistened with perspiration, and wisps of her wild hair clung to her forehead and cheeks.

"Come in, come in." Pamela retreated to the middle

of the entry and beckoned Coco to follow. "Are you okay?" she added. "Do you want some water?"

"Water, yes please." Coco nodded and batted at the tendrils of hair that the nodding had set in motion.

Pamela led her to the kitchen, settled her at the table, and slid an ice cube tray from the freezer. A few minutes later, she and Coco were seated facing each other with frosty glasses of ice water before them.

"It's the journal," Coco said after refreshing herself with two long swallows of ice water. "I was thinking about it after you left, and it sounds so interesting I'd love to see it."

It occurred to Pamela that Coco had worked herself into quite a state over a request that was easily enough granted. She fetched the journal from the coffee table in the living room and handed it to Coco, who had been watching tensely as Pamela reappeared in the kitchen doorway and made her way across the floor. Pamela sat back down and took a sip of ice water.

Coco opened the little book to a page midway through. She studied the drawings for a few moments and then began leafing forward, scanning each new page carefully. When she got to the images of the pink flower, the butterfly, and the bee, she lingered, and she lingered over subsequent pages too, especially those featuring the cocoon.

"It seems very personal," she said at last, looking up. She leafed through more pages, until only the calendar week that included Christmas and New Year's Eve was left, whereupon she looked up again, saying, "I guess that's all . . . the end of 1985."

"Not quite." Pamela reached across the table and

turned over the last calendar page to reveal the "Notes" page, with its step-by-step depiction of a butterfly emerging from a cocoon.

Coco bent her head toward the page until all Pamela could see was the top of her head and unruly hanks of salt and pepper hair shadowing her cheeks.

"Ingrid deserves her privacy," was the pronouncement when she'd completed her study of that page. She closed the little book and covered it with both her hands. "What are you going to do with this?" she asked. Her expression was that of a person waiting for bad news.

"I'm going to pass it along to Eilert, of course," Pamela said. "It belongs with the other materials from Ingrid's archives, and he might want to study it as part of his research."

"Mari should have final say." With her hands still covering the book, Coco pulled it closer. "Ingrid deserves her privacy," she repeated, "and her daughter should decide what gets released to the public and what doesn't."

Coco stood and clutched the book to her chest. "I'll give it to her, the next time she comes to work on clearing out the house." She was nodding spasmodically. "I really will. I promise."

"Well . . . okay . . ." Pamela stood too, and together she and Coco advanced toward the entry.

She herself had no claim on the journal, Pamela reflected. She could assert a claim in order to secure it for Eilert, but if Coco was going to pass it on to Mari, it would likely end up in Eilert's hands anyway. It appeared that Mari trusted Eilert with her mother's legacy. She knew about the materials Ingrid had handed over to him before her death, after all, and she had invited him to photograph Ingrid's most recent batch of tapestries.

"Your house is lovely," Coco observed as they approached the front door and she reached for the doorknob. "I'll see myself out." And with that she was gone.

Pamela had bought cod at the Co-Op, now destined for that night's dinner. Salmon, her usual choice of fish, required only to be baked, but cod required something more. Herbs, she decided, and tomatoes, and garlic of course, and lots of olive oil, in a sort of Mediterranean style, and served with rice.

On her back porch, she studied her collection of herbs. The fresh green shoots of oregano that had appeared as soon as the weather changed were now crowding the pot. The thyme had survived the winter too, as a dense thicket. There was plenty of rosemary, and the new basil seedlings could spare a few more leaves.

She went inside to get a small bowl and a pair of scissors, and when she stepped back out on the porch, she noticed that the thyme had been visited by a bee. It had already flowered, though the flowers were quite unassuming—delicate clusters of the tiniest white blossoms. Bees, however, were relentless in their quest for nectar and pollen. This bee, ungraceful though its flight was with such a cumbersome body, nevertheless darted to and fro searching the thyme blossoms for a sip of sweetness.

Pamela let the bee continue its explorations while she clipped basil leaves, oregano sprigs, and a spike of rosemary, slipping them into the bowl. Waiting for the bee to go on its way, she stepped aside and surveyed her yard. Her gaze was drawn to Richard Larkin's yard, too—and then to Richard Larkin himself. He was standing near the back edge of his yard, apparently studying the perennial border.

He didn't seem dressed for gardening, though. Instead of distressed jeans, he wore slim, dark pants and with them a chambray work shirt. Suddenly, from somewhere, a voice said, *What are you waiting for? Invite him to dinner.* The message was so clear that she looked around, expecting to see that Bettina had crept up on her.

She was alone on the porch, however, except for the bee on its nectar quest, and she realized the voice had come from her own brain. The voice had timed the suggestion well—a dinner like the one she had in mind deserved to be shared. She pictured the pale cod filet, sharing a sauté pan with a gently simmering sauce, herby, garlicky, and featuring chunks of fresh tomato.

How big was the cod filet, though? When she'd browsed the Co-Op fish counter, it was with dinner for one in mind. Before issuing the invitation, it would be wise to check. Back in the house, she opened the refrigerator and hefted the plastic bag that contained the fish, still wrapped in its fish-counter waxed paper. The label, visible through the plastic, said it weighed a pound and three ounces. She always bought more than needed when she shopped while hungry—but in this case, a pound and a bit more would be exactly right.

A lurch in the region of her heart as she headed down the hall to the back door caused her to stop for a moment and revisit the uncertainties that swirled around the idea of Richard Larkin. Almost since the first time she met him, his appeal had been so visceral, and he'd made it clear he was attracted to her. She took a deep breath and rested a hand, which she noticed was shaking, on her chest.

I'm cooking some fish, she whispered to herself, *and there's going to be enough for two. So if you're free, I'd love for you to join me*. Or maybe just, *So if you're free, you're invited for dinner*.

She flung the back door open and reached the steps leading down from the porch in two long strides. And . . . Richard Larkin was gone. But her heart was thumping now, and such resolve was not to be wasted. She crossed her driveway, edged through the low shrubbery that marked the boundary where her yard met his, and continued across his lawn till she reached his driveway.

She'd ring his front doorbell rather than tapping at his back door. Making her way down the driveway, she rounded the side of his house—just in time to see his olive-green Jeep Cherokee poised in the middle of Orchard Street as he shifted into drive after backing out. She watched the maneuver, on the point of dashing forward. But she didn't dash forward.

Casually inviting him to dinner as he contemplated his perennial border was one thing. Chasing his car as it pulled away was another. Besides, he was probably en route to a dinner engagement, maybe with a woman. He'd been dressed as if for more than a run-of-the-mill errand.

Pamela waited until the Cherokee disappeared up the block. Then she continued on to the sidewalk and circled around to her own backyard, where she climbed the steps to her porch. There, she found herself staring at the pot that held the thyme, looking for the industrious bee. Like Richard Larkin, it too was gone—but something about its buzzing and its fuzzy black-and-yellow-striped body had jogged a recollection. Recollection or not, she still needed to pick a few sprigs of thyme, and she could do that now without hazarding a sting.

CHAPTER 19

A few hours later, Pamela had settled into her customary spot at the end of her sofa with Catrina in her customary spot as well. Even in warm weather, it was comforting to have a cat sprawled at one's side, and the vibrating purr emanating from Catrina's furry body made her presence all the more welcome.

On the screen before her, a documentary from the nature channel unfolded. The topic was Icelandic volcanoes, and the inhabitant of a town being threatened by lava flow was being interviewed. Pamela was only half-watching, however, as focused as she was on the knitting in her lap.

She was still working on the back of the sweater that was her current project, but she had reached the point where the cobalt blue of the sweater's body yielded to the orange-yellow-chartreuse ombre yarn that would form a yoke around the upper back, upper chest, and shoulders. The effect, it occurred to her, was like that achieved with complicated multicolor patterning in the style of sweater often called "Icelandic," but it took much less concentration to achieve. It was fun to watch the alternating colors on the strand of ombre yarn create their own unpredictable pattern as each row presented different juxtapositions, stripes here, patches of solid color there.

As she worked, her mind settled into a meditative state, aided by the rhythmic motions of her fingers, the soft drone of Catrina's purring, and the soothing (despite the alarming nature of the topic) voices from the documentary—punctuated by the melodic lilt of the Icelandic language. The purring was rather like a buzz, low and sustained, and her thoughts returned to the bee. Did it range as far as Ingrid's yard? she wondered. Was it one of Honey Hurley's bees? Somebody's nickname was Buzz—she'd recently seen or heard that, but where?

She'd come to the end of another row and held the swath of knitting up to study it, quite pleased with the contrast to the deep cobalt blue provided by the ombre yarn. Then she lowered it back to her lap, turned it over to start a new row, and switched the empty needle to her right hand.

Monday morning, breakfasted and dressed, Pamela was in her office checking over the three copyedited articles that were due the next day. At the sound of the doorbell's chime, she transferred Ginger from her lap to the floor, stepped into the hall, and advanced toward the stairs. From the landing, she could see the front door and the figure visible beyond the lace that veiled the door's oval window. She'd had a premonition that Bettina would be paying a call that morning, because Monday morning was when Bettina met with Detective Clayborn. On that account, she had ground extra coffee and slipped a fresh filter into her carafe's filter cone after preparing and drinking her own usual two cups.

The premonition turned out to be correct, and she opened the door to admit her friend and the fragrance of May flowers in bloom. As Bettina entered, the foot that landed on the worn parquet floor of Pamela's entry was shod in a dainty lavender slingback pump. The lavender echoed the color of the linen skirt Bettina had paired with a silky flower-print blouse in shades of lavender and pink. She was carrying a loaf-shaped object encased in aluminum foil, which she handed to Pamela.

"This isn't from the Co-Op bakery," Pamela said, hefting the object, "but I suspect it's very edible."

"Friends of the Library bake sale," Bettina replied. "It was yesterday, and I did an article on it for the *Advocate*."

Pamela led the way to the kitchen, past Catrina enjoying her customary morning nap in her sunny spot on the thrift-shop carpet. As she moved around the little kitchen, measuring water into the kettle, lighting a burner under it on the stove, and transferring the fresh grounds from the coffee grinder into the filter cone, Bettina was busy too. She set the table with wedding-china plates, cups and saucers, silverware, and napkins. She unwrapped the foil from the loaf, put the loaf on a wooden cutting board, and transferred the cutting board to the table. And she poured heavy cream into the cut-glass cream pitcher, then placed it and the matching sugar bowl on the table, nearer to her side than Pamela's.

Meanwhile, the kettle had begun to whistle. Pamela tilted it over the filter cone, and the aroma of coffee, dark and seductive, arose from the carafe.

"Honey cake," Bettina announced after Pamela had filled the coffee cups and taken her seat. "Homemade by one of the Friends." She had already cut several slices, revealing the fine, moist crumb of the amber-colored loaf's interior.

Bees, whispered a buzzing voice in Pamela's brain, but she willed it to silence because Bettina had things to report. Well, *one* thing, anyway.

"Nestor wasn't killed in the garden shed," she declared. "That's the latest from the county, based on the CSI report. Other than that, Clayborn didn't have anything new to tell me."

"Do they know *where* he was killed?" Pamela inquired after sampling her coffee, which was still too hot for a prolonged sip.

"Somewhere else," Bettina said, "then dragged to the shed. My guess is Ingrid's yard, but it's so overgrown that I'm not surprised the crime-scene unit might find it daunting to search for evidence there."

She used her fork to ease a piece of honey cake onto her plate. Instead of tasting it, though, she sat up straight, squinted, and cocked her head in the direction of the entry.

Saying, "My phone, I think," she scooted her chair back from the table, leaned on the table to push herself to her feet, and hurried toward the kitchen doorway. After a moment, her voice drifted in from the other room, and Pamela could tell from Bettina's half of the conversation that the call did not bring good news.

"No!" Bettina exclaimed. "You poor thing!" Then, after a pause, "Of course you're disappointed. He's a beast!" Another pause. "I'm coming. Don't do anything rash."

Bettina reappeared, striding across the floor, the very picture of righteous indignation with her delicate brows reshaped into a scowl and her jaw rigid.

"Simon!" she hissed. "He's leaving, and Coco is beside herself."

"I heard you tell her you were coming," Pamela said. "Before or after we eat the honey cake?"

"Some things are more important than honey cake." Bettina was carrying her handbag, which was lavender, like her pumps. "Coco sounds desperate."

Pamela returned the honey cake from her and Bettina's plates to the cutting board and tented the cast-off aluminum foil over it. As she did so, the buzzing voice in her brain whispered *bees* again.

"Your car's handier," Bettina said after they stepped out onto the porch.

Pamela agreed, and once they were underway, she was just as glad it was she who was behind the wheel, given Bettina's tendency to let excitement interfere with her driving.

"I never really trusted him," Bettina said, leaning forward and straining against her seat belt as if to urge the car forward. "And now, after leading Coco on, he's told her that he's going back to Connecticut for good and she's not invited. He's across the street right now loading things into his car, and she's sitting at her kitchen table crying." Bettina turned to look at Pamela. "Coco is even older than you, so this might have been her last chance at love."

She immediately inhaled a sharp gasp, like a backward sigh, and raised a hand to her mouth. "I didn't mean it," she squeaked, "about you, being old . . ."

But Pamela hadn't been paying attention. She *knew* why Simon was leaving.

She'd been driving, yes, but automatically—guiding the car up Orchard Street, making the left turn onto Arborville Avenue, turning left again at Serpentine Way. Her mind had been elsewhere, though, revisiting scenes that had unfolded over the past few weeks, ever since Ingrid Barrick's body had been discovered by the mail carrier. She and Bettina had met people, overheard conversations, observed interactions. Now, out of all that . . . *data*, one might say, her mind had selected the bits that explained who had killed Ingrid and Nestor—and why.

The process had been rather like walking into the Timberley yarn shop and being dazzled by the variety of yarn in every possible color and texture, and then paging through books and knitting magazines presenting every possible style of knitted garment. So much to consider, and so confusing! Somehow, though, she inevitably walked out of the shop with a clear sense of just what she planned to make, and with a bag containing pattern and materials for exactly that.

Pamela pulled to the curb in front of Coco's house, turned off the ignition, and faced Bettina, about to reveal what she had realized in the brief time they had been in the car. But Bettina's expression was disconcerting. A worried knot had formed between her brows, and distress tugged at the corners of her mouth. Before Pamela could open her mouth, she reached out and seized both of Pamela's hands.

"I hurt your feelings, didn't I?" she moaned. "I could tell while we were driving over here that you were thinking about what I said. You looked so serious, and I didn't really mean that *you're* old, just that Coco is old . . . and I—"

Bettina gulped as if she was about to cry, and she squeezed Pamela's hands so hard that Pamela winced.

Pamela, for her part, couldn't suppress a laugh. "It's okay," she said. "I wasn't thinking about what you said. I was thinking about Simon, and why he's *really* leaving. And I'm thinking about why Coco came to my house yesterday and asked me to give her that little appointment calendar repurposed as a pictorial journal."

"You're not mad at me?" Bettina transformed back into her cheery self and squeezed Pamela's hands again.

"Of course not." Pamela returned the squeeze. Then she sketched out for Bettina the explanation for Ingrid and Nestor's deaths.

Coco was halfway to the car by the time they clicked the doors open and stepped out. With her abundant hair in disarray, her eyes wild, and her long, gauzy dress clinging to her legs as she ran, she could have been a character from a Greek tragedy in flight to evade the Furies.

"Bettina! Bettina!" she gasped when she reached them, engulfing Bettina in an embrace.

Bettina squirmed until she was able to free her arms, then she wrapped them around Coco's waist. Her hands fluttered as she attempted a few comforting pats.

Pamela glanced toward the house across the street, Simon's parents' house, where he had been staying. There was no sign of Simon, but the aged SUV that she recognized as his was in the driveway, and through its back windows, cardboard boxes and bulging plastic bags were visible.

Bettina disengaged herself from Coco and drew away, but her hands now rested on Coco's arms. "Let's go inside," she whispered. "You don't need to let him see that you're upset."

"He knows I'm upset," Coco wailed. "And how could I not be, after the way he led me on?"

"Come on, come on. We'll sit down inside, and you'll feel better." Bettina was still whispering. She steered Coco back toward the steps that led to her front porch.

Pamela followed, noticing as they approached the house that the neat rows of impatiens seedlings had been trampled nearly into oblivion, and she wondered whether that was the doing of Coco or Simon.

Once they had stepped across Coco's threshold, Bettina turned to Pamela with a questioning look. Pamela mouthed the words "hibiscus tea," and they continued into the kitchen. There, Coco's battered kettle was waiting on the stovetop. Pamela filled it with water and rummaged in cupboards until she found mugs and a package of loose hibiscus tea. The pottery teapot of Asian design that she remembered from previous visits to Coco's was sitting on the counter, still containing damp tea leaves from a recent brewing. Meanwhile, Bettina had coaxed Coco to take a seat at the kitchen table, then joined her there.

As Pamela worked, emptying the teapot and sifting in fresh tea, she was listening to the conversation between Coco and Bettina.

"This always happens!" Coco pounded the table's aged wood surface, and the sound echoed. "It always, always happens—every time I think I've finally found a man who really cares for me."

Pamela heard a creak and tipped her head to see that Coco had straightened. Her arms were folded across her chest.

"It's me, isn't it?" she said grimly. "Something about me that's . . . unappealing."

Suddenly her features convulsed. She lowered her head to the table, and yowls of misery took the place of speech. Bettina hopped to her feet and stationed herself behind Coco's chair. Leaning forward, she began to massage Coco's shoulders.

"It's all right, it's all right," she murmured. "You're not unappealing at all."

A plume of steam had begun to emerge from the kettle's spout. Pamela clicked off the burner and tipped the kettle over the teapot.

"That's not why he's leaving," Bettina went on. "It's not why he's leaving at all."

"Why, then?" Coco reared up and spun around, nearly

tipping her chair. Her face was blotched with spots of red, and moist with tears. "Tell me why he's leaving!" she wailed.

Bettina sat back down. "He has to," she said, and she began to rehearse the explanation for Ingrid and Nestor's deaths Pamela had presented to her.

"No!" Coco shrieked when Bettina had finished. "He *used* me! He sent me to fetch the appointment book because he knew what the contents meant, and he knew that sooner or later someone else would figure that out and you *did* . . ."

She sprang from her chair and elbowed Pamela aside as she reached toward the knife rack above the counter. From it she seized the largest and most lethal knife, while Pamela and Bettina gazed at one another, stunned into inaction by Coco's sudden shift of mood.

Coco dashed past them into the hall that led to the front door. Pamela was the first to give chase, depositing the kettle on the table as she passed. Ahead of her, Coco clattered across the wooden porch and hurtled down the steps, her arm raised, with the knife in her hand and the gauzy dress flowing behind her as if she were now the avenging Fury.

CHAPTER 20

"Wait! Wait!" Bettina panted at Pamela's heels.
With Coco still in the lead, Pamela gaining on her, and Bettina bringing up the rear, the urgent procession crossed Serpentine Way. Coco started up the driveway, veering off the asphalt onto the scrubby lawn when she neared the spot blocked by Simon's SUV. She remained on the lawn as she headed for the porch. When she was within a few yards of the steps, the front door opened, and a man emerged. The man was carrying a huge cardboard box, so huge that it obscured his face. Only a forehead, crowned by gray hair like a shaggy mop, was visible.

Coco seemed certain of her quarry, however. She lurched up the steps, brandishing the knife and shrieking, "You were just using me, you scum! But you're going to pay for it because I have nothing more to lose!"

The figure *was* Simon. That was made clear when

he faltered and the box slipped from his grasp. As it fell, it tipped forward, and the top flaps, which had been unsecured, swung outward. From the box poured a cascade of . . . things: a catcher's mitt, a tennis ball, one ice skate, a set of measuring cups, an eggbeater, a potato masher—and there would have been more ex cept that the box landed on its side on the porch floor. A few more tennis balls, their neon-green color lively against the aged wood, bounced down the steps.

Simon nearly tripped over the box after it landed, but he edged around it, apparently distracted enough by the mishap to be momentarily unaware of the threat posed by Coco. But now she was herding him along the porch with menacing flourishes of the knife, whose blade was at least a foot long. Reacting to each flourish, he retreated farther and farther away, cutting himself off from an escape back into the house or down the steps.

Bettina had reached Pamela's side. "Pamela!" she squeaked, and Pamela turned. "We can't let her stab him." Bettina's voice was urgent. "She's not the one who should be arrested. We should—" She looked down and then back up, aghast. "My phone is across the street in my handbag!"

Without waiting for Pamela to respond, she spun around and—faster than Pamela had ever seen her move—tore across the lawn.

Simon had reached a front corner of the porch and was backed against the railing. He wrapped an arm around the wooden pillar that supported the roof and held the other hand out in a beseeching gesture.

"Coco-puss," he whimpered, "what's this all about?

You knew I was planning to go back to Connecticut. That doesn't mean we can't keep in touch . . ."

"And I'd want to keep in touch with you because?" Coco thrust the knife toward Simon's chest.

"Because we're . . . because we're . . ." His voice faltered, and he shrank away.

"You're a murderer!" Coco stamped her foot, and the porch shuddered. "You killed Ingrid, and you killed Nestor, and Pamela and Bettina know it, and now I know it."

"I . . . I . . ." Simon looked around, as if hoping deliverance might be at hand. "I . . . why would I do that?"

"You were jealous," Pamela cut in. "Understandably so, in a way, because you are actually Mari's father—but that doesn't excuse what you did."

"Meredith!" Simon's tone was suddenly assertive. "Her name is Meredith, not that stupid *mariposa* idea of Nestor's. The guy was obsessed with butterflies."

"You didn't stick around though, after she was born," Pamela said.

"Ingrid and I had fun together, she as much as I, and I never promised her it would be anything more. And the Nestor thing was on again, off again, and he didn't stick around forever either."

"Did you mean to kill Ingrid?" Pamela asked.

Coco still stood with the knife leveled at Simon's chest and a fierce expression on her face. Perhaps in an effort to postpone a result that seemed inevitable, he began to elaborate on the details of his crimes.

"No, no! Of course not!" he said. "I begged! I *begged* her to tell Mari that I was her real father. I'm getting old. My parents are old, and I see them getting older and older, and I'll get older and older, and there comes a time when you just want to . . . *settle* things. Ingrid wouldn't agree to do it, though, and I got angry. She could be very excitable, and she got angry too. We argued. She pushed me away. I pushed back, and she fell and hit her head on the hearth."

He lifted a trembling hand to his face, closed his eyes, and bowed his head.

"I didn't mean to kill her, really." His voice was trembling too. "I just wanted my daughter to acknowledge me. That wasn't so much to ask . . . was it?" He looked up, his expression desperate, and addressed Coco. "When I learned about the journal and realized it was all going to catch up with me, the last thing I wanted was for you to have to witness my arrest."

Simon sank to his knees, and Coco hopped backward. He rocked forward then, burying his face in his hands. Huge sobs emerged from behind the tangle of unruly hair disarranged by the motions of his head.

"Simon!" The word erupted from Coco's throat, sounding more like a sob. She cast the knife aside and knelt beside the crouching figure.

Pamela had been switching her attention back and forth between the drama playing out before her and the street, watching for Bettina to return and waiting for a sign that the police were on their way. The clatter of the knife onto the porch floor pulled her focus back to Coco and Simon. Without thinking, she edged forward. With her foot, she nudged the knife toward the front door, where the contents of the box Simon had dropped lay scattered about. She stopped nudging when it came to rest next to a cheese grater.

"Simon, Simon!" came Coco's voice. "I forgive you! Tomorrow is the first day of the rest of our lives! Everything will be all right!"

As if to punctuate the statement—or, more accurately, contradict it—the thin wail of a siren whipped through the air.

Simon reared up onto his knees. "Everything won't be all right," he moaned. "I'm a murderer—and my motive is there for anyone to see in that journal, in the pictures Ingrid drew! That's why I wanted you to get it away from Pamela. Then I realized the damage had been done, and I had to disappear."

Coco was kneeling too. She reached out to embrace him, and then, both leaning on the porch railing, they pulled themselves to their feet. The siren was drawing closer, the pitch shrilling high and then falling, again and again, until it cut off with a hiccup mid-shrill and a police car came to rest at the curb. At the same time, Bettina was hastening up the driveway, veering around Simon's SUV, and cutting across the lawn.

The driver's-side and the passenger-side doors of the police car opened in unison, and two uniformed officers lunged out, one male and the other female. They rushed toward the porch, arriving at the porch steps just as Bettina did. Bettina edged aside to let them pass.

"I thought you were leaving because you didn't love me," Coco said. She reached up to stroke Simon's cheek.

"I *do* love you, Coco-puss." He guided her hand to his mouth and kissed it. "But now I've ruined everything, and we can never be together because I'm a murderer."

Both officers had made their way onto the porch and

were standing a bit behind Pamela. She had recognized Officer Sanchez and Officer Anders as they dashed across the lawn, and now she could hear them panting.

"Why did you have to kill Nestor too?" The words popped out before Pamela realized they'd taken shape in her mind.

"He wouldn't believe I was Meredith's real father. It was an accident, just like with Ingrid . . ."

Simon's voice trailed off as he seemed to notice that his audience had grown to include two people with particular reason to be following his story with interest. He turned slightly to glance at Coco, then he stepped forward to meet his fate.

"I'm so glad she didn't stab him," Bettina commented a few hours later from a comfortable perch on the sofa in Pamela's living room.

Officer Sanchez had called for backup to take Simon away, and then she and Officer Anders had taken statements from Coco, Pamela, and Bettina. After all the drama had subsided, Bettina stayed behind to comfort Coco, and Pamela drove home. Now Bettina had joined her.

"Dorcas is with Coco now," Bettina added. Then, in a shift of topic, she inquired, "What did you do with the knife?"

"It's with the other kitchen things," Pamela said, "next to the cheese grater. It's just as well Coco dropped it before the police got there."

"Monday." Bettina sighed. "Of course this had to happen on Monday, *after* my weekly meeting with

Clayborn. Now Marcy Brewer will get all kinds of juicy details, and people will read about it in the *Register* tomorrow morning, and everyone will know everything by the time the *Advocate* comes out on Friday."

Pamela's sigh echoed Bettina's. "Bettina," she said, "you were *there*. You can report on the story from first-hand experience. Marcy Brewer can't say that!"

"No." Bettina sighed again, but a little less mournfully. "I don't guess she can."

Bettina went on her way then, with Pamela waving from the porch. Back inside, Pamela felt at loose ends. The morning's events had been so unexpected and dramatic, but all the questions surrounding the deaths of Ingrid and Nestor had been answered. Work for *Fiber Craft* could always be counted on to focus the restless wanderings of her mind, but she had finished copyediting the current batch of articles, and there was no immediate pressure to return them. The upcoming Knit and Nibble meeting was at her house, but that wasn't until tomorrow.

She had remained standing in the entry after coming inside. Now, as she glanced around, her gaze landed on her knitting bag on the floor near her accustomed spot on the sofa. A minute later, she had occupied that spot, and the knitting bag was in her lap. Much remained to be done on the piece currently in progress—the piece that would form the back of the cobalt sweater with the contrasting yoke knit from ombré yarn.

Anticipating the pleasure to come, she extracted from her knitting bag the skein of ombre yarn, with its shadings from orange to yellow to chartreuse and back again. Soon she was enjoying the smooth whisper of the yarn against her fingers as her needles danced around each other, and the alternating colors of the yarn created unexpected patterns.

Once in the meditative state produced by the rhythmic motions, Pamela's thoughts returned to the scene that had played out on Serpentine Way that morning. Simon Malbourne, though revealed as the killer, had struck her as oddly sympathetic. He'd watched his parents getting older and older and realized he was getting older too. "There comes a time," he had said, "when you just want to *settle* things." That meant in his case, she supposed, that he didn't want to live out the remainder of his years unacknowledged by a child who had turned out to be the only child he would ever have.

An hour, or more, passed and the sweater's back grew under her fingers. As the angle of the sun shifted, the patch of sunlight that beamed through the east-facing window in the morning appeared on the carpet below the west-facing window. Precious descended from the cat climber to luxuriate in its warmth, and the sunlight set her pale fur aglow. The thrift-shop clock on the mantel, recently repaired and now in working condition, signaled the hour with six faint chimes.

Pamela put her knitting aside, arched her back to ease the kink in her spine, and stood. An image had been forming in her mind, an image that involved catching sight of Richard Larkin as he arrived home from work, strolling across the lawn for a casual conversation, and extending a spur-of-the-moment invitation to share dinner.

Ignoring the *thump* in her chest and a feeling of breathlessness, she advanced toward the door, twisted the knob, pulled the door back, and crossed the threshold. From the vantage point of the porch, she could see that, as she had hoped, Richard Larkin's driveway was empty. The moment his familiar Jeep Cherokee pulled in, she'd descend the steps and quickly collect the recycling bin from the side of the house.

Then she'd make her way toward the street, recycling bin in tow, pausing at the end of the driveway to wave at Richard Larkin. He'd move a bit closer to return the greeting, she'd move a bit closer, and . . . an olive-green vehicle was heading down Orchard from Arborville Avenue. *Thump* went her heart again.

She hurried down the steps, veered to the right and to the right again, and continued on to where the tall, wheeled bins waited. She seized the middle one by the handle. With the bin rattling behind her on the driveway, she headed for the street. As she reached the end of the lofty hedge that divided her front yard from Richard's, she turned to look toward the spot where the Cherokee usually parked.

He had already parked. She bent forward to peer closer, but she could see no one behind the wheel. It hadn't taken that long to fetch the bin, but it seemed the chance of a casual encounter had come and gone. She advanced farther and turned again to get a view of his porch. The front door was just closing. Some yards behind her on the sidewalk, though, someone else's gamble on a chance encounter had just paid off.

"Ms. Paterson, Ms. Paterson!" came an insistent voice.

Pamela remained where she was, immobile, and closed her eyes. She recognized the voice. Had she been inside, she would never have opened her front door—no matter how insistent the doorbell's chime—if her caller was Marcy Brewer. But Marcy Brewer had caught her outside, and her escape route up her front walk was cut off by Marcy Brewer's photographer, who was even now aiming a camera at her.

Parked at the curb was a vehicle bearing the logo of the *County Register* on its door, and Marcy Brewer was heading toward her from that direction. The high-heeled boots visible beneath her chic pants seemed chosen to compensate for her small stature. The smartly tailored jacket lent an air of authority, as did the unrelenting confidence of her smile, highlighted by her bright lipstick.

"Just a few comments, Ms. Paterson." As she uttered the request, Marcy tilted her head and gazed into Pamela's eyes, expectant and unblinking. One hand held her smartphone, already recording, Pamela was sure. "According to the police, Simon Malbourne, who was arrested this morning for the murders of Ingrid Barrick and Nestor Flavin, was in mid-confession when they arrived, summoned by Bettina Fraser." Still unblinking, she added, "Would you have any idea what elicited the confession?"

"Guilty conscience?" Pamela suggested.

"You and Colette Dalrymple were the other people present, and Ms. Fraser, before she left to summon the police," Marcy said. "What happened before Mr. Malbourne started to confess?"

Pamela had given a statement to Officer Anders that morning. She hadn't found it necessary to mention Coco's dash across the street to confront Simon with a kitchen knife. She hadn't lied either, but simply allowed a bit of vagueness in her answer to the question of when she'd arrived on the scene.

"He and Coco—Colette—reconciled."

"They reconciled?" Marcy raised herself onto her tiptoes and peered deep into Pamela's eyes. "Could you explain?"

"There had been a misunderstanding, and they had broken up, but then they reconciled." The photographer had moved from his post on Pamela's walk. Pamela addressed Marcy. "Is that enough? It's all I have to say."

Trusting that her legs were longer than Marcy Brewer's, not to mention that she wasn't wearing high-heeled boots, she sprinted for her porch and was soon inside. Through the lace that curtained the oval window in the front door, she watched Marcy Brewer shrug at the photographer and turn toward the car with the *County Register* logo.

CHAPTER 21

A casual chat in the early evening could lead naturally to a dinner invitation. But first thing in the morning, while wearing robe and pajamas and with the kettle about to whistle on the stove . . .

No, Pamela decided the next morning, even though Richard Larkin was now advancing toward his Jeep Cherokee and was even waving at her. She waved back and bent to scoop the *Register*, in its protective plastic sleeve, from the dewy grass at the edge of the curb. Richard Larkin was now in his car, and in the process of backing out of his driveway, so she paused a moment, despite the robe and pajamas, to extract and unfold the paper.

Many Arborville minds were no doubt being put to rest at that very moment by the bold headline, two columns wide, that dominated the front page: ARREST MADE IN ARBORVILLE MURDER CASES.

What they made of the smaller sub-headline beneath was another question. It read, KILLER CONFESSES WHEN LOVE SOFTENS HEART.

Stepping back into her house, Pamela was happy to hear the kettle's whistle. She'd already provided the filter cone with a paper filter and fresh grounds, and it would be but a minute or two before a steaming cup of coffee was ready for sipping. Absorbing Marcy Brewer's report on Simon's arrest, sure to feature the interview Pamela had been ambushed into, was going to require courage and a bracing infusion of caffeine.

While the boiling water dripped through the grounds, which now resembled damp, dark sand, Pamela lowered a slice of whole-grain bread into the toaster. As she waited for the metallic *chunk* that would signal the toasting was complete, she gazed at Richard Larkin's kitchen window. Her thoughts had no time to roam, however. Soon the toast had been retrieved from the toaster and buttered, the coffee had been poured, and Pamela was seated at the kitchen table with the front page of the *Register* before her.

No photograph of a startled-looking Pamela Paterson illustrated the article on page one. Before reading even the first sentence, she turned to the inner page where the article continued and was grateful to see that no photograph appeared there either. At least she had been spared having a candid shot of her, with recycling bin in the background, appear as an accompaniment to the story of Simon Malbourne's arrest. Doubtless, though, Marcy owed the "love softens heart" angle to the hasty words Pamela had uttered in her eagerness to escape to her own house. She returned to page one.

The first few paragraphs of the article were straight-forward, beginning with the information that Simon had confessed to the killings, and giving the details—such as they were now known—based on his confession. The part about Ingrid's death overlapped with what Pamela (and Coco too) had heard firsthand on the porch of Simon's parents' house.

Apparently his willingness to confess had continued under questioning by Detective Clayborn at the police station. Even with Ingrid dead, he had explained, he was determined that Mari—or Meredith, as he called her—know he was her actual father. To that end, he determined to persuade Nestor to acknowledge that his and Ingrid's on-again, off-again relationship was off at the time she became pregnant.

The encounter took place in Ingrid's yard and quickly escalated from angry words to angry actions. Simon hadn't intended his rage to be murderous, but in the event, it was. Panic-stricken, he hid Nestor's body in Dorcas's garden shed, which was conveniently located just past the border of Ingrid's property.

Not content with presenting the facts of the case, however, Marcy turned then to the "exclusive interview with Pamela Paterson" that would shed light on the killer's motivation to confess. Pamela was described as a "close friend" of Colette Dalrymple, and Marcy said that Pamela and Bettina had been summoned to comfort Coco on the occasion of her breakup with Simon. Pamela, she went on to say, had then been on hand when Coco made her distress about the breakup known to Simon, and Pamela had witnessed the result when Simon realized that only by admitting his guilt could he be worthy of the woman he had loved for so long.

"Well!" Pamela spoke out loud, and Ginger looked up from the bowl of food she was still nibbling. "That's one way of looking at it, I suppose!" Detective Clayborn, she imagined, was happy to have obtained a confession that tied all the details of the two cases together in a sensible way. Any motive for the confession, as long as the confession wasn't coerced, would have no bearing on prosecuting the crimes.

She'd been ignoring her toast, which had gotten cold, but she applied herself now to finishing her breakfast and browsing through the rest of the *Register*. Before delving into the Lifestyle section, she poured the rest of the coffee from the carafe into her cup and then spent a happy ten minutes reading about a local woman who ran a business stitching authentic-looking eighteenth-century garments for Revolutionary-era reenactors.

After dressing and making her bed, Pamela crossed the hall to her office, where she addressed an email to her boss at *Fiber Craft* and attached the three copy-edited articles due back. She sent the email off, freed her mouse to rest on its mouse pad, and quickly left the room. No doubt a new assignment would arrive momentarily, but Knit and Nibble was coming that evening. There was housecleaning to do and a nibble to prepare.

All three cats disappeared up the stairs as soon as Pamela switched on the vacuum cleaner. Vacuuming was meditative work, aided by the white-noise effect of its purring motor, and she was soon absorbed in guiding the vacuum over the stylized flowers and foliage that patterned her living room carpet. A ferocious pounding intruded on her reverie, however, and she switched the vacuum off to get a sense of where it was coming from. The source, it turned out, was her own front door.

"Why so desperate?" Pamela murmured to herself, parking the vacuum and crossing to the entry. Even more puzzling was the fact that the figure behind the lace that curtained the oval window in the front door was clearly Bettina. "Isn't the bell working?" she inquired as she opened the door.

Bettina responded with a question of her own: "'Exclusive interview with Pamela Paterson'?"

She gazed at Pamela as if to extend a challenge, her lips forming an unhappy closed-mouth smile. The expression suggested that she was keeping a laugh—a sarcastic laugh—in reserve for an explanation likely to be unconvincing. The moment was awkward enough that Pamela almost closed the door. Instead, she closed her eyes and bowed her head. After a few moments, she looked up.

"I wasn't trying to avoid you," she explained. "The sound of the doorbell was drowned out by the vacuum."

"I realized that," Bettina said. "I could hear the vacuum."

"Knit and Nibble is coming tonight. I was cleaning."

"Whatever you're going to serve, you don't need to make enough for me." Bettina crossed her arms across her chest, a gesture that highlighted the way the deep pink of her manicure exactly matched the roses in the print of her blouse. "I won't be there," she added, as if the implications of her first statement hadn't been clear enough.

"It's going to have bananas and strawberries in it." Pamela, in her entry, was still facing Bettina across the threshold. She took a few steps backward and nudged the door into a fully open position.

"I'm not coming in," Bettina said. "I'm not even staying on your porch. I just . . . I just don't understand how you could do such a thing." Her voice faltered as her earlier defiance slipped away. "If you were going to give an interview about Simon Malbourne's arrest to someone, why of all people did you give it to Marcy Brewer?"

"She trapped me."

Bettina uttered a sharp laugh. "Trapped you? Why did you answer the door?"

"I didn't answer the door," Pamela said. "I was already outside."

"Why did you even go outside? You know how Marcy is when she's on the trail of a story . . . coming around and pestering people."

"I didn't see her"—Pamela studied Bettina's face—"because, if you must know, I was looking for Richard Larkin."

"You were?" Bettina squealed.

Pamela was standing far enough back from the threshold that only a few retreating steps were necessary to avoid a collision when Bettina lunged forward. Nearly toe to toe with Pamela after the lunge, she tilted her head to meet Pamela's eyes. No trace remained of her earlier defiance—or the disappointment that had replaced it. Instead, she gazed at Pamela with delighted anticipation, like a devotee of a streaming series who has just keyed up the newest episode.

"Did you find him?" Bettina asked in response to Pamela's nod.

"He'd just gotten home, but he was already inside by the time I collected the recycling bin . . ." Pamela began backing toward the kitchen doorway.

"What on earth did collecting the recycling bin have to do with looking for Richard Larkin?" Bettina took a step forward, and then another and another.

"I wanted it to seem casual"—Pamela shrugged—"like I just happened to be in my yard when he got home from work, and I was going to maybe invite him—"

Bettina grabbed Pamela's hands. They were in the kitchen now. "Yes! Yes!" She fairly shouted it, and her expression matched the enthusiasm in her voice. Then her features relaxed, and quietly, she asked, "Why now?"

Pamela eased herself free of Bettina's grip and lowered herself into her customary chair at the kitchen table. Taking the hint, Bettina sat down too.

"Simon Malbourne?" Pamela said. "The impulse to *settle* things?" She tipped her head forward and hid her face in her cupped hands. "Or Coco? *She's* certainly not afraid to be in love. Or Penny, moving so far away and leaving me alone here."

"It's time." Bettina's nod was barely seen by Pamela, whose hands still covered her face.

"You've been saying that for years." Pamela couldn't suppress a smile. She lowered her hands to let that be known.

"It's been true for years." Bettina rose. "See you to-night."

After Bettina left, Pamela returned to her vacuuming, maneuvering the vacuum into the dining room and then circling back to go over the carpet in the entry. Dusting was next, and she worked her way around living room, dining room, and entry to dust every wooden surface, as well as the vintage treasures from thrift shops and estate sales that decorated shelves, cabinets, and tables. The last step was to arrange the needlepoint pillows in a neat row on the sofa, making sure the needlepoint cat was upright and not standing on its head.

Pamela's plan for the evening's nibble was to make a variation on the classic banana pudding, traditionally called "pudding," though it was actually a trifle-like creation that included pudding as but one ingredient, layered with vanilla wafers, sliced bananas, and whipped cream. Her version, however, would include strawberries, in a nod to the season. A layer of strawberries would also add a pop of color to a dessert that was otherwise quite monochromatic. And to bring out the flavor of the strawberries, she would cut them up, add a bit of sugar, and stew them into a quick fresh-strawberry jam like the one Wilfred had made for his strudel.

In the kitchen, Pamela washed the strawberries that had been sitting on the counter in their cardboard container since the trip to the Co-Op on Sunday. Reaching for the paring knife from her knife rack reminded her of the scene in Coco's kitchen and Coco's frantic dash across Serpentine Way with a much larger knife in hand. The small paring knife made short work of the strawberries. She quartered each one, slicing through the deep-red surface, textured with the berry's tiny seeds, to reveal the pale interior, then divided each quarter into two or three chunks.

Soon the saucepan waiting beside the cutting board was half full of the berries, red and white alternating in a fragrant mosaic. She sprinkled on a tiny bit of water—the berries would release liquid as they stewed—and a few tablespoons of sugar, then covered the saucepan, transferred it to the stove, and lit the burner beneath it.

The next step was to make the pudding. The recipe started with sugar, cornstarch, and a pinch of salt blended together in the top of a double boiler. Pamela didn't have a double boiler, so she improvised with a saucepan that fit inside a slightly larger saucepan. To the larger saucepan she now added water to a depth of a few inches and set it to boil. She then poured three cups of milk into the smaller saucepan and thoroughly blended in the sugar, cornstarch, and salt. When the water had come to a boil, she lowered the smaller saucepan into the larger saucepan and stirred the milk mixture again.

The cornstarch would cause the milk mixture to thicken slightly. At that point, three egg yolks would be added. Keeping an eye on the double boiler, she cracked each egg on the rim of a custard cup and captured the yolk in half the shell while the translucent white slithered away into the cup beneath. She stirred the milk mixture and paused, waiting and watching, and stirred again until she judged the time had come to add the egg yolks, which were waiting in a second custard cup.

They couldn't be added as they were, though, because the heat of the milk mixture would quickly hard-boil them. A few spoonfuls of the hot milk mixture had to be blended into the yolks to temper them. That step completed, Pamela used a rubber spatula to coax every bit of the tempered yolks out of the custard cup. They joined the contents of the double boiler as dribbles of yellow against the pale surface. The pudding continued to thicken, smoothed by vigorous stirring, and then Pamela lifted out the top saucepan, set it aside, and turned off the burner.

Both jam and pudding had to cool before the final assembly could take place. While she waited for them to be ready, Pamela climbed the stairs to her office. Seated at her desk, she awoke her computer monitor from its sleep by guiding her mouse over its mouse pad and spent the next ten minutes responding to an email from her sister.

Back in the kitchen, she embarked on the most fun part of the recipe. The strawberry-banana pudding would be served in a grand, footed compote, clear glass with a filigree design etched around the rim. She had found it at the St. Willibrod's Church rummage sale a few years earlier. The clear glass would allow the layers to be seen, and she expected that the stripes of red where the strawberries were layered in would add an appealing contrast to the less-assertive tones of the other components. She fetched the compote from the sideboard in the dining room and set it on the counter.

The bananas intended for the recipe, four of them, had been ripening on the counter since Sunday. The green streaks had faded, and the bananas were now a uniform bright yellow. Pamela chose one, bent the stem back to breach the thick peel, and tugged away a long strip of peel to expose the creamy fruit beneath. Once all four bananas were peeled and lined up on a cutting board, she sliced them into even rounds and set the cutting board aside.

Next, the heavy cream had to be whipped, with a few tablespoons of sugar added before the mixer did its work. When the pool of cream in the bottom of the bowl had expanded into an airy drift that threatened to overflow the bowl's rim, she turned the mixer off, used the rubber spatula to coax the whipped cream clinging to the beaters back into the bowl, and set the bowl aside.

The first layer of the banana pudding was composed of vanilla wafers, store-bought, in a box. She opened the box and then the waxed paper bag within and shook a pile of the cookies onto a dinner plate. She covered the bottom of the compote with them, side by side, like small, domed tiles dusted with crumbs. Next came half the pudding, smoothed over the cookies with the rubber spatula. Two bananas' worth of slices came next, arranged in a single layer. She spooned half the strawberries over the bananas, covering the pale rounds with the rich red jam. Whipped cream formed the top layer, a layer thick enough to hide the bright accent of the jam.

The compote was half full now, and Pamela tipped her head to study her creation from the side. As she had imagined, the red jam stripe offered a bright contrast to the layers of cookies, pudding, and bananas below it and the whipped cream above it. The whole sequence would be repeated now, starting with cookies placed in concentric circles until the first layer of whipped cream was totally hidden.

As she worked, she contemplated the Knit and Nibble meeting to come. Holly would suspect there was more to Simon's surprising confession than the explanation with which Pamela had deflected Marcy Brewer's inquisitiveness. And there *was* more—the little journal with the drawings that had revealed the link between Simon and Ingrid, the link that made sense of so much.

She added the pudding layer, and the rest of the bananas, and the rest of the jam, and she finished off with the rest of the whipped cream in a splendid drift across the top. The compote would go into the refrigerator now. The bananas would meld with the pudding, and the pudding would soften the cookies until they became almost pudding-like themselves. The strawberries would add a bright note of fresh-picked fruit, and the whipped cream would blend the whole into a rich and smooth delight.

The strawberry-banana pudding was too impressive a sight in its footed glass compote to remain hidden at break time. Rather than serving individual portions in the kitchen and delivering them to the Knit and Nibblers assembled in the living room, she would spread a lace tablecloth on the dining room table and arrange all the cups, saucers, dessert dishes, silverware, and napkins there. As soon as Roland announced that eight o'clock had arrived, she would invite the knitters to the dining room, where she would present the strawberry-banana pudding and scoop portions from the compote into the dessert dishes.

When she finished preparing the table, she surveyed the effect, mentally picturing how it would look with the layered compote as the focal point. Very pleased, she returned to the kitchen to face the clean up chore that awaited.

CHAPTER 22

Bettina was the first to arrive, beaming as if suppressing a delightful secret—or perhaps it was just that, in contrast to the Bettina who had shown up at the door that morning, she was once again her cheerful self.

"Holly is parking," she announced, "and Karen is with her. Nell is probably walking." She stepped across the threshold, placing a foot shod in a high-heeled sandal, pale green, on the worn parquet floor and added, "Roland's car is here"—she veered off to glance toward the living room—"but where is he?"

"Probably double-checking the alternate side of the street parking signs." Pamela laughed. "He's always sure they've been changed since the last time we met at my house or yours."

"Do you need help in the kitchen?" Bettina asked. The pale green sandals had been chosen to accent a linen sheath in the same shade, mid-calf length and wide-collared. A triple strand of pearls filled in the neckline.

"It's all done," Pamela said. "I even ground the cof-fee beans and put the tea leaves in the teapot."

As they stood there, footsteps echoed on the porch, and the doorbell chimed. A few moments later, Holly and Karen had joined them in the entry.

"I *know* there's more to the story of Simon Mal-bourne's confession than what you told Marcy Brewer," Holly whispered, "but Nell will be here any minute, so it will have to wait."

The door had remained ajar, and Nell's voice drifted in, calling, "Hello, hello!" The gap between door and door frame widened, and Nell stepped through. Her vigorous walk had disarranged her white hair and brightened her eyes. "Hello, hello," she repeated. "Roland said to tell you he'll be a few minutes late."

After a brief hubbub of greetings, everyone but Pamela proceeded through the arch that divided the entry from the living room and settled into their usual spots: Bettina, Holly, and Karen lined up on the sofa, and Nell in the comfortable armchair at one end of the hearth.

Heavy steps on the porch announced another arrival, and a moment later, the doorbell's chime echoed. With the front door still ajar, Pamela could see that it was Roland who had rung the bell. She pulled the door open all the way and said, "You could have just come in."

Without responding to that comment, Roland raised his left wrist, stretching his arm and wiggling his hand to expose the watch that lurked beneath his flawlessly starched shirt cuff.

"Five minutes past seven," he said. "I apologize for my tardiness, but I wanted to make sure I was on the legal side of the street. Why is there only one alternate-side parking sign on the whole block?"

"Because it's been the same for ten years or more," came Bettina's voice from the sofa.

"Visitors don't know that," Roland responded mildly as he made his way toward the hassock at the other end of the hearth. In his hand was the elegant leather brief-case he used in place of a knitting bag.

With all the Knit and Nibblers present and accounted for, Pamela took her own seat, in the rummage-sale chair with the carved wooden back and needlepoint seat.

No surprises were revealed as people took out their projects. Bettina was still working on the bright yellow pullover for her grandson, and Nell on the cheery red pullover for her husband. Holly and Karen's knitted bathing suits had progressed considerably but were still incomplete. And Roland still juggled the four needles and multiple bobbins required for his current argyle sock. Pamela had only several more rows of ombre to go on the piece that would form the back of her sweater project. She'd be finished, she expected, just in time to start the coffee and tea for the break.

Bettina, sitting at the end of the sofa near the chair Pamela occupied, was silent, inspecting the few inches of knitting that hung from her needles. Farther down the sofa, Holly and Karen had been talking about an upcoming playdate planned for Lily and one of her friends, but that topic had been exhausted, and no new topic had taken its place. Nothing had been said by

Nell once she had settled into the armchair, and Roland hadn't seemed inclined to elaborate on how scarce Orchard Street's alternate-side parking signs were.

In contrast to the kind of silence that characterizes mutual contentment with satisfying work, however, this silence seemed pregnant, as if people were longing to speak . . . about something very specific. As Pamela glanced from face to face, the silence stretched on, and the impression intensified. Holly could usually be counted on to do her sociable part, but at the moment she was concentrating on her nearly finished bikini top.

Roland was surveying the room, too, his fingers uncharacteristically still. "I'm not a criminal defense lawyer," he said suddenly, a statement that immediately made him the focus of five pairs of eyes. Even Nell's curiosity appeared to have been aroused, to judge by her attentive stare.

Roland went on placidly, seemingly unaware that his audience was rapt. "I'm not a criminal defense lawyer," he repeated, "and based on what I read about the arrest of Simon Malbourne in the *Register* this morning, I'm glad I went into corporate law."

"Oh?" Several voices uttered the same syllable at once.

Roland allowed himself a carefully rationed smile. "It would be unusual for a corporation to blurt out its guilt for no apparent reason. What's a lawyer supposed to do with a client when that happens?"

"There *was* a reason," Holly said. "Love softened his heart."

"Corporations don't have hearts." Roland's lean features settled back into their usual stern intensity, and he resumed knitting.

But after a few moments, he lowered his knitting to his lap again and looked up. "I'll grant you that love can soften a human heart," he observed, "but how would a softening of the heart cause a man to confess to murder in the presence of the woman he loves? Wouldn't that be a secret he'd want to keep hidden?"

Holly directed a dimpled smile across the room. "You're curious, too, aren't you, Roland? It's obvious that there's more to this story than what Marcy Brewer reported in the *Register*."

Pamela glanced at Nell and noted that her face had remained expressionless during this exchange—no pursing of lips or puckering of brow to indicate her disapproval of the topic. There certainly *was* more to the story, beginning with the bees that Ingrid had doodled almost obsessively in the days leading up to her death. It was Bettina who spoke, however, starting nearer to the end of the story than the beginning.

"Coco thought Simon was leaving because he had never loved her, but the real reason was that he'd killed Ingrid and Nestor and he suspected the crimes were about to catch up with him."

"I wonder what put that into his mind." Holly leaned forward, her lips quivering with mischief, and turned to address Pamela in her chair near the other end of the sofa.

"Simon was the father of Ingrid's daughter, Mari," Pamela said. "That much was included in Marcy's article. Not included in Marcy's article was the fact that Ingrid had left a record of her relationship with Simon—not in words, but in her art."

"That makes sense," Holly murmured, "given that she was an artist."

"She turned a little appointment book for 1985 into a pictorial journal," Pamela explained, "and she revisited some of the same themes in a recent group of tapestries. In her mind, Nestor was a butterfly, and Simon was a bee. A neighbor on Serpentine Way who knew the Malbourne family when Simon was still a boy even mentioned that his childhood nickname was 'Buzz.'"

"A bee!" Holly exclaimed. "That sounds threatening."

"Simon *was* threatening at the end," Pamela agreed. "He was pressuring Ingrid into acknowledging that he was the father of her daughter, and she had bees on her mind to the point that she was doodling them in odd moments. But she'd had a romantic fling with him in 1985, when he was a college student spending school vacations with his parents on Serpentine Way."

"The yellow-and-black-striped sweater!" Surprise and admiration mingled in Bettina's voice as she gazed at Pamela. "In that photo of Coco and Simon and their friends in front of the old van covered with peace signs, Simon was wearing a yellow-and-black-striped sweater. We both looked at the photo, but I didn't make the connection."

Pamela nodded. "And one of the last tapestries Ingrid made juxtaposed a yellow-and-black-striped sweater with a large, three-dimensional cocoon and the word *conception*. The cocoon appeared in the pictorial journal, too, as the climax of a sequence in which a butterfly and a bee alternated visits to a deep-pink flower."

Roland had taken up his knitting again, but his fingers were moving more slowly than usual, and he was clearly interested in Pamela's explanation. "So," he said, "the journal and the tapestries revealed the connection between Ingrid and Simon, the fact that he was the father of her daughter. That's all interesting, but I don't see that as an automatic motive for killing her, or Nestor."

Pamela nodded. "I didn't either," she responded, "but I happened to mention to Coco that I thought the flowers and the butterflies and the bees in the journal were real people. Simon overheard me. He apparently thought the contents of the journal were more incriminating than they actually were, and he decided his guilt was about to be revealed. But it was really he who revealed his own guilt."

"By deciding to rush back to Connecticut," Bettina cut in. "Coco was beside herself because she thought he was hurrying to get away from her, but he was actually trying to spare her being associated with a murderer."

"What made him decide to confess, though?" The question came from a surprising quarter, the armchair in which Nell was sitting.

"You don't mind that we're talking about it?" Holly sounded pleased and relieved.

A corner of Nell's mouth twitched in a furtive smile, and she said, "Marcy Brewer obviously didn't ask the right questions."

"She didn't have time." Pamela laughed. "I was running for my house."

"The confession was my doing," Bettina said, "indirectly at least. Pamela told me what she'd figured out about Ingrid and Simon and Nestor from studying the journal—and that Simon had sent Coco to ask for the journal, with the supposed aim of returning it to Mari. Then yesterday morning, Coco called me while I was at Pamela's, beside herself because Simon was leaving. Pamela and I went to her house to comfort her in person, and I told her what Pamela had figured out from the journal. She was furious at the idea that he'd used her to get the journal out of Pamela's hands, and she decided his supposed love for her had been a ruse the whole time. We were sitting in her kitchen, and she jumped up and—"

Bettina left off speaking as Pamela tapped her on the knee and made a face—eyes wide and lips compressed—that blended warning with distress.

"And?" Holly whispered from her spot on the sofa.

"She ran across the street," Bettina went on. "Simon was just stepping out onto the porch, and Coco was yelling at him, and she backed him into a corner and . . ." Bettina looked at Pamela.

"Love softened his heart," Pamela said. "It was sudden, and very odd."

"No question about that," Roland murmured. He had been knitting steadily the whole while. Now his fingers slowed and then stopped as he flexed his wrist to sneak a discreet glance at his watch. Bettina had apparently been keeping track of the time too. She set her work aside and whispered, "I'll get the water started boiling."

Pamela was in mid-row and nodded her thanks. She continued to ply her needles, watching the neat stitches form and enjoying the juxtapositions as chartreuse gave way to yellow and yellow gave way to orange. Just as she reached the end of the row, movement at the far end of the hearth drew her attention. Roland had rested his project on the briefcase at his side and was studying the face of the impressive watch peeking from beneath his flawless shirt cuff.

"Eight o'clock," he intoned, climbing to his feet. Pamela's thrift-shop clock chimed from the mantel to confirm the time.

Bettina's voice followed a minute later, from the arch between the living room and the dining room. "Coffee and tea are ready," she sang out, and the aroma of coffee reinforced the announcement. "There's a nibble too . . ." she added, "somewhere."

Pamela hopped to her feet and headed for the kitchen via the entry as the others made their way toward the arch, and the dining room table beyond.

"You didn't forget about the nibble, did you?" Bettina had retreated to the kitchen through the door that led from the kitchen to the dining room. Standing next to the little table, whose top was bare of all but a tablecloth, she seemed genuinely alarmed.

"Of course not." Pamela laughed and reached out to open the refrigerator.

The door swung back to reveal the strawberry-banana pudding, bathed in the shadowless light of the refrigerator's bright interior.

"Oh, my goodness!" Bettina sighed. "That is the most beautiful thing I have ever seen."

Pamela bent forward and reached for the pudding. Cradling the compote with both hands, she removed it from the refrigerator and carried it to the doorway that linked the kitchen with the dining room. A few more steps took her to the table, where she set the compote on the lace tablecloth among the wedding-china cups and saucers, and cut-glass dessert dishes. The chandelier cast a welcoming glow over all and made the cut-glass facets of the dessert dishes sparkle.

The Knit and Nibblers had obediently heeded Bettina's summons and were gathered near the table. Bettina followed right behind Pamela, bearing the carafe and the teapot, and she applied herself first to filling cups with tea for Nell and Karen. Pamela, still stationed next to the compote, picked up the serving spoon. As she stood with the spoon poised over the pale drift of whipped cream that formed the pudding's surface, Holly stepped closer. Her expression made her admiration obvious even before she pronounced the pudding to be *awesome*.

"It's banana pudding, with all the traditional layers," Pamela said, "but I added strawberries to make it more colorful and because they're in season."

It seemed almost a shame to disturb the pudding, with the subtle color gradations, accented by the dramatic vein of red, clearly visible through the glass of the compote. Pamela nevertheless scooped out a portion and transferred it to one of the cut-glass dessert dishes. Holly was standing right in front of the pudding, but she stepped aside and nudged Nell forward.

"No more, please!" Nell raised a hand as Pamela launched another scoop. "This is just right."

Pamela handed the dish over and continued scooping and serving as Bettina moved on to pouring coffee from the carafe. By the time all six dishes had been filled, the layered chunks of pudding remaining in the compote evoked a stratified landscape disrupted by a seismic upheaval.

Soon people were back in their seats, bowls of pudding in their hands and coffee or tea nearby on the coffee table or hearth. Pamela slowly maneuvered her spoon along the edge of her serving, seeking to include a bit of each pudding component in her first bite. Exclamations of pleasure, however, indicated that others had been more impulsive.

"Amazing!" was Holly's verdict, and Karen concurred.

"My mother made banana pudding," Nell said. "It was a popular summer dessert because, except for the actual pudding part, no cooking was required. Everybody didn't have air-conditioning back in those days."

Bettina's approval was obvious from the fact that her bowl was nearly empty, and despite the fact that the sugar bowl and cream pitcher were at hand, she hadn't yet begun the ritual that made her coffee drinkable.

"There's plenty more." Pamela nodded toward Bettina's bowl.

"I couldn't, really." Bettina shook her head.

"It wouldn't have to be strawberries," came Roland's voice from across the room.

"It often isn't," Nell responded. "The classic recipe just uses bananas for the fruit."

"I like the berries, though." Holly illustrated her comment by holding aloft a spoon containing a dollop of the strawberry jam streaked with whipped cream. "Blueberries could be good too, or raspberries . . ."

"Why would there have to be bananas at all?" Roland inquired.

"Without bananas, but with other fruit, it would be more like trifle . . ." That voice was Nell's.

"Trifle needs pound cake . . ."

"No! Ladyfingers . . ."

"Instant pudding . . ."

"Peach preserves . . ."

The voices ebbed and flowed—Holly, Karen, and Nell, yielding occasionally to Roland's measured tones, as Bettina stirred sugar into her coffee and then cream. Pamela was happy to let the discussion swirl around her, relieved that no one had wanted to revisit the topic of Simon's arrest. What would become of poor Coco? she wondered. Perhaps she'd be content, in a way, knowing that Simon's love had been real, though he'd likely spend the rest of his life paying for his crimes, rather than sharing it with her.

The conversation was subsiding now, and the sofa was being vacated as Bettina, Holly, and Karen rose to clear away cups and saucers and dishes. Nell took up her needles and patted the skein of yarn at her side. Roland checked his watch, glanced at the mantel clock, then retrieved his knitting from the top of his briefcase. He soon set to work, as did the other knitters when they returned from the kitchen.

*   *   *

The mantel clock chimed nine, interrupting a lively discussion about the best shore towns for vacations with small children. Nell stowed away her needles, partial sleeve, and cheery red yarn as Roland snapped open the latch on his briefcase. Holly and Karen, still chatting, tucked their in-progress bathing suits into their knitting bags. Bettina, too, collected her yarn, needles, pattern, and project.

Soon everyone was gathered in the entry, thanking Pamela and bidding her a good night. The first to leave was Roland, heading for the curb where his white Porsche glowed in the light from the streetlamp. Holly, Karen, and Nell left together, after Nell reluctantly agreed to accept a ride home. Bettina remained poised near the door with her knitting bag in her hand.

"There's more of the pudding," Pamela said. "It doesn't keep well because the bananas turn brown, and you know you want some." Bettina seemed curiously unresponsive to the offer, and Pamela bent forward to study her expression. Bettina at that moment edged toward the door and peeked through the lace curtain.

"I'll have some with you," Pamela added. "It really doesn't keep well."

Bettina continued to peek through the curtain.

"You can't see much that way," Pamela said. "Go ahead and open the door."

Pamela herself reached for the knob and gave it a twist. Bettina hopped back as the door swung open, then she circled around Pamela and stationed herself in the open doorway. She gazed silently at the street for a long minute.

Suddenly she twisted sideways to look at Pamela.

"It's a beautiful night," she exclaimed. "Walk out to the street with me."

"You're sure you don't want some pudding?" Pamela inquired. "Or you could take some with you, for you and Wilfred to share."

"No, no, really!" Bettina resumed gazing at the street.

"Didn't you like the pudding?" Pamela asked. "You acted like you liked it."

Bettina twisted sideways again, seized Pamela's arm, and stepped over the threshold. With an urgent, "Come on!" she tugged Pamela after her, across the porch and down the steps. "Look," she said, pausing at the bottom of the steps. "The stars are out, and we can probably see them even better from the curb."

"Why?" Pamela squirmed, but Bettina continued down the front walk, clinging tightly to Pamela's arm and hauling her along, one step at a time. *What on earth has come over Bettina?* Pamela wondered.

They reached the curb, and Bettina relinquished her grip. She tilted her head until Pamela feared she would tip over backward and pointed at the sky. "Now, look," she said, "isn't that—" But she broke off to glance sharply to the side.

Pamela was still gazing upward, following Bettina's instruction. The stars *were* clearly visible, like pinpricks of light shining through a dark canvas. Then her contemplation was interrupted by Bettina's voice. Instead of enthusing about the celestial spectacle, however, Bettina was focused on something much closer at hand.

"Well, hello, neighbor!" she crooned. "What a coincidence running into you at this time of night—and here are Wilfred and Woofus too!"

The voice that responded was that of Richard Larkin. "I just stepped out to fetch my recycling bin," he explained, "and Wilfred and Woofus came along and stopped to chat."

"Yes." That voice was Wilfred's. "Meeting Rick like this was a coincidence for me and Woofus too. We usually take our evening walk much later, but tonight we just happened to venture out . . . and here you are, dear wife, on your way home from Knit and Nibble, and here's Pamela too . . ."

"It all seems very *very* coincidental," Pamela commented, "almost *too* coincidental." Her tone was dry as she uttered the words, but that tone, with its implication of emotion withheld, didn't reflect what was going on in the region of her heart.

Richard Larkin was standing with his back to the streetlight, nearly looming over her, his face in shadow. She tilted her head as if to make eye contact, though she couldn't see his features clearly. The loud *thump*s within her chest must be audible, she thought. They nearly drowned out the soft murmurs coming from Bettina and Wilfred, and the jingle of Woofus's leash, as couple and dog retreated toward the Frasers' house across the street.

"The tree," Richard Larkin said after what seemed like a long pause. "Did you mean what you said about the tree?"

"About your tree? The tree that shades my yard?"

"That tree, yes. Trimming it?" He bent forward, and eyes in a shadowy face peered into her own.

"Yes," she said, her own voice seeming barely audible above the pounding of her heart. "I would like you to trim it." She thought for a moment then added, "I'll cook you dinner as a thank you."

KNIT

Doll Sweater with Intarsia Butterfly

Intarsia is a knitting technique that allows the knitter to create patterns involving blocks of color on a background of another color. The name derives from a similar, and very old, woodworking technique in which designs are created by inlaying one type of wood into a solid background of another type. Intarsia knitting is easy and fun to do once one gets a bit of practice, and what better way to practice than on something small, like this charming doll sweater with an intarsia butterfly on the front?

For a picture of the finished Butterfly Sweater being modeled by a cloth-body doll from an estate sale, as well as some in-progress photos, visit the Knit & Nibble Mysteries page at PeggyEhrhart.com. Click on the cover for *Last Wool and Testament* and scroll down on the page that opens. References below to in-progress photos are to this page.

Directions are scaled to fit a doll about 15" tall and 10" around the torso. Use yarn identified on the label as "Medium" and/or #4, and use size 7 or 8 needles. With this yarn and these needles, you will average about four stitches to the inch, so if your doll is a different size, you can measure the doll and modify the pattern to fit. The sweater requires about 62 yards of yarn in the main color and 5 yards of yarn for the butterfly. You will also need graph paper to work out your butterfly design, or you can use my design (see below).

If you've never knitted anything at all, it's easier to learn the basics by watching than by reading. The internet abounds with tutorials that show the process clearly, including casting on and off. Just search on "How to Knit." Most of the sweater is worked in the stockinette stitch. To create the stockinette stitch, you knit one row, then purl going back the other direction, then knit, then purl, knit, purl, back and forth. Again, it's easier to understand "purl" by viewing a video, but essentially when you purl, you're creating the backside of "knit." To knit, you insert the right-hand needle front to back through the loop of yarn on the left-hand needle. To purl, you insert the needle back to front.

The sweater is created from four rectangles.

Make the back.

With your main color, cast on 24 stitches using the slip-knot method. Casting on is often included in internet "How to Knit" tutorials, or you can search specifically for "Casting on." After you've cast on, start creating the ribbing that will form the sweater's lower edge. Ribbing is normally knit 2, purl 2, but because the sweater is for a doll, the scale is smaller. For your first row, knit 1 stitch, then purl 1, then knit 1, purl 1, and continue like that to the end of the row. On the way back, knit 1, purl 1, and so on again. If you've cast on a multiple of 2 (which 24 is), you'll see that now you're doing a knit where you did a purl, and vice versa. This is what creates the effect of ribs. After you do a few rows, you will see the ribs starting to form, and this concept will become clearer.

One important note: After you knit the first stitch of the ribbing, you must shift the yarn you're working with to the front by passing it between the needles. After the purl stitch, you must shift it to the back, and so on back and forth. If you don't do this, extra loops of yarn will accumulate on your needles. Do the knitting and purling for 3 rows, then switch to the stockinette stitch, beginning with a knit row, and continue for 23 rows. Cast off. Casting off is often included in internet "How to Knit" tutorials, or you can search specifically for "Casting off."

Make the front.

To create your butterfly on the sweater front, you will be working from a design drawn or printed on graph paper, with each square corresponding to one stitch. On the page devoted to *Last Wool and Testament* on my website, you will find a link to a PDF for the pattern I used. It will print as the correct size on an 8½-by-11-inch sheet of paper.

If you want to create your own design, rule off a

square 24 squares (width) by 26 squares (height) on a sheet of graph paper. Mark off the bottom three rows of the little squares. These will be your ribbing. Centering your design in the remaining space, draw your butterfly. Place an X in each square that falls within the outlines of the butterfly. Each horizontal row of squares corresponds to one row of knitting (or purling). As you knit or purl each row, put a checkmark at the edge of that row of squares on the graph paper. When you get to the first row that contains Xs, you will switch over to the color you are using for your butterfly.

You will need a way to keep your separate strands of yarn from tangling as you work. You can measure off the lengths of yarn you need for each color and wind them on bobbins, or you can improvise, making balls and securing them with rubber bands, as shown in one of the photos on my website. For my butterfly design, you need a length of the main color 13 yards long, another of the main color 3 yards long, and a length of the butterfly color 5 yards long.

With the larger ball of your main color, cast on 24 stitches using the slip-knot method. Create three rows of ribbing as described above. Continue, beginning with a knit row and using the stockinette stitch, until you reach the first row that contains Xs. Start the row with your main color. When you get to the first X, you will graft in your butterfly color. Begin that stitch as usual, inserting the right-hand needle into the stitch waiting on the left-hand needle. Make a loop of the butterfly color, leaving a tail of about three inches, and slip the loop over the right-hand needle. Complete the stitch in the usual way. For the next stitch, insert the right-hand needle into the stitch waiting on the left-hand needle and use the butterfly color, but pull the butterfly color to the right *under* the main color and pass it to the left *over* the main color before completing the stitch. You need to do this to link the section with the butterfly color to the section with the main color. There are photos on my website illustrating this process, and the process is the same on a purl row.

If you are using my design, you can work the first row that includes the butterfly color all the way across using the same ball of your main color because there are just a few stitches using the butterfly color and the main color can float across the back of them. When you get to the next row, however, you will need to graft in the 3-yard ball of your main color when you get past the section using the butterfly color. To do that, follow the process described above.

Continue to work, following your chart and switching from main color to butterfly color and back. If you're using my design, you'll be grafting in an extra bit of the main color in the middle at the very top; a photo on my website shows how this works. When you get past the rows that use the butterfly color, go on with the main color until you get to the last row of the chart. Cast off. Using a yarn needle—a large needle with a large eye and a blunt end—hide the tails left from switching colors. Do this by working your yarn needle in and out of the loops left from linking the new color to the old one and/or the backs of stitches. There are photos on my website illustrating this process.

Make two sleeves.

With your main color, cast on 14 stitches using the simple slip-knot method. Create 3 rows of ribbing, as described above. Continue, beginning with a knit row and using the stockinette stitch, for 19 rows. Cast off. Repeat the process for the other sleeve.

Assemble the sweater.

There are photos on my website illustrating this process.

To assemble the sweater, thread your yarn needle with your main color or use the tails left from casting on and off. Lay the sweater front on top of the sweater back, wrong sides together. Use pins if necessary to make the top edges line up smoothly. Sew the top edges together for an inch on each side, leaving an opening in the middle for the sweater's neckline. To make a neat seam, use an overcast stitch and catch only the outer loops along each side.

Open the front-back piece out flat, right-side up. Arrange a sleeve, flat, on each side, with the middle of the sleeve's top edge lined up with the shoulder seam you have just sewn. Sew each sleeve to the front-back piece. Again, to make a neat seam, use an overcast stitch and catch only the outer loops along each side.

Fold the front-back piece, with sleeves now attached, along the shoulders and smooth it flat. Use pins if necessary. Sew the sweater's sides and sleeves in one long seam, up the sides and along the bottoms of the sleeves.

Hide the tails left from casting on and off and from

sewing the sweater together. To do this, thread your yarn needle with each tail, work the needle in and out of the knitted fabric at an edge or in a seam for half an inch or so, pull the tail through, and cut off the bit of yarn that's left. There are photos on my website illustrating this process.

NIBBLE

Strawberry-Banana Pudding

May is strawberry season, and it's fun to use them whenever possible—as the various cooks who make strawberry-based goodies in *Last Wool and Testament* demonstrate. When Pamela hosts the Knit and Nibble group at the end of the book, she makes this variation on classic banana pudding, the layered creation involving vanilla wafers, vanilla pudding, bananas, and whipped cream. She serves it in a footed compote, clear glass, the better to show off its layered construction—and she's serving six people, so she can be sure that most of it will be quickly eaten.

That's fortunate, because banana pudding, with or without strawberries, doesn't survive very well as left-overs. The sliced bananas soon become brown and mushy, so in the recipe below, I suggest making individual servings of the Strawberry-Banana Pudding. The recipe will make four generous servings or six small servings. To make more, for eight generous servings, or to layer in a compote or medium-sized bowl, just double everything in the recipe but the strawberries. A pint of strawberries will make plenty of jam.

If you're making the recipe when strawberries are really in season, use fresh strawberries and follow my instructions for turning them into a quick jam. The jam will add a more intense strawberry flavor than if you just used sliced strawberries, and homemade jam keeps the fresh berry taste when they are actually in season. In seasons when you can't get strawberries that actually taste like strawberries, you can substitute good-quality strawberry jam from a jar.

The Strawberry-Banana Pudding is best when assembled on the day you plan to serve it and chilled for a few hours. The vanilla pudding and the jam, however, can be made a day or so in advance and refrigerated.

For pictures of the Strawberry-Banana Pudding, as well as some in-progress photos, visit the Knit & Nibble Mysteries page at PeggyEhrhart.com. Click on the cover for *Last Wool and Testament* and scroll down on the page that opens.

Ingredients

For the vanilla pudding:
⅜ cup sugar
2 tablespoons cornstarch, generous
⅛ teaspoon salt, generous
1½ cups milk
2 egg yolks, slightly beaten
¾ teaspoon vanilla

For the strawberry jam:
1 pint strawberries
1 tablespoon water, scant
2 tablespoons sugar

For assembly:

    1 cup heavy whipping cream
    1 tablespoon sugar
    24 vanilla wafer cookies
    2 bananas, cut in 1/4-inch slices

Make the pudding.

Mix sugar, cornstarch, and salt in the top half of double boiler. If you don't have a double boiler, you can improvise with a larger pot and a smaller pot. I include a photo of my improvised double boiler with the photos for this recipe on my website.

Add the milk and blend well. Bring water to a boil in the bottom half of the double boiler, put the top half in place, and cook the mixture over boiling water, stirring frequently, until it starts to thicken—10 to 15 minutes.

Add a few spoonfuls of the milk mixture to the egg yolks and stir, then add the egg yolks to the milk mixture and blend well. Continue cooking and stirring until the mixture becomes thick enough to coat a metal spoon. There's a photo of this step on my website. Turn the heat off and stir in the vanilla. Transfer the pudding to a bowl and let it cool.

Make the strawberry jam.

Slice or quarter the strawberries and place them in a small saucepan. Add a scant tablespoon of water and the sugar. Cook and stir over medium heat until the consistency becomes jam-like—about 15 minutes. They will produce a lot of liquid as they cook, and you might need to raise the heat at the end to thicken the mixture. Transfer the jam to a bowl and let cool.

Assemble the individual pudding servings.

In a small bowl, whip the heavy cream with the sugar until it forms soft peaks. Use clear glass dessert dishes, stemmed or not. Put three vanilla wafers in the bottom of each dessert dish. Add a few tablespoons of vanilla pudding, four slices of banana, a few tablespoons of strawberry jam, and a scoop of whipped cream. Repeat the layers, using up the rest of your banana slices by tucking extras in here and there. End with the whipped cream layer. If you are assembling the Strawberry-Banana Pudding in a compote or bowl, you can use extra vanilla wafers to fill out each layer.

Some strawberry jam might be left over. It keeps for a week or so in the refrigerator and can be used with yogurt or ice cream.

Chill the pudding in the refrigerator for a few hours or longer before serving.

BONUS NIBBLE

Roland's Magic Cake

Roland describes the cake he serves when the Knit and Nibblers meet at his house as "magic"—and the recipe, indeed, seems magical. Four simple ingredients combine, and then separate while baking, to form a three-layer creation: custard-like on the bottom, soft and creamy in the middle, and light as a soufflé on top. It's an old French recipe, and like many French desserts, it's not overwhelmingly sweet. Its simplicity makes it a great backdrop for berries or other fruit.

For a few pictures of Roland's Magic Cake, visit the Knit & Nibble Mysteries page at PeggyEhrhart.com. Click on the cover for *Last Wool and Testament* and scroll down on the page that opens.

Ingredients

 ¾ cup flour
 ¾ cup sugar
 4 cold eggs, separated
 2 cups milk

Line a square cake pan, 8 x 8 inches, with parchment paper.

In a large bowl and using a wire whisk, mix flour,

sugar, egg yolks, and ½ cup milk until smooth. Mix in the rest of the milk to make a thin batter. In a smaller bowl, beat the egg whites with an electric mixer until stiff. Fold the beaten egg whites into the batter, a third at a time, making sure no liquid is left at the bottom of the bowl.

Pour the mixture into the cake pan and bake at 325 degrees for 45 to 50 minutes. The cake is done when a wooden toothpick inserted in the middle comes out clean. It should cool for an hour or more before cutting into squares and serving. It can be served at room temperature or chilled. Top each square with sugared berries, strawberry or other, if desired. It's also good sprinkled with powdered sugar.

Visit our website at
KensingtonBooks.com
to sign up for our newsletters, read
more from your favorite authors, see
books by series, view reading group
guides, and more!

BOOK **CLUB**
BETWEEN THE CHAPTERS

Become a Part of Our
Between the Chapters Book Club
Community and Join the Conversation

Betweenthechapters.net